WIPED
OUT

WIPED OUT

A Charlotte LaRue Mystery

Barbara Colley

WHEELER
CHIVERS

This Large Print edition is published by Wheeler Publishing, Waterville, Maine USA and by BBC Audiobooks, Ltd, Bath, England.

Published in 2005 in the U.S. by arrangement with Kensington Books, an imprint of Kensington Publishing Corp.

Published in 2005 in the U.K. by arrangement with Kensington Publishing Corp.

U.S. Softcover 1-58724-951-0 (Cozy Mystery)
U.K. Hardcover 1-4056-3328-X (Chivers Large Print)
U.K. Softcover 1-4056-3329-8 (Camden Large Print)

The text of this Large Print edition is unabridged.
Other aspects of the book may vary from the original edition.

Set in 16 pt. Plantin by Carleen Stearns.

Printed in the United States on permanent paper.

British Library Cataloguing-in-Publication Data available

Library of Congress Cataloging-in-Publication Data

Colley, Barbara.
    Wiped out : a Charlotte LaRue mystery / by Barbara Colley.
        p. cm. — (Wheeler Publishing large print cozy mystery)
    ISBN 1-58724-951-0 (lg. print : sc : alk. paper)
    1. LaRue, Charlotte (Fictitious character) — Fiction.
2. Women cleaning personnel — Fiction.   3. New Orleans
(La.) — Fiction.   4. Large type books.   I. Title.
II. Wheeler large print cozy mystery.
PS3603.O44W57 2005
813'.6—dc22   2004030864

For April, Charles, and Cristi —
my children.

ACKNOWLEDGMENTS

I would like to express my sincere appreciation to all who so generously gave me advice and information while I was writing this book: the New Orleans coroner's office; René Schmit, county agent with the LSU Agricultural Center; my wonderful friends and fellow writers, Rexanne Becnel, Jessica Ferguson, Marie Goodwin, and Karen Young.

I also want to thank Evan Marshall and John Scognamiglio. Their support and advice are invaluable.

Chapter 1

Watch out for that woman. She's not someone you want to cross. Like a nagging toothache that just wouldn't go away, Bitsy Duhe's dire statement about Mary Lou Adams came to mind yet again as Charlotte LaRue drove down Prytania.

Monday morning traffic had slowed to a crawl, and as Charlotte inched along in her van, she found herself growing more frustrated with each passing minute. The traffic jam was bad enough, but what Bitsy had said had haunted her all week . . . and worried her.

The last thing that Charlotte had wanted was to listen to one client gossiping about another client, especially a brand-new client whom she'd never met except through a phone conversation. She'd always preferred to form her own opinions about the people she cleaned for. And truth be told, Bitsy, bless her old heart, was one of the biggest gossips in New Orleans. Any little tidbit of information was fair grist for Bitsy's gossip mill.

As usual, though, Bitsy had ignored Charlotte's attempts to change the subject, and she'd filled her ears with information about Mary Lou and Gordon Adams.

According to Bitsy, Mary Lou was a social butterfly, but a butterfly with the sting of a wasp. As for Gordon Adams, his one obsession in life was becoming even wealthier than he already was. He had not only expanded his car dealerships to include South Louisiana but had ventured into Mississippi as well.

Behind Charlotte a car horn blared and she jumped. "Okay, okay, for Pete's sake!" She glowered in the rearview mirror at the driver behind her, then eased her van forward. Both of them were going nowhere fast, so she didn't see what the big deal was about lagging a few feet behind the car in front of her.

Still irritated at being honked at, she ventured a quick glance at the dashboard clock. Five minutes. She drummed her fingers impatiently against the steering wheel. She still had five minutes to get to the Adamses' house before nine.

The line of vehicles in front of her stopped again, and with a groan of frustration, Charlotte craned her neck in an attempt to see past the SUV ahead of her. Half a block down was a side street. If she could just reach the side street, she could get around the traffic jam altogether.

A few minutes later, Charlotte sighed with relief when she finally parked behind an old battered truck alongside the curb in front of the Adamses' house. From the looks of the contents in the bed of the truck, she figured that today was most probably the day for the gardener as well as the maid.

Charlotte glanced at the dashboard clock again. "You're late," she grumbled to herself. *Just five minutes. So what?* her inner voice chided. *It's highly doubtful that Mary Lou Adams is sitting in front of a clock and counting the minutes, Charlotte.*

Feeling a bit foolish for worrying so much about the time, Charlotte quickly unloaded her supply carrier and vacuum cleaner from the back of the van.

A black cast-iron fence surrounded the house, and as she let herself in through the ornate gate, she paused a moment to admire the beautifully preserved home and the well-manicured grounds.

The huge house was magnificent, probably built in the late 1800s, she decided.

Like many of the old homes in the New Orleans Garden District, she could tell that it had been altered over the years, the end result that the style was a combination of Greek Revival and Victorian. But the landscaping was what really caught her eye. She'd worked in the Garden District for more years than she cared to count, and she'd be willing to rate the grounds of the Adamses' home as one of the most fascinating that she'd seen. It was filled with exotic plants. A couple of the plants she recognized — Tibouchina, the Sago Palm — but there were many more that she didn't.

Charlotte's long experience working as a maid exclusively in the Garden District had made her somewhat of an expert on architecture and furnishings, and she was well aware that only someone very wealthy could afford the upkeep on such an extravagant old home.

Mary Lou and Gordon Adams were indeed wealthy. Not only did Gordon Claiborne Adams III own a conglomerate of car dealerships that stretched over the entire state of Louisiana, but according to Bitsy, he came from old New Orleans money as well.

Charlotte climbed the steps to the lower

gallery and approached the double entry doors. Each oak door contained beveled leaded glass, and above the doors was a transom made of the same type of glass as well. A large brass door knocker was located to the side of the doors and was shaped in an oblong circle; within the circle was an ornate *A*.

"*A* for Adams," Charlotte murmured as she lifted the door knocker and banged it a couple of times. She waited several minutes. When no one came to the door, she banged the door knocker again.

After a moment, Charlotte frowned and tapped her foot impatiently. *The gardener.* Maybe the Adams woman was outside in the backyard with the gardener. Still she hesitated. Should she take the supply carrier and vacuum cleaner with her or not? Not, she decided. Neither was that heavy, but both together were a bit unwieldy, and besides, there was no use lugging them all over creation if she didn't have to. She set the supplies and vacuum cleaner down on the porch, then went in search of her new employer.

As Charlotte neared the back of the house, she heard voices. One was the low, gravelly rumble of a man's voice. Probably the gardener, she figured. Though Charlotte had never met her newest client face-to-face, she had talked to her for just a few minutes over the phone, and there was no mistaking the other voice, with its imperious, higher-pitched tone, as belonging to Mary Lou Adams.

When Charlotte rounded the back corner of the house, she glanced around in awe. The landscape of the backyard was just as amazing as the front and side yard had been. The entire property in the back was encased in a wall of well-manicured Photina that served as a living privacy fence. At the far back corner of the property was what looked like a small greenhouse. Beneath a portico attached to the main house was a large brick terrace, which Charlotte suspected was original to the house. Flanking the terrace were even more exotic plants, and in the center of the terrace was a circular brick planter containing ferns and a Venetian urn.

Charlotte stared at the small urn and shuddered. Though not nearly as large as the urn that one of her former clients Patsy Dufore had owned, Charlotte doubted that she would ever be able to look at another urn again without remembering the harrowing experience she'd had when she'd worked for Patsy.

With another shudder, Charlotte forced herself to turn her attention to the middle-aged, scruffy-looking man and the tall, slim woman near the edge of the property.

Her first impression of Mary Lou Adams was that the woman's appearance fit her voice. Her dark brown hair was long and brushed straight back in a seemingly effortless style that revealed a high forehead; finely arched brows; a straight, narrow nose; and full cupid lips. She was a tall woman, probably in her midforties, and though she appeared to be dressed casually, even from a short distance Charlotte suspected that the aqua-colored blouse and matching slacks she wore were made of silk because of the drape of the fabric.

Charlotte herself was only five feet three with short, gray-streaked, honey brown hair, which she liked to think was cut stylishly, and she still wore a size nine. But compared to Mary Lou Adams, she felt downright frumpy.

It's the age difference, she consoled herself. She figured that she was probably almost twenty years older than the other woman. And, of course, there was no way her plain blue polyester uniform could compare to Mary Lou's silk outfit.

Silk, just the thing to wear while mucking around in the heat and dirt. The moment that the sarcastic thought popped into her head, she felt the chiding prick of her conscience. *Shame on you. Judge not lest ye be judged.* Promising herself that she would try to be less critical in the future, she walked briskly toward where the couple was standing.

"This is the one." Mary Lou pointed out a small tree that was all but naked of leaves. What few leaves that were left on the scrawny tree were brown and shriveled. "I want it dug up, roots and all." She gave Charlotte a cursory glance, and continued her instructions to the gardener. "After you get it all up, I need you to prepare this area for a small flower bed. About three feet by ten feet should be plenty of room." Without waiting for a question or comment from the gardener, she turned her back on him and faced Charlotte. "You must be Charlotte." She thrust out a hand with perfectly manicured and polished fingernails.

Charlotte nodded and shook her hand. "And you must be Mary Lou," she said with a smile, noting that although the handshake was brief, the other woman's grasp was strong and firm.

16

"Yes, I am. But for goodness sake, call me Mimi. It's a nickname I've had so long that I probably won't answer to anything else."

Again, Charlotte nodded. "I'll try to remember that." Charlotte motioned toward the small tree. "Termites or the heat?"

"Neither," Mimi retorted. "The poor thing was murdered, outright killed on purpose by Sally Lawson, that awful woman who lives next door. It's the second one she's killed in less than a year."

Charlotte wasn't quite sure how to respond. All she could think of to say was, "But why?"

"Humph! Why indeed. Because Sally is a selfish, vindictive woman who loves nothing more than to make my life miserable. And all because of her stupid pool."

"Her pool?"

"She has a swimming pool just on the other side of the hedge. Pathetic creature that she is, evidently her pool parties are her only form of social entertainment." She glared toward her neighbor's house. "Her *noisy* pool parties," she added in a loud voice as if hoping that Sally Lawson were listening. She turned back to Charlotte. "She's already cut down a couple of trees in her own yard — beautiful old live oaks that had to be over a hundred years old. And all because they shaded her pool. So now she's poisoning my tree."

Mimi suddenly laughed. It was a wicked sound that matched the sly expression on her face. "But I've found a delicious way to get even." She motioned for Charlotte to follow her and led Charlotte to the small greenhouse. Near the opening of the greenhouse were several large containers grouped together. Inside the containers were what appeared to be flowers, but Charlotte personally thought they looked more like weeds. From a distance, the plants, with their pale green stems, large leaves, and purple, funnel-shaped blooms, were rather pretty, but by the time Charlotte and Mimi got within a few feet of the plants the putrid, rotten-egg smell was overpowering. Charlotte wrinkled her nose and tried not to breathe too deeply.

"Don't they smell just awful?" Mimi said with a grin, her hands on her hips. Charlotte nodded, and Mimi laughed and bent down to gently caress one of the stinky blooms. "These are my little revenge."

She stood upright, pulled a small package of hand wipes from her pocket, and, using one of the wipes, scrubbed at her hands. Then, to Charlotte's horror,

Mimi dried her hands by rubbing them on the legs of her silk pants. "Actually, they're classified as weeds," Mimi continued.

If it looks like a weed, then it must be a weed, Charlotte thought.

"But you'd never know from the looks of them," Mimi said.

Charlotte had to bite her tongue to keep from voicing her thoughts on that one.

"A friend of mine came up with the idea," Mimi told her. "Instead of planting another tree for Sally to kill, I'm going to plant these. With enough of them growing along that fence, I'm banking that the awful smell will drive her and her noisy friends crazy or, at the very least, ruin her parties."

"But won't the smell bother you as well?"

Mimi shrugged. "Just a small price to pay. Besides, we don't entertain back here hardly at all. And I can always get rid of them eventually."

Charlotte found herself at a loss for words. The capacity for one human being to hurt another never ceased to amaze her, nor the lengths someone would go to. For most of her life, she had always tried her best to live by the Golden Rule of "repay no one evil for evil" instead of the "eye for an eye, tooth for a tooth" philosophy. Finding herself really uncomfortable with the whole conversation, she decided that about now would be a good time for a change of subject.

Charlotte cleared her throat. "Well, I guess I'd better go get busy and leave you to your gardening before it gets too hot. I left my cleaning supplies on the front porch, though, so if you'll unlock the door, I'll get to work."

Mimi gave her a curious look, and then, with a whatever shrug, she pointed toward the back door beneath the portico. "You can go in that way. That door isn't locked, and there's a key in the dead bolt on the inside of the front door."

With a nod and eager to get away from the awful smell of the flowers, Charlotte forced a quick smile, did an about-face, and gladly headed for the portico.

As Charlotte approached the terrace, the stench of the flowers still lingered in her nostrils, and unbidden, Bitsy Duhe's warning about Mary Lou Adams came to mind. *Watch out for that woman. She's not someone you want to cross.*

Charlotte reached inside her apron pocket and pulled out a tissue. She could hardly wait to get inside and blow her nose, and the moment she closed the door behind her, she did so. It helped, but a bit of the stench still lingered. She wadded the tissue and shoved it back inside her pocket. As far as Charlotte was concerned, Mimi's little feud was just plain ridiculous. Regardless of what Sally Lawson had or had not done to the silly tree, Charlotte didn't think it justified what Mimi was doing. Besides, there were always two sides to an argument, two sides to every story, weren't there?

So what was Sally Lawson's side?

Chapter 2

The back door of Mimi Adams's house opened into a short hallway leading to the kitchen. And what a marvelous kitchen it was, Charlotte thought, as she took a quick inventory of the top-of-the-line appliances, the granite countertops, and the oak plank floor. In spite of the dirty dishes sitting in the sink, the Viking stovetop being splattered with grease, and the floor needing a good wax job, she decided that whoever had planned and decorated the room had been a genius of design. Though modern in every respect, the room still retained an ambiance in keeping with the era of the house.

As in most of the Garden District homes built in the 1800s, the ceiling heights were a good fourteen feet. As Charlotte made her way to the front entrance hall, she caught her breath when she saw the elaborate plasterwork, the hand-painted ceiling, and the brass and crystal chandelier that hung from an intricately carved medallion.

Antique tables with petticoat mirrors and chairs flanked the walls, and every detail of the decor looked to be authentic and had been beautifully preserved.

"Gorgeous, just simply gorgeous," she whispered. It was going to be a real delight and a challenge to keep the old house clean.

Once Charlotte had retrieved her supply carrier and vacuum cleaner from the front porch, she took her lunch bag into the kitchen and placed it on the counter. Then, she inspected the house from top to bottom, just to get an idea of what needed to be done.

Downstairs contained a huge double parlor. Across the wide entrance hall opposite the parlor were a small library and a grand dining room. The kitchen; a laundry room; and a small, more modern family room were located along the back of the ground floor. A half bath was tucked beneath the grand staircase, and at the top of the stairs was a central hall that opened to five bedroom suites, each suite containing its own private bath.

Though somewhat orderly, the house needed a thorough cleaning, and the more Charlotte explored, the more curious she grew about the Adams family. As a maid, she often saw things that others missed, and she learned things about the people she worked for from cleaning up after them.

Mimi was a die-hard garden enthusiast and a stickler for authenticity, Charlotte decided, as she straightened a stack of preservation and gardening magazines addressed to Mimi in the library. Also, a vast array of books on the same subjects filled the floor-to-ceiling bookshelves opposite an antique desk. And, of course, there were the well-manicured grounds, the various plants inside and outside of the house, and the greenhouse in the backyard.

Mimi's husband, Gordon, was another matter, though. The designer suits in the master suite closet indicated that he liked nice clothes, and the expensive brand of men's cologne on the dresser also suggested that he liked to be well groomed. But other than the suits and cologne, and several miniature car reproductions done in pewter and displayed in the family room, there was nothing else to indicate that he even lived there. No golf clubs, no hunting paraphernalia, nothing that gave her a clue as to his interest or his hobbies . . . if he had any. Was it possible that the man had no interest or hobbies outside of his car dealerships? Strange . . . strange indeed.

Usually Charlotte worked her way from the upstairs on down, but since the second floor was in pretty good shape, she decided that today she would strip the beds first, and she'd start cleaning on the ground floor while the sheets were washing.

After Charlotte put the sheets in to wash, she tackled the kitchen. Once she'd loaded the dirty dishes into the dishwasher and finished everything except the floor, she quickly dusted and straightened the rest of the downstairs rooms, saving the double parlor for last.

Before she began cleaning the parlor, she transferred the sheets from the washer to the dryer. In the corner of the laundry room she spotted a small stepladder that she decided would be just the right height for dusting the mirror in the parlor.

With the help of the ladder, Charlotte was able to give the gilt and lacquered mid-nineteenth-century mirror frame above the fireplace mantel a really good cleaning. After she wiped down the frame, she Windexed the mirror. Then she gave her attention to the Italian marble mantelpiece.

The mantelpiece was lined with an array of small framed photos that she assumed were of the Adams children. The different photos showed a progression of age, the earliest being baby pictures, the latest being graduation pictures, and each one was in desperate need of a good cleaning.

Because of the way the photos were arranged and as best as Charlotte could tell, Mimi and her husband had two children, a boy and a girl. Both were sun-bleached blondes, and in all of the pictures the girl was knockout beautiful and the boy was truly handsome. Going by the most recent-looking photos and judging from the decor in two of the bedrooms that she'd inspected earlier, she figured that both children were probably away at college.

Charlotte finished dusting the last photograph, and set it back on the mantelpiece. Then she dusted and straightened the rest of the room.

The most time-consuming chore was waxing the hardwood floors. Though doing so was hard on her knees and required application by hand, Charlotte still preferred using a paste wax to the liquid kind. She had waxed all of the downstairs rooms except for the double parlor, when the stiffness in her knees along with the shooting pains up her thighs dictated that it was time for a short break.

In the parlor, she picked up the step-ladder, and with intentions of getting herself a nice tall glass of water first, then putting away the ladder and checking on the sheets in the dryer, she headed for the kitchen. She had just poured the water and was taking a long drink when she heard the back door open.

Mimi entered the kitchen first and was followed by another woman who looked to be a few years younger than Mimi. Though the other woman was almost as tall and slim as Mimi, she was the complete opposite in appearance with her long blond hair, fair skin, and turquoise-blue eyes.

"It's hot as blue blazes out there," Mimi complained, as she walked straight to the sink, scrubbed and rinsed her hands, then yanked off a paper towel from the towel rack. She dried her hands, and, as she delicately blotted her face, she motioned toward the woman who had come in with her. "Charlotte, this is my good friend, June Bryant. June lives three houses down on the other side of the street."

Charlotte smiled at the other woman and placed her glass inside the dish-washer.

"Nice to meet you, Charlotte," June said.

"Same here," Charlotte responded, as she closed and locked the dishwasher door.

Mimi motioned at the stepladder propped against the cabinet. "I see you found the ladder." She glanced around the kitchen. "And I see you've been really busy. The kitchen looks marvelous, especially the floor."

"Thank you," Charlotte said. "Except for the floor in the front parlor, I've finished most of the downstairs. After I wax the parlor I'll be ready to start on the upstairs after lunch."

Mimi glanced at her watch. "I'm impressed." She tapped the crystal of her watch. "It's only eleven-thirty. You work fast."

There was something about the way Mimi had said "work fast" that bothered Charlotte. It was her tone of voice, she decided, almost as if she equated "work fast" with a sloppy job, and it was hard to tell if the woman was being snide or truly paying her a compliment.

Mimi smiled a tight little smile that could have meant anything. "Now, don't let us interrupt you," she said. "June is more like family than company, and mostly drops by to save me from having heat-stroke since she knows that I'm usually working in the greenhouse."

"Someone has to make you behave," June teased her friend. "I swear," June said to Charlotte, "the woman just doesn't know when to quit. It must be close to a hundred degrees, and just look at how she's dressed. If I didn't come by once in a while and drag her out of that greenhouse, she'd make herself sick."

"Shall I get you ladies something to drink before I get back to work?" Charlotte offered. "Maybe a nice glass of iced tea?"

Mimi shook her head. "Goodness no. You've got enough to do. But thanks for offering." She motioned at the ladder. "Just leave that, and I'll put it away for you."

"That's not necessary," said Charlotte. "I need to get the sheets out of the dryer anyway, so I'll put it away."

As Charlotte took the sheets out of the dryer and folded them, she could hear the clink of ice being dropped into glasses, and then the scrape of chairs. The last thing that Charlotte wanted was to eavesdrop, but the house was quiet and sound carried.

"What am I going to do?" she heard June

ask Mimi. "I thought that age would mellow him, but instead of better, he seems to be getting worse."

"What's Fred done this time?"

"Humph!" June grunted. " 'This time' is certainly the right way to put it. But that's my point. There always seems to be a 'this time' where Fred's concerned. Ever since Johnny got into that trouble, Fred's been determined to send him away to military school. He's already enrolled him and made arrangements for him to leave next week. Bad enough Fred went back on his promise to buy Johnny a car, and who knows, if he hadn't broken his promise, maybe Johnny wouldn't have made that little mistake —"

"Now, June, writing five bad checks to the tune of five thousand dollars and forging his father's signature is not just a 'little mistake,' and you know it."

In the laundry room Charlotte folded the last pillowcase, and though she really dreaded getting back down on her knees, she dreaded having to walk back through the kitchen where the two women were even more. She didn't want to appear to be eavesdropping, but surely they had to realize that she could hear every word they were saying. But what if they didn't?

Maybe if she walked fast and didn't look at them. . . .

Charlotte picked up the stack of sheets and pillowcases, took a deep breath, and headed for the kitchen, just in time to hear June say, "But, Mimi, I'm sure Johnny didn't realize —"

As she hurried past the women, she felt foolish for worrying in the first place. She might as well have been a piece of furniture, she decided, since neither of the women paid the least bit of attention to her.

"Aw, come on, now, June," Mimi chided. "Who are you trying to kid? Remember, this is your old friend Mimi you're talking to. Johnny is what now? Fifteen? Believe me, Johnny knew exactly what he was doing. Why, if that had been Justin or even Emma, Gordon would have reacted in the same way."

Justin and Emma. In the entrance hall, Charlotte placed the stack of bed linens on a table near the staircase. Justin and Emma had to be the names of the Adamses' son and daughter, she decided.

"But, Mimi," June argued, "if Gordon had promised them a car, he would never have gone back on his promise."

"Well, duh." Mimi laughed. "Gordon is

in the car business."

A brief moment of complete silence passed; then June burst into laughter. "That's not what I meant, and you know it," she told Mimi. "A promise is a promise."

In the parlor, Charlotte grinned. She could still hear the women, but just barely, and her grin quickly turned into a frown as she lowered herself onto her knees. Wincing, she began rubbing the wax into the hardwood floor as she made a mental note that the next time she had to wax Mimi's floors, she'd make sure she brought her knee pads.

"Yes, I know what you meant," was Mimi's reply. "But all I'm saying is that you've always had a blind spot when it comes to Johnny. And, after all, Fred has had experience with raising boys and maybe military school will be good for him."

"Oh, yeah, he's got experience alright. He's always throwing up his other kids in my face. He's forever comparing them to Johnny, and poor Johnny always comes out second best. But it's not just the way he treats Johnny. It's how he treats me, too. You just don't know how lucky you are. Unlike that tightwad husband of mine, your Gordon has always been generous with Justin and Emma. And with you," she added. "Why, do you realize that I have to account for every penny I spend. I have to show Fred receipts for everything."

"Maybe it's his age," Mimi offered. "He's what, sixty-five or so?"

"Sixty-four," June grumbled.

"Then maybe it's the money. Maybe his law firm isn't doing as well as it used to."

"That's not it, not with the client load he's had lately."

Mimi cleared her throat. "Ah, I don't know quite how to say this, but do you think it's possible that he's having an affair?"

"I don't think so," June answered.

There was a brief moment of silence as Charlotte finished the last few feet of the hardwood floor near the doorway to the hall.

"But I suppose anything's possible," June continued. "Hmm, maybe I *should* have listened to my mother when she warned me about marrying him. She said that he was too old for me and had too much baggage. She also told me that any man who would cheat on one wife would cheat on another one too. But, silly me, I thought love would conquer all."

In the entrance hall, Charlotte put the lid on the wax and placed it and the cloth she'd used inside her supply carrier. She glanced in the direction of the kitchen. She'd intended on taking her lunch break after waxing the parlor. Normally, when she worked she preferred to eat her lunch outside when the weather was nice, but if it was hot, she always sat in the client's kitchen and read a bit while she ate.

"Not silly," Charlotte heard Mimi say. "And stop being so hard on yourself. Do what I do. Go get a massage, and then treat yourself to a facial and a new hair style."

Since Charlotte had no desire to brave the heat, she decided to just keep working for the time being and hope that June didn't stay too much longer. She picked up the stack of sheets and her supply carrier and trudged up the stairs.

"Try out that new place that just opened on Magazine," she heard Mimi tell June. The women's voices faded, and June's reply was inaudible once Charlotte reached the second floor.

A few minutes later, Charlotte was smoothing down the comforter on the bed in the master bedroom when Mimi walked into the room. "I was beginning to think that June was never going to leave, poor thing. I hated to do it, but I finally had to tell her that I had plans for lunch."

The only thing that Charlotte could think to say was, "She seems like a nice lady."

"Oh, she is, and I love her dearly — we've been friends for almost ten years now — but June is one of those women who are never satisfied no matter what they have." Mimi waved a dismissing hand. "But never mind all that. I'm sure you must be starving by now. I know I am. Why don't you go ahead and take your lunch break? I need to get a quick shower, and then I have a luncheon date. But I'll be back before it's time for you to leave," she added.

Charlotte smiled. "I'll be in the kitchen if you need anything."

It was almost three-thirty on the dot when Mimi returned from her luncheon date. Charlotte was loading her vacuum cleaner and supply carrier into the back of the van when Mimi drove past her, waved, then turned the corner leading to her driveway. If nothing else, her new employer was punctual, Charlotte thought, as she slammed the door to the van. It was a trait that Charlotte admired and adhered to herself.

By the time Charlotte finished putting her things away, Mimi was already waiting for her in the kitchen. "Would you like to inspect everything before I leave?" Charlotte asked.

Mimi shook her head. "Heavens, no. I'm sure everything is just fine. But I would like to ask if you'd mind staying late on Friday. A group I belong to — the HHS — is meeting here Friday afternoon."

"Is that the Horticulture Heritage Society?"

Mimi smiled. "You've heard of it?"

Charlotte nodded. "It's a garden club that specializes in the propagation and preservation of heritage plants, isn't it? At least that's what the write-up in the *Picayune* said."

"Well it's good to know that someone actually read that article. And you're right. That's exactly what we do."

"I always try to attend the annual spring and fall charity sales each year," Charlotte said. "I've picked up some really nice plants in the past and always look forward to it." Charlotte laughed. "But then I should have guessed that you would be involved." She spread her hands out as if to encompass the house and grounds. "You have such beautiful landscaping and so many lovely plants inside and out."

Mimi beamed. "Why, thank you. I don't really like to brag about it, but I actually founded the HHS." She momentarily averted her eyes as if embarrassed by the admission. Then, she glanced back at Charlotte. "Guess that's what I just did, though, didn't I? Brag about it, I mean." She laughed and waved a dismissive hand. "Anyway, we're having a meeting on Friday afternoon. It starts at two, so do you think you'll be finished cleaning by then?"

"Shouldn't be a problem," Charlotte answered. "Today took a little longer because I waxed the floors, but I won't be waxing every week."

"Good. I really could use some help during the meeting. We're electing officers, but we also have to decide on a charity to sponsor for our fall event." She paused, her brow wrinkled, and then she said, "I have to confess that I'm a bit nervous about this particular meeting. For the first time in the almost ten years that I've been president, there's actually someone running against me." Her expression turned fierce. "I still can't believe it. And after all the time and money I've spent." She shook her head and sighed. "In any case, I've got a really bad feeling that I'm going to need all the help and support that I can get."

Chapter 3

Fifteen women showed up for the HHS meeting at Mimi's house on Friday afternoon. Charlotte knew there were fifteen because, at Mimi's request, she'd been instructed to greet each one of them at the door and escort them to the front parlor.

With the arrival of each member, it quickly became obvious that the women had been there before and already knew their way to the parlor. Greeting Mimi's guests at the front door was one thing, but personally escorting each one into the parlor was an unnecessary and pretentious gesture at best, simply a way, Charlotte realized, for Mimi to show off her new maid.

By the time she had escorted the last two women into the parlor, her face ached from maintaining a smile, and the decibel level in the parlor had risen sharply.

The noise reminded Charlotte of a swarm of bees, each trying to outbuzz the other. Buzzing bees was a fitting description, she decided, as she placed cups and saucers on the buffet in the dining room for the refreshment break. After all, the HHS was an organization for the propagation and preservation of heritage plants, and bees helped propagate plants, didn't they?

Snickering at her private little joke, Charlotte checked the silver coffee urn, made a mental note that it could use a good cleaning and polishing, and then arranged the crystal wine glasses that she'd set out earlier on the buffet. Charlotte held up one of the delicate, paper-thin glasses to the light. The pattern of the crystal was one that she recognized as being very old and rare . . . and very expensive.

Carefully placing the wine glass back on the buffet, she frowned. Mimi had only set out one bottle of wine. One bottle wouldn't go very far. As she made a mental note to search the pantry for more, she turned to inspect the table one last time.

Like most of the other furnishings in the house, the buffet, the china cabinet, and the table and chairs were beautifully preserved antiques that fit the era in which the house was built.

An ivory-colored, intricately crocheted tablecloth covered the large, oblong table.

In the center of the table was a large vase overflowing with zinnias, marigolds, and salvias that Mimi had grown in her greenhouse and arranged herself that morning.

At one end of the table Charlotte had placed linen napkins, crystal dessert plates, and silver forks. At the other end she'd set out two small crystal bowls: one she'd filled with mixed nuts, and the other, mints. She'd purposely left both sides of the table clear for the trays of pastries she had yet to prepare.

Satisfied with the appearance of the table, Charlotte headed back to the kitchen. Though the voices in the parlor were somewhat muted, even in the kitchen she could still hear bits and pieces of the chatter.

On the cabinet countertop were several white boxes from Gambino's Bakery, filled with assorted pastries. Beside the boxes were four crystal platters.

Charlotte had just finished arranging the fourth platter when the sound of the back door opening gave her a start. With a puzzled frown, she turned to see June Bryant enter the kitchen. In June's arms was a bulky sack.

"Hi, Charlotte," June said. "Hope I didn't startle you."

"Just a little," Charlotte admitted, with a forced smile. "I guess I just assumed that the back door was locked."

June laughed and set the sack down on the table. "It probably should be, but Mimi rarely locks it when she's home." She pulled a bottle of wine out of the sack. "I was supposed to have brought these over earlier, but I've been running late all day long." She removed two more bottles. "I figured that the meeting would already be well under way by now, but judging by the noise, I guess they haven't gotten started yet."

June pointed at a drawer near the sink. "The corkscrew is in there," she said. "Just uncork these, if you don't mind, and put them on the buffet. The bottle of white wine should go in a wine bucket with ice. I think Mimi has one stored in the cabinet beneath the sink. I'd do it myself, but I'm sure that Mimi's probably having fits wondering where I am."

"I'll take care of it," Charlotte told her.

"Great! And thanks." June folded the sack, then shoved it into the trash can. "Now —" She dusted her hands and drew in a deep breath. "Guess I'd better get in there before Mimi has heart failure."

At least the wine problem was solved,

Charlotte thought, as she watched June hurry from the room. Charlotte stepped over to the drawer that June had pointed out, and, sure enough, there was a corkscrew inside, along with various serving implements.

"So what about the red wine?" she murmured. "I thought red wine was supposed to have time to breathe." At least that's what she'd heard. She inserted the corkscrew into the cork of the first bottle. When she'd twisted most of the cork out, she placed a dish towel over the top of the bottle and finished working the cork out with her fingers. A soft pop sounded, and Charlotte repeated the process on the second bottle. Charlotte was working on the cork of the third bottle when she heard a loud rapping sound in the parlor. The abrupt silence that followed was startling and a bit eerie after all of the noise.

Charlotte raised an eyebrow. Evidently, as June had indicated, Mimi *had* been waiting for her friend's arrival before calling the meeting to order.

With a shrug, Charlotte finished uncorking the last bottle and carried the two bottles of red wine into the dining room. As she placed them on the buffet, Mimi's commanding voice broke the silence in the parlor and carried into the dining room.

"The monthly meeting of HHS is now called to order, and since I don't see any visitors who need welcoming, we'll move on to the reading of the minutes and the financial report. I'd like a motion to dispense with both."

Charlotte heard June make the motion and another voice seconded it.

"Good," Mimi said. "Thank you. Our next order of business for the day is our presidential election. After the election we'll take a short refreshment break before tackling the rest of our business. Nominations for president of HHS are now open."

There were a few moments of complete silence, and then a crisp voice with a no-nonsense tone spoke up. "I nominate Rita Landers for president."

Almost immediately, a second, more vigorous voice chimed in. "I second the nomination."

As Charlotte headed back toward the kitchen, she heard June Bryant speak up. "I nominate Mimi Adams for president."

In the kitchen, Charlotte iced down the remaining bottle of wine in a silver wine bucket, and when she returned to the dining room with the wine and the first platter of pastries, Mimi was talking again.

"Are there any more nominations?" A short silence followed; then she continued. "Voting will be by secret ballot. Our vice president, June Bryant, is passing those out now. And since there are no more nominations, we'll vote. When you've finished marking your ballot, give it back to June and she'll count them."

A murmur of protest broke out. "That doesn't seem quite fair, Mimi." It was the same voice that had nominated the woman named Rita. "We all know that you and June are friends, and besides, she was the one who nominated you."

"Are you insinuating that I would cheat?" June challenged.

Personally, Charlotte thought that the woman had a valid point, so why on earth was June being so defensive? In spite of herself, Charlotte's curiosity overcame her common sense. With her ears tuned to the goings-on in the parlor, she made a show of straightening the forks on the table while she waited to hear how the woman would respond to June's question.

There was a slight hesitation before the woman finally answered June, and even to Charlotte's ears, she sounded embarrassed. "No, June," she said. "Of course I don't think you would cheat. Sorry . . ." Her voice trailed away.

Charlotte rolled her eyes. June's intimidation tactic had worked. The woman had given in. The woman might as well have said nothing at all if she hadn't been prepared to back it up. Instead, all the poor thing had done was humiliate herself. Too bad, Charlotte thought, as she headed back to the kitchen for the remaining platters of pastries.

A few minutes later, when Charlotte returned to the kitchen for the last platter, June was standing by the kitchen table. On the table were two stacks of small square pieces of paper.

"Just counting the ballots," June said absently, as she thumbed through the first stack. With a frown, she counted the same ballots again. Then, after only a moment's hesitation, she wrote something down on a notepad.

Charlotte picked up the last platter and carried it to the dining room. When she returned to the kitchen, June was tearing one of the ballots into little pieces. Startled by Charlotte's return, June glanced up with the look of someone who had been caught with her hand in the cookie jar. Then, with an expression of relief and a tight smile, she picked up her notepad and pen and walked over to the trash can. She dropped the pieces inside, and without a word, she marched out of the kitchen.

Once June had disappeared through the doorway, Charlotte tilted her head and stared at the trash can. There was only one reason why June would have torn up one of the ballots.

"Oh, for pity's sake," she muttered. Though she couldn't be certain, she was pretty sure that June had just rigged the election to make sure Mimi won. More than likely, she'd forged a ballot to take the place of the one she'd destroyed. Charlotte shook her head in disgust. Too bad the woman who had protested had been such a coward and hadn't stuck to her guns when she'd challenged June about counting the ballots.

Charlotte turned to stare at the dining room doorway. There was no good reason to return to the dining room since everything was ready and waiting for the ladies to take their refreshment break. "Nope," Charlotte muttered, "no reason at all." But then she didn't really need a reason, did she? Still, she hesitated.

Mind your own business.

Ignoring the voice of reason in her head, she grabbed a feather duster from her supply carrier and marched into the dining room. The moment she entered the room, she heard June's announcement of the voting results.

"The winner and new president of HHS is Mimi Adams."

"Who didn't know that?" Charlotte grumbled to herself in the dining room.

With June's announcement, a murmur of disbelief broke out in the parlor, then, above the chatter, a louder voice. "Ah, excuse me please. Excuse me." The noise died down. "I don't mean to sound like sour grapes," the woman said, "but I would like to know what the ballot count was."

Had to be the other candidate, Charlotte figured, as she brushed the feather duster along the edges of the buffet. Rita something or other was her name if she remembered right.

"Of course, Rita," June answered. "The vote was eight for you and nine for Mimi."

Charlotte winced. Even to her ears, June's tone dripped with condescension.

"It was a close vote," June continued. "But we all know that 'close only counts in horseshoes and hand grenades.' "

"Or when there's cheating going on," Rita shot back. "May I please see the ballots."

Rita's own condescending tone more than matched June's, and Charlotte could just imagine the hateful looks bouncing back and forth between the two women.

"Gladly," June retorted. "Here, count 'em yourself."

Several moments passed, and the parlor was so quiet that Charlotte fancied she could hear the rustling of the ballots being counted by Rita. For all the good it would do her, Charlotte thought. The fix was in. June had made sure of it.

"Well?" June demanded. "Are you satisfied now?"

"Not by a long shot," Rita snapped back. "Winning by only one vote is just a bit obvious, don't you think, especially when you went slinking off to the kitchen to count the votes all by yourself. Without any witnesses, I might add."

"Now you just hold on there," Mimi cried. "June would never —"

Rita interrupted with a shout. "No, Mimi, *you* hold on! Secret ballots are one thing, but this is carrying things too far. And anyone with any scruples at all would offer to let everyone vote again and count the votes in the presence of everyone — which is what should have been done to begin with."

The silence was deafening. Charlotte held her breath, waiting to see if Mimi would give in to Rita's demands. But Mimi didn't say a word, and after a moment it was Rita who finally spoke again. "That's it! I'm out of here. I don't like cheaters. Never have. And you know exactly what you can do with your election and your precious HHS," she added.

"Hey, Rita, wait for me," a voice called out. "I'm going with you."

"Me too," another voice chimed in.

"Me three," yet another voice spoke up.

Mere seconds later, the front door slammed so hard that the sound echoed throughout the house. There was a brief moment of dead silence, and then the room burst into an uproar.

Buzzing bees, thought Charlotte. *Angry* buzzing bees. But no, not bees. Bees were much too tame by comparison. It was more like Rita had stirred up the mother of all hornets' nests.

Several loud raps sounded. "Order, please," Mimi cried, but the women ignored her. "Ladies!" Mimi rapped sharply again and kept rapping until the chatter finally died to a low murmur. "I think that now would be a good time for our break," she said, her voice quivering with emotion.

"There's coffee, wine, and pastries in the dining room across the hallway. We'll reconvene in about twenty minutes."

Uh oh. Suddenly realizing that her presence in the dining room could be construed as eavesdropping, Charlotte tucked her feather duster beneath her arm and hurried back into the kitchen. She was bent over her supply carrier when Mimi entered the room only seconds later. Charlotte straightened. Mimi's face was pale, and she looked as if any minute she were going to burst into tears.

"Charlotte, I'm going upstairs for a few minutes," Mimi said, an edge of desperation in her voice. "Would you please make sure that everyone has what they need?" Without waiting for Charlotte's answer, she turned and fled the room.

Charlotte wanted to feel sorry for Mimi, and she did, but only up to a point. In Charlotte's opinion, Mimi had no one but herself to blame for the fiasco with Rita. She could have let the group vote again, as Rita had requested. That would have been the gracious thing to do, the fair thing. But she hadn't, and because she hadn't, and because of what June had done, Charlotte just couldn't sympathize as much as she would have under other circumstances.

With a sigh, Charlotte wandered into the dining room to check on things. Whether she agreed or disagreed with what Mimi and June had done didn't matter in the long run. What mattered right now was that Mimi was her employer, and she still had a job to finish.

Even with a dozen women milling around, the dining room was large enough that it wasn't overly crowded. Charlotte paused just inside the doorway and glanced around. She spotted June almost immediately standing near the buffet with a glass of wine in her hand. Looking as innocent as a newborn lamb, she was laughing and talking to a small group of women. Almost as soon as Charlotte saw June, June glanced up and saw Charlotte. June abruptly excused herself from the group and made a beeline for Charlotte.

When she reached Charlotte, she took her by the arm and pulled her just inside the kitchen. "Do you know where Mimi got off to?"

Charlotte didn't appreciate the accusatory tone in June's voice at all — a tone that insinuated that Mimi's disappearance was Charlotte's fault. She firmly pulled her arm from June's grasp and fought the urge to rub it, not from pain, but simply because she also didn't appreciate being manhandled by anyone, least of all someone who was almost a complete stranger. Using all the self-control she could muster, she said, "Mimi went upstairs for a few moments."

June's face wrinkled with concern. "Did she say why?"

"No, she didn't."

"Hmm, maybe I'd better go check on her, just to make sure she's okay." She narrowed her eyes. "I don't know how much of what went on in there you heard" — she waved toward the parlor — "but we had a little altercation with one of the members — a slight misunderstanding — and, well, the member got upset, and Mimi — poor thing — takes everything to heart."

A slight misunderstanding? First the woman manhandles her, and now she was insulting her intelligence. Charlotte felt her temper rise.

"Anyway," June continued, "I won't be gone but a moment, so just make sure everyone has what they need until I get back."

Yes, ma'am; no, ma'am; right away, ma'am. Or maybe she should just stand at attention and salute. Charlotte swallowed hard. June's intimidation tactics might work on some people, but she had another thing coming if she thought Charlotte was going to put up with it. Charlotte forced a tight little smile. "*Ms.* Bryant," she said, "I've already assured *Mimi* that I would take care of things. And I will," she added pointedly.

June gave her an odd look but nodded once. "Of course," she said, her tone chilly. Then, with a slight lift of her chin, she stuck her patrician nose in the air, turned, and hurried toward the doorway leading to the central hall.

As Charlotte watched June weave her way through the other women, she took several deep breaths in an attempt to calm her racing pulse. Good thing she didn't have trouble with high blood pressure.

After a moment, she felt a bit calmer. She returned to the dining room and busied herself with picking up the dirty dishes and tidying the table. All around her, conversations centered on Rita and continued as if Charlotte weren't even there. But, then, no one ever paid attention to the hired help. It was a fact that Charlotte had learned early on when she'd first started up Maid-for-a-Day, and it was the very reason she insisted that the women who worked for her adhered to her client confidentiality policy.

Once Charlotte had cleaned up as much as she could for the time being, she slipped into the kitchen. As she stood at the sink hand washing one of the crystal dessert plates, she tried to concentrate on what she was doing instead of the conversation between the two women standing just inside the dining room doorway. But ignoring what they were saying proved to be impossible, and she got an earful.

Chapter 4

Both of the women looked to be in their early forties, and each had a glass of wine. The taller of the two had a whiny, nasally voice and was the one who did most of the talking.

"It's a shame that there's such bad blood between Mimi and Rita," she said.

"Bad blood?"

"Has been for a while now."

Charlotte glanced over at the two in time to see the shorter woman wrinkle her brow. "How come? I thought Mimi and Gordon were really good friends with Rita and Don."

"They were, once upon a time, but not any more. I can't believe you haven't heard about it. Why, that was just an awful scandal."

"Scandal? What scandal?"

"Well, I'm not exactly sure, but I heard that Rita accused Mimi of having an affair with Don."

The shorter woman gasped, and Charlotte almost dropped the plate she was rinsing. She cleared her throat loudly, hoping that when the women realized she could hear everything they said, they would stop their gossiping.

"Why, that's just plain ridiculous," the shorter woman said.

So much for trying to be discreet, Charlotte thought.

"Mimi would never cheat on Gordon," the shorter woman continued. "And she certainly wouldn't cheat on him with the likes of that awful Don Landers."

"Well, you and I know that," the taller woman whined, "but, evidently, Rita thought differently."

Shades of Bitsy Duhe, Charlotte thought, as she tried again to tune out the women's malicious gossip session, but again it was no use. Whether she liked it or not, she was a captive audience.

"Anyway," the taller woman continued, "no matter how many times Mimi denied it, Rita just couldn't get past it. And we both know that Rita is not exactly the soul of discretion. She claimed that she'd caught 'em in the act."

"Nooo," the shorter woman drawled in a tone of utter disbelief.

"Oh, yeah," the other woman replied.

"But if she caught them doing it, then it must be true."

The taller woman shook her head. "Not hardly. Rita has been known to lie. Regardless, Rita, like a ninny, went and blabbed it to anyone and everyone who would listen."

"Aw, come on now. Why on earth would she do that? You'd think she'd be too humiliated to want anyone to know."

"I kid you not. That's exactly what she did, mostly, I suspect, to humiliate Mimi and cause her problems with Gordon. Of course, poor Mimi found out. But even worse, Gordon found out what Rita had done, and woe to anyone who upsets his Mimi. Suffice it to say, Rita's little scheme backfired. Gordon didn't believe any of her gossip, and since he couldn't get back at Rita directly, he got back at her through Don.

"Why, Don was Gordon's right-hand man," she continued. "But after Gordon heard what Rita had done, he made Don's life a living hell. First he fired him. Then he made sure that no other dealership in the city would touch him with a ten-foot pole." With a sigh, she added, "Needless to say, the two couples aren't friends any more, and ever since, Rita has had it in for

Mimi. And you can mark my words, that's the only reason that Rita wanted to be HHS president to begin with. Just her little way of getting back at Mimi."

The shorter woman shook her head. "Poor Don. That's just awful."

Charlotte washed the last of the dirty dessert plates and rinsed it. In her opinion, *Awful* was too tame a word. More like cruel and downright nasty.

"But what on earth made Rita think that she could win against Mimi in the first place," the shorter woman continued, "especially after all that Mimi's done for HHS over the years?"

The other woman shrugged. "Who knows," she said, as she swirled what was left of the wine in her glass. "But I'm here to tell you, you can bet your prize roses that's not the end of it. No siree, not by a long shot."

"Why would you say something like that?"

The taller woman glanced around the room, then leaned closer to her friend and lowered her voice. "I overheard Doreen Mires tell Karen Douglas that if Rita didn't win, Rita and some of her cohorts were going to quit and form their own garden club."

"Shh, the others might hear you," said the shorter woman, as she glanced around, but the taller woman waved away her concerns.

"They're probably in the parlor," she said.

The shorter woman frowned. "So how come Doreen and Karen know so much?"

The taller woman shrugged. "Maybe they're in on it. Maybe they've hooked up with Rita."

"But if I recall correctly, don't Doreen's and Karen's husbands work for Gordon too?"

The taller woman nodded. "Yep, they each manage one of his dealerships."

"Well, if what you said about what Gordon did to Don is true, then Karen and Doreen had better watch their step if they know what's good for them. I know I would."

"You're right about that," the other woman agreed. "If Gordon thought for an instant that Doreen and Karen were in cahoots with Rita or had turned on Mimi, he'd do the same to their husbands as he did to Don in a New York minute. Why, I heard —"

"Hey, you two." Another woman approached the two gossips, and they both plastered fake smiles on their faces. "I think our twenty minutes are up," she said. "Everyone is heading back to the parlor."

To Charlotte's relief, the two gossips followed the other woman, and within moments, the rest of the women in the dining room wandered back to the parlor.

In the kitchen, Charlotte stood at the sink and stared at the dirty wine glasses stacked on top of the cabinet. Had what she'd just overheard been vicious gossip, or was it true? If it were true, then what she'd heard had been a far different picture of Gordon Adams than the one that June had painted in her conversation with Mimi on Monday. According to June, Mimi's husband was the salt of the earth — generous, loving, and protective. But if the gossip were true, then Gordon Adams was a ruthless, vindictive man, a man who shouldn't be crossed.

And what about Mimi? Was Mimi just an innocent victim, a woman who was the object of another woman's unfounded jealousy, a woman in need of the protection of her powerful husband?

Charlotte thought back to the first day she'd met Mimi . . . the dead trees . . . the stinky flowers she'd been planting to get back at her neighbor . . . Charlotte shook her head. Hard to imagine that the woman she'd met that day needed anybody to protect her. So which was the real Mimi, and which was the real Gordon?

Who knows and who cares. Just mind your own business, do your job, and for Pete's sake, stop wasting time.

"Okay, okay, enough already," Charlotte muttered in response to the voice of reason in her head.

A minute later, the now familiar rapping sound of Mimi's gavel echoed from the parlor. Evidently, she had finally rejoined the group and was calling the meeting back to order.

"Thank goodness," Charlotte whispered. She glanced at her watch and wondered how much longer the rest of the meeting would take. As far as she was concerned, the sooner it was over, the better. She rubbed her lower back and grimaced. For one thing, she was tired, and being on her feet for the past hour without a break had made the dull ache in her back grow more painful. Visions of a nice long soak in a hot tub of water danced through her head.

"So get busy," she told herself. If she could get the dining room and kitchen cleaned up now, once the meeting was over, straightening the parlor should only take a few minutes. Then she could finally go home.

The water in the sink had grown cold, so Charlotte drained the sink, refilled it with hot sudsy water, and placed the dirty wine glasses in to soak. Then, she headed for the dining room to collect the remaining dishes.

Since she'd already cleared out most of the plates and platters, all that were left were a few coffee cups and saucers. Clearing off the buffet was her first priority, and as she stacked the cups and saucers that hadn't been used back into the china cabinet, she heard Mimi announce that the group needed to decide on which charity would be the recipient of the proceeds from the upcoming fall plant sale.

"I think that new women's shelter in the warehouse district would be a good place to sponsor," one woman said. "It's a worthy cause and would gain HHS a lot of respect in the community, not to mention a lot of publicity."

"I agree with Doreen," another voice chimed in. "It's only been open for a couple of weeks, and I heard that it's almost full already."

"That's certainly a worthy project, Karen," Mimi said, "but I had another project in mind. The renovations on the old Hebert plantation upriver near Luling are just about finished, and since our group's function is the preservation of heritage plants, I was hoping that the money we raise could be used to help with the landscaping. We could also donate some of the plants that are needed." Mimi paused, then continued, "If there aren't any other projects you all want to consider, then I'll open up the discussion for the two that have been proposed."

Charlotte only caught bits and pieces of the discussion that followed as she moved between the kitchen and the dining room, but what she did hear was heated and fraught with tension. If nothing else, the women were passionate about their convictions. And they were divided right down the middle, with one faction supporting Mimi's plantation project, and one supporting Doreen and Karen's women's shelter.

Charlotte was polishing the buffet in the dining room when Mimi called for a vote. "We'll vote by a show of hands," she told the group.

In the dining room, Charlotte nodded her approval as she removed the crocheted tablecloth. *Live and learn. No secret ballots this time.*

"Okay, then," she heard Mimi say, "it's agreed that the Hebert plantation will be the beneficiary of our annual fall sale."

"Ah, excuse me, Mimi." Charlotte recognized the voice as that of the woman who had suggested the women's shelter. If she remembered right, the woman's name was Doreen.

"Karen and I have an appointment and are going to have to leave."

"But, Doreen, we still have a lot of planning left," Mimi argued.

"That may be, but I'm sure that you all can finish planning everything just fine without us."

"But —"

"Are you coming, Karen?" Doreen asked pointedly.

"You betcha," Karen answered. "I've had just about as much of this as I can stand for one day."

Either play the game my way, or I'll just take my ball and go home. In the dining room, Charlotte shook her head as she recapped the lemon oil and placed it back into her supply carrier. These women are unreal, she thought. Just like a bunch of children.

The moment the front door closed, the bees in the parlor began buzzing with a vengeance. Then the rapping of Mimi's gavel started.

"Ladies," Mimi cried. "Ladies, please come to order."

With another shake of her head, Charlotte headed for the kitchen to wash and dry the last of the wine glasses. Once that was done and she had put them away, the only chores left were washing the coffee urn and cleaning the parlor.

Once again she noted that the silver urn needed polishing, but that would be a job for another day, she decided. For today, a good washing would have to suffice.

She glanced toward the direction of the parlor. Maybe she could go ahead and get started on the parlor even though the women were still meeting. If nothing else, she could pick up any cups and saucers and wine glasses that might be in there.

Should she or shouldn't she? she wondered, but as she reached for the coffee urn, a sudden, unexpected wave of weakness came over her, and she gripped the edge of the sink instead.

Low blood sugar. She grimaced. It wasn't the first time she'd experienced the feeling, and she immediately recognized it for what it was. Being a borderline diabetic wasn't a problem most of the time as long as she took her little pill each day and stuck to her diet. But sometimes, like now, for whatever reason, her glucose level would plummet, leaving her shaky and weak.

Charlotte sighed. She'd learned to keep a supply of glucose tablets handy for just such rare occasions, but naturally, she was out. She had intended to get some — she really had — but never got around to it.

"So much for cleaning the parlor," she muttered. Besides, Mimi might not appreciate the interruption while the meeting was still in progress. What she needed at the moment was a jolt of sugar and a few minutes to recover. Maybe now would be a good time for a break.

Charlotte eyed the coffee urn again. More than likely a bit of caffeine with a half teaspoon of sugar would give her what she needed. And there was probably just enough left in the urn for a cup. Charlotte poured the coffee into a cup and spooned in a bit of sugar, then seated herself at the kitchen table. As she sipped the coffee, she noted that at least the pain in her back had eased to a dull throb.

Low blood sugar, backaches . . . "You're turning into a sickly old woman," she complained, as she took a few more sips of coffee.

Charlotte had just finished her coffee and was feeling somewhat better when she heard a commotion in the hallway. Maybe the meeting was finally over, she thought. If it was over, she figured that by the time she washed the coffee urn, the women should be cleared out of the parlor. And once she straightened the parlor, she could finally go home.

When Charlotte entered the parlor, only Mimi and June were left. Mimi, looking a bit tired and drawn, had slipped off her shoes and was sitting on the sofa with her feet propped up on the coffee table. In her lap was a spiral notebook and pen. June was sitting in a winged-back chair adjacent to the sofa.

With a brief glance around the room, Charlotte surveyed the damage. There were a few wine glasses and cups and saucers that needed clearing away, and once she returned the extra chairs to the dining room, the only thing left to do would be to vacuum.

Other than a brief smile and nod to acknowledge Charlotte's presence, Mimi's attention was on the notebook in her lap. "I had hoped to finish up today," Mimi told June. "But what with all of the mess going on, there was just no way."

"We still have a couple of weeks," June offered. "And hopefully everyone will show up on Monday again."

Mimi frowned. "That reminds me." She glanced over at Charlotte. "I'll need you to stay late again on Monday, Charlotte. Is that going to be a problem for you?"

"I'll have to check my calendar," Charlotte told her, "but it shouldn't be a problem."

June leaned forward. "Ah, Mimi, I hate to bring this up, but . . ."

"But what?"

"It's about Rita."

Mimi groaned. "Do you have to? I'm so sick of that woman I could scream."

"Me too," June agreed. "And you know I wouldn't even mention her name if I didn't think it was important."

Charlotte began gathering the cups and saucers and wine glasses. Maybe June was going to confess to rigging the election, and if she did confess, then that would mean that Mimi wasn't in on the fix.

"Okay, okay," Mimi said. "Let's have it and get it over with."

"First of all, I heard some talk that she's forming her own garden club."

Mimi shrugged. "More power to her, but I doubt if she can dig up any members —

any who have money, that is. She simply doesn't have the right social connections."

"Don't be so blind, Mimi. She already has nearly half the members of HHS for a following — the vote count proved that. And I suspect that half includes Karen and Doreen. But neither has committed herself yet, at least not openly. They're both afraid of what Gordon might do if he finds out."

"I've halfway suspected as much about those two all along," Mimi replied. "But they had better watch their step. If I find out for sure that they're in cahoots with Rita — or I should say, if Gordon finds out — then their husbands could find themselves standing in the unemployment lines along with Don Landers. That woman has caused us enough misery and embarrassment already, and I won't have her infecting anyone else with her lies."

"Ah, speaking of lies." June grimaced. "That brings me to the other thing I wanted to discuss. You heard that pointed remark she made about cheaters?"

Charlotte's ears perked up, and no matter how many times she told herself to go about her business and ignore the two women, her curiosity got the best of her. Glancing at the tray full of dirty dishes, she began rearranging them. Only so they would be balanced evenly, she told herself, and not just because she wanted to hear Mimi's response.

Mimi sighed deeply. "Yeah, I heard it, and you and I both know she meant more than just the election."

"Exactly," June agreed. "And so did everyone else. I hate to be the bearer of bad tidings, but she's still spreading those awful rumors about you and Don. I heard that she swore she'd seen the two of you together just last week."

"Oh, pu-lease," Mimi groaned. "The woman is obviously a nut case. Anyone with a brain can see that. And she's jealous," she added. "She's so jealous that she can't see straight." She shook her head. "Don is a nice enough man, and I had considered him a friend once upon a time, but that was before Rita became obsessed with the idea that he and I were having an affair. Why, the woman would have to be crazy to think that I'd risk everything I have with Gordon for someone like Don."

So much for a confession from June about the votes, Charlotte thought, as she picked up the tray and headed for the kitchen. But maybe June didn't need to confess. Maybe Mimi had known about the fix all along.

Judge not lest ye be judged, so just stop it, Charlotte.

Once in the kitchen, Charlotte unloaded the tray and washed and dried the remaining glasses, cups, and saucers. She was putting the last wine glass away in the china cabinet when Mimi entered the dining room, a check in her hand.

"All that's left is to vacuum the rug in the parlor," Charlotte told her. "Then I'll be leaving." She closed the door to the china cabinet and faced Mimi.

Mimi shook her head and waved a dismissing hand. "That's okay. Don't bother vacuuming. The rug is fine. Besides, it's getting late." She handed Charlotte the check. "I included a little extra for all of your help today."

Charlotte smiled. "Thank you."

Mimi nodded. "You earned it, and don't forget, I need you to stay late on Monday again. We've still got some details to iron out about the fall charity sale."

"See you Monday then," Charlotte said, and within minutes, she had gathered her supply carrier and vacuum from the kitchen and was headed out the door.

All day the van had been baking in the heat. When Charlotte opened the back door of the vehicle to load her supplies, the heat inside hit her like a blast from a furnace.

Any other time, Charlotte would have opened all of the doors to release some of the heat before getting inside, but she was so thoroughly disgusted by all that she'd heard and witnessed the past two hours that all she could think of was getting home.

At home she could forget about Mimi, June, Rita, and HHS. At home she could take a shower and relax and savor the peace and quiet.

Chapter 5

The weekend had passed much too fast, Charlotte decided, as she knocked on the Adamses' front door on Monday morning.

Saturday had been filled with her own household chores, as well as making out the payroll for Maid-for-a-Day and recording receipts. She'd attended church services and the weekly family lunch afterward on Sunday. And thanks to spicy jambalaya at lunch, she'd battled indigestion all night.

Charlotte heard the click of the deadbolt lock. With a sigh of weariness and hoping that she looked better than she felt, she stiffened her back, squared her shoulders, and forced a smile of greeting.

When the door swung open, Charlotte was shocked at Mimi's appearance. She was still wearing a nightgown and robe, her face was bare of makeup, dark circles ringed her bloodshot eyes, and her hair looked as if she'd just crawled out of bed. Was she ill?

Mimi nodded a greeting, stepped aside, and motioned for Charlotte to come in. "I'm afraid you have your work cut out for you today," she said. "The house is a wreck." She closed the door and locked it. "My son and daughter both decided to come home this weekend," she explained. She turned and walked down the hallway toward the kitchen, and Charlotte followed. "June just got here," Mimi said over her shoulder. "We're having tea in the kitchen."

"I'll start in the dining room and parlor then," Charlotte offered.

Mimi shrugged. "Whatever."

"Ah, Mimi, excuse me, but are you feeling okay?"

Mimi paused and faced Charlotte. "Just tired," she said, "but thanks for your concern."

Charlotte's normal routine for cleaning a room was to begin at the top and work her way down. In the dining room that meant first dusting the elaborate crystal and brass chandelier and the padded cornice boards over the tops of the windows. Whether she liked it or not, though, because the dining room was next to the kitchen, she was going to be privy to the conversation going on in there.

Charlotte slipped off her shoes, and armed with her feather duster, she climbed onto one of the dining room chairs near the chandelier.

"Okay, Mimi, what's wrong?" she heard June ask.

"I really don't want to talk about it," Mimi responded, her tone lackluster.

"Well, something's wrong. You've been moping around since I got here. Is it Emma or Justin? Are they okay?"

"Emma and Justin are just fine."

"Then it must be Gordon. That's it, isn't it? I can tell by that look on your face. Something's going on with Gordon. Oh, dear. Don't cry. Here — here's a tissue."

"S-sorry," Mimi stammered, "but I really don't want to talk about it."

"Talk about what? Come on now. Sometimes talking helps."

"It's just that-that I still can't believe it myself."

"Believe what?"

"I think Gordon is having an affair."

"Uh-uh, no way," June argued. "Not Gordon."

In the dining room, Charlotte froze. *Another* affair? What in the devil was wrong with all these people? First June's husband

76

was supposedly having an affair; then Rita thought Mimi was having an affair with her husband, Don; and now Mimi thinks her husband is having an affair.

"Yes, way," Mimi declared tearfully. "He's been coming home later and later each night, and he's never in his office anymore. And-and I found lipstick on his shirt collar."

"But I'm sure there's a perfectly good explanation for all of that."

"Yeah, and Rita is her name."

Charlotte almost fell off the dining room chair with shock. These people needed some serious counseling, she decided, as she climbed down. The longer she thought about the counseling idea, the funnier it became, and in spite of herself, she felt a fit of silly giggles coming on. Group therapy. That's what they needed. She snorted, then clapped her hand over her mouth and prayed that neither Mimi nor June had heard her.

To give June credit, she protested, "Aw, come on, Mimi. That's ridiculous. Gordon wouldn't do such a thing, not with Rita of all people."

"Why not? What better way for Rita to get back at me for the so-called affair I had with Don?"

"Nope, I don't believe it, not for a moment. For one thing, you're not giving Gordon enough credit here. He's got better taste in women than someone like Rita. You're just still upset over what happened on Friday."

Charlotte couldn't take it any longer. The whole mess was pathetic and sordid, not really funny at all, but she couldn't seem to help herself. And if she didn't do something fast, she was going to make a fool of herself and get fired to boot. Grabbing her supply carrier, she fled to the parlor.

A few minutes later, Charlotte heard the back door shut; then she caught a glimpse of Mimi on the staircase.

"I'm going to my room, Charlotte," she called out, "and I don't want to be disturbed."

To Charlotte's dismay, Mimi stayed holed up in her bedroom for the rest of the morning. Charlotte had cleaned all of the rooms downstairs and upstairs, all except the master bedroom. She'd hoped to clean it as well before lunch, but since Mimi was still in the room, Charlotte decided that she might as well eat lunch a bit early. She only hoped that Mimi would come out in time for her to clean the room before she had to begin preparing for the HHS meeting that afternoon.

Charlotte was sitting at the kitchen table eating the last few bites of the salad she'd brought from home when Mimi finally came downstairs. The change in Mimi's appearance from earlier was astounding. Charlotte knew she was gawking, but she couldn't seem to help it.

Mimi had swept her dark hair up and back into a French twist, a style that showed off her high cheekbones. Makeup had made the dark circles beneath her eyes disappear, and she was wearing a figure-hugging dress that only someone with her tall slim figure could get away with wearing.

"Clean up pretty good, don't I?" Mimi quipped, with an amused expression. "A little makeup, the right hair style, and the right dress can do wonders."

Still amazed at the transformation, Charlotte finally managed to say, "You look stunning."

"Thank you." Mimi glanced around the kitchen, her gaze pausing when she spied the brownies that Charlotte had arranged on one of the crystal platters and covered with Saran Wrap. "I see you found the brownies that June brought over this morning."

"I didn't see anything else, so I figured they had to be for your meeting this afternoon."

Mimi nodded. "Yes, they are, and they're homemade. It was June's turn to furnish refreshments, and she wanted to try out a new recipe. That's why she was here so early." Mimi's forehead wrinkled in a frown. "She made me taste test one. Did you try one?"

Charlotte shook her head that she hadn't. She'd been tempted, though. The brownies had looked and smelled wonderful, and next to pecan pralines, fudge brownies were her favorite sweet. But she'd resisted.

Mimi grimaced. "I didn't want to hurt June's feelings, but between you and me, the one I ate didn't taste all that good, a bit too much chocolate maybe. But then I'm not exactly a chocolate lover either." She glanced at Charlotte's salad. "If you're finished with your lunch, I'd like your opinion."

Charlotte's mouth watered. "I'm a borderline diabetic," she said. "I really shouldn't." She paused as her better judgment warred with her salivating taste buds.

"But maybe just one little bite wouldn't hurt, though."

Mimi grinned knowingly. Slipping one of the brownies from beneath the plastic wrap, she pinched off part of it and handed it to Charlotte. Charlotte popped the piece into her mouth.

"Well?" Mimi asked, a moment later. "What do you think?"

"I think I should have the rest of that." Charlotte pointed at the partial brownie still in Mimi's hand. "Wouldn't want it to go to waste now, would we?"

Mimi laughed and handed Charlotte the rest of the brownie. "Guess my taste buds were off," she said. "And speaking of food, I'm going to be late if I don't get a move on." She grinned. "Gordon called and wants me to meet him for lunch. It's so rare that he —" She waved a dismissing hand. "Never mind. The HHS meeting doesn't start until two, so I should be back in plenty of time." She motioned toward the dining room. "Just set everything up like you did on Friday."

"Enjoy your lunch," Charlotte told her. So that's why Mimi had undergone such a drastic change from earlier that morning, she thought, as she watched the younger woman head for the back door. All it had taken was a bit of attention from her husband.

How sad, Charlotte thought. Then, she shook her head and sighed. Time to get to work.

When Mimi returned from her luncheon appointment, it was almost one-thirty, and Charlotte was placing the last of the wine glasses on the buffet.

"Everything looks lovely, Charlotte," Mimi said.

Charlotte smiled. "Thanks. One thing, though. I'm not sure you have enough wine. I only found a couple of bottles in the pantry."

Mimi groaned and rolled her eyes. "I knew there was something that I'd forgotten. I think it was either Rita or Karen's turn to furnish the wine, but after Friday, it's not likely that either of them will show. I meant to pick some up on my way back from lunch." Her expression grew thoughtful; then she shrugged. "Oh, well, too bad and too late. Just make sure there's plenty of coffee."

The sound of the door knocker echoed throughout the house, startling both women. Mimi frowned and glanced at her watch. "No one's ever this early."

Assuming that she would have door duty again, Charlotte took a step toward the door leading to the hallway, but Mimi waved her off. "I'll get it," she said.

A moment later, Charlotte heard the front door open, then Mimi exclaiming, "Rita! Karen? Doreen?"

Rita laughed. "Don't look so surprised. We come in peace. And we've come to apologize. Here —"

"What's this?" Mimi asked.

"It's a peace offering, if you'll accept it, a Mauro 1998. The clerk at Martin's Wine Cellar assured me that it's your favorite. And we've brought a couple more bottles of the plain stuff for the meeting."

"Well, ah . . . I-I don't know quite what to say," Mimi stammered.

"Well, I say we pop the cork and have a glass, that is, if you'll forgive us. We all acted like a bunch of selfish children and we are truly sorry. So — can we let bygones be bygones? Will you forgive us?"

After what Mimi had told June about Rita that morning and after all of the commotion the women had caused on Friday, Charlotte expected Mimi to tell the three women to take a flying leap. Charlotte did notice that Mimi took her time giving an answer, but after several long, silent moments passed, she finally said, "Why don't y'all come on back to the kitchen, and I'll get Charlotte to bring us some glasses. That way, if anyone else shows up early, we won't be disturbed."

There was a clatter of footsteps in the hallway; then Mimi poked her head in the dining room. "Would you please bring four wine glasses to the kitchen, Charlotte? And if anyone else shows up early, just escort them into the parlor."

Charlotte figured she had ten, maybe fifteen minutes before the HHS members began arriving, just enough time to change the sheets on Emma's and Justin's beds. She quickly stripped Emma's bed first, and just as she finished stripping Justin's bed, she heard the muted raps of the door knocker downstairs. *Great. Someone else is early too.*

Bundling up the sheets and pillowcases, she dumped them into the laundry basket that she'd left at the top of the stairs, then hurried down to answer the door.

Before the next group arrived, Charlotte had just enough time to retrieve the laundry basket and put the linens in to wash. Then, for the next fifteen minutes or so, she spent the time answering the door.

With each additional arrival, the noise level rose.

Buzzing bees. The thought made Charlotte grin as she guided what she figured had to be the last of the HHS members into the parlor, then made sure they had a seat. When she turned to leave, Mimi, followed by Rita, Doreen, and Karen, entered the room.

Reasonably sure that most of the members except June had arrived, Charlotte eased out of the parlor, then dashed back to the laundry room to switch the linens from the washing machine into the dryer. She figured that if she timed it just right, she could have clean sheets on the stripped beds before the refreshment break or, at the very latest, before the meeting adjourned.

After putting the linens in to dry, she headed back toward the kitchen.

When Charlotte entered the kitchen, she caught sight of Rita, just before she disappeared around the hall doorway. Thinking that Rita must have come back to retrieve something she'd left earlier, Charlotte walked over to the sink to rinse her hands. As she reached for the hot-water spigot, her hand froze in midair. Sitting in the dish drainer on top of the cabinet were the four wine glasses that the women had used, four *sparkling clean* wine glasses.

Charlotte frowned. Had Rita returned to the kitchen just to wash up the wine glasses? Surely not, especially since she knew good and well that there was a maid on the premises. But then again, maybe she had; maybe she was trying to be helpful, yet another apologetic gesture.

With an oh-well shrug, Charlotte rinsed her hands and dried them. As she gathered up the wine glasses to return them to the buffet in the dining room and contemplated what to do with the half-empty wine bottle that Mimi had left on the cabinet, she heard the back door open and then close. She turned just in time to see June enter.

"It's just me," June said and laughed as she hurried through the kitchen. "As usual, I'm late," she called over her shoulder.

Didn't the woman ever use the front door? Charlotte wondered.

Charlotte decided against adding the wine that Rita had brought to the other three bottles on the buffet. Rita had said it was Mimi's favorite, so Charlotte figured Mimi would want to save it for herself.

In the dining room, as Charlotte placed

the glasses on the buffet, she heard the sharp rap of Mimi's gavel in the parlor.

"The meeting is now called to order." She banged it again. "Ladies, please, we have a lot of business to take care of today."

When the buzzing died down, Mimi said, "Yes, Rita? Did you want to say something?"

"First, I'd like to apologize to the members for my outburst on Friday. I really have no good excuse, and I *am* sorry." A low murmur broke out, then Rita said, "And, second, I want to make a motion that we have more discussion about the charity that will benefit from the funds we raise at our annual fall sale." The murmurs grew louder.

"And I second the motion," a voice chimed in.

The buzz grew, and Mimi rapped her gavel. "But-but, we've already decided that issue," she cried. The room abruptly grew quiet.

"In that case," Rita said, "I make a motion that we donate the proceeds of the plant sale to the new women's shelter instead of the Hebert plantation."

"And I second the motion." The voice belonged to Karen.

"All in favor?" Rita asked. "One, two, three . . ." Charlotte could hear Rita counting the votes out loud. "Ten for and six against," Rita said. "The women's shelter wins."

Charlotte shook her head and rolled her eyes. "Talk about your Judas," she whispered. *Beware of a Greek bearing gifts.* With another shake of her head, she decided that now would be a good time to check on the linens in the dryer.

In the laundry room, Charlotte folded the sheets and pillowcases as she took them out of the dryer. She could tell from the noise that the women were taking their refreshment break. She placed the items in the laundry basket, picked up the basket, and carried it into the kitchen.

When she entered the kitchen, she was surprised to see Mimi standing by the sink, one hand gripping the edge of the cabinet, the other hand holding a full glass of water.

"Are you looking for me?" Charlotte asked.

With one hand still gripping the cabinet, Mimi turned to face her and shook her head. "Just thirsty."

One look at Mimi's pale face and dilated pupils set off alarm bells, and Charlotte immediately dropped the laundry basket and rushed over to her. "Are you okay?"

Mimi shook her head again and blinked several times. "Don't-don't feel so good," she said. "My head's killing me — maybe a virus or something. Could you get me the aspirin? It's in that cabinet by the refrigerator."

"Maybe you should cut the meeting short, either that or let someone else take over for you."

Mimi shook her head. "Can't — still too much to do. Just get me the aspirin."

Seconds later, aspirin bottle in hand, Charlotte asked, "How many?" She twisted off the cap.

"Two — no, make that three."

Charlotte shook two out of the bottle, then paused. "Are you sure you want three?"

Mimi glared at her. "I said three, didn't I? Why would I say three if I didn't mean three? Just give 'em to me."

"Okay, okay." Charlotte shook out a third aspirin. "Here."

Mimi snatched up the tablets, popped them into her mouth, and washed them down with the water. When the glass was empty, she refilled it with more water, and drank all of the second glass as well.

"Mimi?" June entered the kitchen. "I've been looking for you," she said.

Mimi slammed the empty glass down on the cabinet and glared at June. "Well, you found me. What do you want?"

June cast a sideways glance at Charlotte, then focused on Mimi again. "Are you okay?"

"Okay! Okay?" Mimi's voice rose. "Now just why wouldn't I be okay? I've just been blindsided, outmaneuvered, and stabbed in the back." She waved in the general direction of the parlor. "Thanks to Rita, Karen, and Doreen, I'm just hunky-dory. With friends like those three, I don't need enemies. That's for sure."

"Hey, just calm down, now."

"I'll calm down alright, but mark my words. Those three are history, and they're going to live to regret this day — that's a promise."

Charlotte was straightening the dining room when the meeting finally broke up. She waited a few minutes to give the women time to clear out, then proceeded to the parlor. As she passed through the main hallway, she saw Mimi at the front door, and standing with her was Doreen Mires.

From the glimpse she got, Charlotte thought Mimi looked even more ill than she had earlier in the kitchen. As Charlotte gathered the cups and saucers in the parlor, she heard Doreen tell Mimi, "I'm so sorry for what happened. I had nothing to do with what Rita and Karen did in there."

When Mimi said nothing in response, Doreen continued, her tone growing more fearful and desperate with each word. "I-I don't know how to say this, but please-please don't hold what happened against George — not because of me. We can't afford for him to lose his job, and I swear I didn't agree to be a part of any of that stuff."

"Yeah, right, Doreen," Mimi retorted. "If that's true, then why did you volunteer with them to head up one of the committees?"

"I-I — I'll quit," Doreen cried. "I'll resign the committee and quit HHS if that's what it takes."

"That's up to you, but —" Mimi suddenly closed her eyes and groaned.

"Are you okay?"

Mimi shook her head. "No, no I'm not, and I can't discuss this right now. I'm sick. We'll have to talk later."

When Charlotte heard the click of the front door, she picked up the tray of dirty dishes. As she stepped into the hallway, Mimi's hand was still on the doorknob, her forehead resting against the door casing, and she heard her mumble something that sounded like, "Traitors. Two-faced traitors."

Then, with a dejected sigh, Mimi squared her shoulders and turned. When she saw Charlotte, she stiffened. "I-I'm going to bed," she said, her voice fragile and shaky. "When you've finished, just let yourself out."

"Do you need any help — up the stairs, I mean?"

Even though she shook her head that she didn't, Charlotte waited and kept an eye on her, just in case. Once she was sure that Mimi had safely negotiated the stairs, she took the tray into the kitchen.

Charlotte had just finished unloading the tray of dishes into the sink when the clatter of the door knocker sounded. "Now what?" she grumbled, but before she'd even taken two steps, she heard the sound of the front door opening and closing. Since she couldn't remember if Mimi had locked the front door after Doreen had left, her sense of caution made her pause.

"Hel-lo!" a voice called out. "Mimi?"

Rita. What on earth did Rita want now? Charlotte released her pent-up breath, scowled, then hurried to intercept Rita. Rita had already advanced as far as the foot of the staircase by the time Charlotte reached her.

"Where's Mimi?" Rita demanded.

"She's upstairs," Charlotte answered.

Rita glanced up the staircase, made a face, then waved an impatient hand. "Never mind. No need to bother her. I only came back because I think I left my rings on the window ledge above the sink."

Charlotte shook her head. "I don't recall seeing any rings."

"Well, I'm positive that I left them there," Rita retorted, and completely ignoring Charlotte, she marched past her, her heels clicking loudly on the hardwood floors.

Charlotte turned and glared at Rita's back until she disappeared through the kitchen doorway. Not only was the woman a back stabber, but she was rude and insulting as well. With a sigh of disgust, Charlotte trudged toward the kitchen.

Charlotte stepped through the doorway just in time to see Rita grab a wine bottle off the countertop and shove it into her tote bag.

When Rita glanced up and realized that Charlotte had seen what she'd done, she said, "I was mistaken about the rings."

Charlotte chose to remain silent, and Rita shifted her gaze from Charlotte to her tote bag, then back to Charlotte. "Guess you're wondering about the wine." She patted her tote bag. When Charlotte said nothing, Rita shrugged and laughed, but it was a forced, nervous sound. "It's not as if I'm stealing it or anything. I figured that after what happened today, Mimi would probably just throw it in the garbage. Why let good wine go to waste?"

The unmitigated gall of some people never ceased to amaze Charlotte, and she decided that Rita had enough for ten people. Before Charlotte could think of a response, Rita sashayed past her and disappeared through the doorway. Charlotte could hear her heels clicking all the way down the hallway.

When the front door snapped shut, Charlotte stepped out into the hallway, just to make sure Rita was truly gone. Satisfied that she was, Charlotte went to the door and secured the dead bolt, then hurried through the remaining chores.

Once Charlotte had finished cleaning, she decided to check on Mimi before leaving. She found Mimi still fully dressed and curled tightly into a fetal position on top of the bed covers in the master bedroom. Her breathing was deep and even, but to Charlotte, she still looked pale, and she looked cold. Charlotte stepped over to the bed and pulled the bottom side of the bed comforter over Mimi's shoulder, then tiptoed out of the room.

Charlotte descended the stairs and checked to make sure that the back door was locked. Then, armed with her supply carrier and vacuum cleaner, she walked back through the house to the front door. With one last, worried glance toward the staircase, she unlocked the dead bolt and then twisted the doorknob lock and stepped outside. As she reached to pull the door shut, she hesitated.

She was tired and ready to go home, but what if Mimi got worse? There would be no one to check on her, not for a while anyway, at least not until her husband got home.

He's been coming home later and later each night. Mimi's complaint popped into Charlotte's head. Maybe if he knew his wife was ill, he might try to get home earlier. Then again, maybe not. If what Mimi suspected were true — that he was having an affair — he might not even care that his wife was ill. And Mimi might not bother to call him.

Charlotte narrowed her eyes and glared at the doorknob. What if she called him? If someone other than his wife called him, for appearance's sake, he might feel obligated to come home and check on his wife.

Mind your own business.

"Oh, for Pete's sake," she muttered. Why was she standing there even debating the whole matter? Besides, hadn't Mimi told her just to let herself out when she was finished? For all she knew, Mimi had already called her husband. Even now he could be on his way home.

Charlotte pulled the door firmly shut.

For most of her life, Charlotte had lived on Milan Street, a narrow, one-way street in the Uptown neighborhood of New Orleans. Charlotte's maid service catered exclusively to clients in the Garden District, and since Milan was just on the outskirts of the Garden District, it was the perfect location.

As her van bumped down the uneven street, thoughts of her newest employer still nagged her. In spite of all reasoning, she still felt as if she should have stayed with Mimi a while longer, just to make sure she was doing okay. Of course, she could always call and check on her.

Charlotte shook her head as she turned the van into her driveway. Calling wasn't really a good idea. The woman was sick, and sick people needed all the rest they could get.

She parked the van, switched off the engine, and for a moment, she simply sat there. It was good to be home . . . finally.

To Charlotte, her home was her sanctuary and her security. The small Victorian shotgun double had been built in the early 1900s. She and her younger sister, Madeline, had been raised in the house and had inherited it after their parents' untimely deaths. Unlike Madeline, who, after her first marriage, had long ago sold her half of the double to Charlotte, Charlotte had never felt the urge or the need to live anywhere else.

On weekdays, Charlotte usually only skimmed the headlines of the newspaper before going to work. On Wednesday morning, she had awakened earlier than usual, though, early enough, she decided, for a leisurely cup of coffee and to actually read the newspaper.

In the kitchen, she switched on the coffeepot. On her way through the living room, she stopped long enough to uncover her little parakeet's cage, and then she retrieved the *Times-Picayune* from the front porch steps.

Once back in the kitchen, she poured herself a cup of coffee. To make sure she allowed enough time to eat breakfast, dress, and get to work, she set the kitchen timer for forty-five minutes. Then she settled at the kitchen table with the newspaper and her coffee.

Charlotte read through a good bit of the paper and then came upon the obituary section. Unlike Bitsy Duhe and others Charlotte knew who always read every word of the death notices, she found the obituaries morbid and depressing. But just as she reached to turn the page, one of the pictures caught her eye.

Charlotte gasped, and a deep hollow feeling settled in the pit of her stomach as she stared at the picture. "No way," she whispered. It just wasn't possible.

Chapter 6

Mimi Adams was dead.

Above the picture of Mimi, the headline read, MARY LOU (MIMI) ADAMS, NOTED COMMUNITY ACTIVIST.

Charlotte quickly scanned the article below the picture. Mimi had died Tuesday of undetermined causes, and funeral arrangements were pending. The article went on to say that she had served on many boards of charitable organizations, among them HHS.

Charlotte squeezed her eyes shut and bowed her head as deep regret washed through her. She should have trusted her instincts and stayed with Mimi until Gordon came home. She shouldn't have left the poor woman alone. If she had stayed, Mimi might still be alive.

She sighed deeply, opened her eyes, and stared at the black and white picture. *Undetermined causes.*

Remembering how Mimi had looked

when she'd first seen her on Monday morning, Charlotte frowned as she read the first paragraph of the article again. Charlotte had thought she was ill, but then later, after Mimi had dressed and left for her luncheon date with Gordon, she'd seemed just fine. It was only during the HHS meeting that she'd truly become ill.

Charlotte shook her head. On the whole, Mimi had seemed healthy enough, and except for not feeling well during the Monday HHS meeting, she hadn't complained of any ailments. She'd also seemed like the type of woman who would be vigilant about medical checkups, the type who would take care of herself. So why didn't they know what she'd died of? And why were funeral arrangements pending? Unless . . .

Charlotte felt a sudden chill. Was it possible? Could undetermined causes mean that the police suspected foul play? Even as Charlotte tried to deny the possibility that Mimi could have been murdered, even as she told herself she was letting her imagination get the best of her, deep in her gut she knew that it was possible.

Stop jumping to conclusions.

What else then? Once again, visions of how Mimi had looked and acted on Monday reeled through Charlotte's mind. *A virus, a rare virus of some kind.* Surely that was the explanation.

The kitchen timer buzzed, and Charlotte jumped. Only then did she realize how long she'd been sitting there lost in a fog of disbelief and numbed by the dreadful realization that her newest client was dead.

What, if anything, should she do? she wondered, still staring at the picture. She could call the Adamses' house.

And say what?

She could express her sympathy to Mimi's husband.

Yeah, right. Just the thing to do. A complete stranger calling in the middle of his grief.

Charlotte squeezed her eyes shut and shook her head. Maybe she could call June Bryant instead.

And say what?

Again she shook her head. What she should do is mind her own business. She should get dressed, go to work, and wait. Surely someone, a member of the family or a friend of the family, would eventually get in touch with her.

Her mind still reeling, by sheer willpower Charlotte pushed away from the table and stood. On legs that felt weighted with lead, she headed for the shower.

★ ★ ★

An hour later Charlotte was ready to walk out the front door when the phone rang. Her hand on the doorknob, she paused. The phone call could be from someone at the Adams household.

Charlotte hurried over to the desk and picked up the receiver on the third ring. "Maid-for-a-Day, Charlotte speaking."

"Have you got a minute?"

Recognizing her son's voice, Charlotte smiled. "Of course, hon."

"You doing okay?"

Charlotte hesitated, tempted to tell Hank about the death of her newest client, and even more tempted to ask him if he could find out what had happened to her. As a doctor, he could inquire about the incident easily enough, but asking for his help would mean explaining all about how Mimi had been acting on Friday.

She glanced at the cuckoo clock on the wall behind the sofa. Explaining it all would take too much time, so she said, "I'm fine, son."

"Carol and I were wondering if you have any plans for Friday evening."

"Hold on a minute, hon, and let me check." She wedged the receiver between her shoulder and chin to free up both hands, then rummaged through her purse until she found her Day-Timer. She flipped through it to Friday's date. "I have an appointment to get my hair cut at four, but other than that, I'm free."

"Good, then how about letting me treat you to dinner? We thought we'd take you to August Moon, if that's okay. We could pick you up around six-thirty or so."

Just thinking about the Chinese restaurant made her mouth water. "Sounds great. Any special reason?"

"Do I have to have a special reason to treat my mother to dinner?"

"No, hon, of course not — I didn't mean it like that. It's just that I know how busy you both are. But listen, no need to pick me up. I never know how long I might have to wait at the beauty shop, so I'll just meet you there."

"Good, see you then. Love you, Mom."

"I love you too, sweetheart."

Just minutes later Charlotte parked her van in front of her Wednesday client's home on Sixth Street. Marian Hebert's house was a small, raised cottage type, and like so many of the Garden District homes, it was well over a century old and had been lovingly renovated as well as updated to accommodate all of the modern conveniences.

Marian was the owner of a real estate company that she ran by herself out of her home. She was a slim, attractive woman in her late thirties with dark hair and a flawless, ivory complexion, and a single mother raising two sons.

Though Charlotte had been working for Marian on Mondays, Wednesdays, and Fridays, at the end of July, Marian had decided that she only needed help once a week, and Charlotte had been left with openings on Mondays and Fridays as well as her regular day off on Thursdays.

At first Charlotte had been reluctant to let it be known that she had openings, but only because she'd been trying to appease her son, who wanted her to cut back on work. In no time, though, she'd grown bored, and since Mary Lou Adams had been the only one of Charlotte's prospective clients who needed a maid on Mondays and Fridays, Charlotte had decided to work for her.

Charlotte unloaded her supply carrier and vacuum cleaner from the back of the van and trudged up the steps to Marian's front door. She still couldn't believe that Mimi was dead — it just didn't seem real

— and she couldn't help wondering how Mimi's death would affect her work schedule now. Would Gordon Adams still want a maid, or would she be left again with Mondays and Fridays open?

Marian left almost as soon as Charlotte arrived and was gone most of the day. Charlotte had just finished wiping off the countertops in the kitchen and was unloading the dishwasher when she heard Marian's car pull in the driveway.

When Marian entered through the back door, Charlotte put the last of the clean dishes into the kitchen cabinet.

"What a day," she told Charlotte. "At least it was productive, though. I sold that old Johnson mansion on St. Charles."

"Well, congratulations," Charlotte said. "That's quite a coup, considering how run-down that place is. Maybe the new owners will renovate that old eyesore."

"I think that's the plan, and with these particular clients, money is no object. So — anything going on here while I was gone?"

Flashes of the headlines and the article about Mimi Adams's death went through Charlotte's mind, but she shook her head. "All's quiet on the home front."

Marian smiled as she approached Charlotte. "Good." Her smile faded, and her expression grew pensive. "Before you leave, Charlotte, I need to talk to you," she said. "Could you come into my office for a moment?"

Charlotte nodded. "Sure." She closed and locked the dishwasher door, then followed Marian into the adjoining room that Marian used as an office.

"Have a seat." Marian motioned toward a chair in front of her desk. Once Charlotte was seated, Marian crossed her arms and perched herself on the front edge of her desk. "I don't know quite how to say this," she said. "And I'm truly sorry, but I won't be needing your services any longer after next Wednesday."

Charlotte was stunned. She'd been cleaning for Marian for a long time and had never had a complaint. Her mind raced, but for the life of her, she couldn't think of anything she could have done to warrant getting fired.

Marian narrowed her eyes. "Now, Charlotte, just get that look off your face and let me explain before you go jumping to conclusions. I won't be needing your services because I've decided to move."

"Move! Where?"

"The boys and I will be moving to the North Shore. Mandeville, to be specific. I've always liked the North Shore, and I really think it will be good for B.J. and Aaron," she replied. "And for my business," she added. "Real estate is still booming there, and I think I could do well."

Charlotte heaved a sigh of relief. "For a minute there, I thought I'd done something wrong."

"Oh, don't be silly, Charlotte. If I thought I could persuade you to move with me, I'd do it in a heartbeat. It's largely thanks to you that I finally realized what was important in life and got myself straightened out these past months. For that I'll always be grateful. Of all the people we know, the boys and I are going to miss you the most."

Relief tinged with a bit of sadness washed through Charlotte. "I'm going to miss them too. They're both great kids." She paused a moment. "But, Marian, are you sure about this? What about your home? I know how much time and effort you and your husband put into this house. And I never would have believed you would leave New Orleans."

"I do love New Orleans," she admitted.

"But renovating this house and living in the Garden District was really Bill's idea; his dream, not mine. If he were still alive, things would be different. But he's not, and I've thought about this for some time now. Moving will be a fresh start for all of us. I thought I could stick it out here, and I've tried, for almost a year now, but —" She shook her head. "Too many bad memories . . ." Her voice trailed away.

Charlotte could see the pain of the past reflected in Marian's eyes. She truly sympathized with the younger woman, especially after all she'd been through: the horrible secret she'd had to live with for years, her battle with alcoholism, and the loss of her husband. And she respected Marian for the progress she'd made getting her life back together. "So — when are you planning on making the move?"

Marian blinked several times, then smiled. "That's the best part of all. I already have a buyer for my house lined up, so I won't even have to put it on the market. I've also gone to contract on a house in Mandeville. I've got movers scheduled for next week. School starts August sixteenth, so that should give me a week to get settled in the new house before the boys start back to school. I figure the movers should be done packing up by Tuesday; then I'd like you to come in and clean up on Wednesday after everything is out. I know it's not much notice, and I'm really sorry about that, but," she shrugged, "things just seemed to fall into place overnight."

Still a little dazed by Marian's announcement, Charlotte rushed to load her cleaning supplies into the back of her van. The sky had grown overcast, and thunder rumbled in the distance.

Charlotte was happy for Marian and her two sons. She truly was. And deep in her bones she felt the move would be good for B.J. and Aaron, especially B.J., after the harrowing experience the teenager had had back in October.

October. Charlotte shivered. At times even she still had nightmares about the sordid mess, and she was a grown woman. It wasn't every day that she stumbled across a dead body, and she couldn't begin to imagine what kind of long-term effect something like that would have on a fifteen-year-old boy.

Charlotte shook her head. *Don't think about it. Think positive.* The positive had been the end results. Marian had finally climbed out of the alcoholic stupor she'd been in since the death of her husband and had gotten her life back on the right track.

Charlotte hefted the vacuum cleaner into the van. Telling herself not to think about the frightening experience and then actually not thinking about it was almost impossible, just as not thinking about Mary Lou Adams all day had been impossible.

Mimi Adams . . . undetermined cause of death.

Charlotte shivered again. How had Mimi died? Had she been murdered? Maybe she'd ask Hank to check into it after all.

Charlotte slammed the back door of the van. For now, though, she needed to think about how the loss of Marian as a client was going to affect Maid-for-a-Day. Losing a client meant a loss of income for her and for her cleaning service, and with the possibility of losing the Adams family as well . . .

Charlotte climbed into the driver's seat just as a streak of lightning lit the sky. "Just in time," she murmured, as she glared at the fat raindrops splashing on her windshield.

Charlotte switched on the ignition, turned on the headlights and the windshield wipers, then checked in the mirrors for oncoming traffic. She was probably worrying for no reason. She and Maid-for-a-Day had a good reputation, and she'd never had a problem getting clients. All she had to do was let it be known that she had an opening. For that matter, all she had to do was tell Bitsy Duhe. Bitsy, bless her gossip-loving heart, was better than taking out a classified ad any day . . . and cheaper.

"Maid-for-a-Day will survive," she muttered, as she pulled out into the street, "and so will you."

By the time Charlotte parked beneath the carport of her house, it was pouring rain. On days like this she was thankful that several years back she'd been able to add the carport and storage room onto the side of her half of the double and could get from the van to the house without getting soaked.

The moment she entered the kitchen, her parakeet began to chatter. "Missed you, missed you."

Leaving her purse and lunch bag in the kitchen, she walked into the living room. Near the window, her little bird launched into his regular routine of chirping and fluttering his wings as he pranced back and forth along his perch in the cage, all designed to get her attention.

"Hey, Sweety Boy. I missed you too," she told the little green bird. "You're such a good little bird." Near the front door, she slipped out of her shoes and stepped into the soft suede moccasins she used as house shoes.

Out of habit she glanced at her answering machine. Sure enough, the light was blinking, indicating that she had a message. Ignoring Sweety Boy's acrobatic antics, she walked to the desk and pressed the PLAY button.

The machine beeped, and a mechanical voice announced that one message had been received at two forty-five p.m. The machine beeped again.

"Charlotte, this is June Bryant." June's voice was flat, without inflection. "I guess by now you've heard about poor Mimi. Please call me as soon as possible at —"

Charlotte grabbed a pen and jotted down the number. As soon as the machine beeped and the mechanical voice said, "End of message," she tapped out June's phone number. The call was answered on the fourth ring by a deep male voice whom she didn't recognize.

"Hi, this is Charlotte LaRue," she said.

"I'm returning June Bryant's call."

"Just a second," the voice told her, and though muffled, Charlotte heard him call out, "June, phone call. Someone named Charlotte LaRue."

A moment later Charlotte heard the click of an extension being picked up. "Charlotte?"

"Yes, hi, June. I got your message. I'm so sorry about Mimi. I know that you two were really good friends."

June sniffed, and with a slight catch in her voice, she whispered, "Thank you." A moment passed, she cleared her throat, and then she said, "I-I can hardly believe it." She sniffed again.

"Is there anything I can do to help?" Charlotte asked.

"Why, yes — yes there is. Gordon asked me to make some calls for him and you were on the list. Now, more than ever, he's going to need someone to come in, someone to keep the place clean, and he was hoping that you'd still be willing to work for him. Same hours, same days."

Charlotte hesitated before answering. One other time, early in her career as a maid, she'd had a man for a client. She was a lot younger then, and she learned a hard lesson. The arrangement lasted only a month before she decided that fighting off the man's amorous advances wasn't worth what he was paying her. But that was then, and she wasn't young and naive any longer. Besides, she figured that the last thing on Gordon Adams's mind would be fooling around with a woman who was probably almost old enough to be his mother.

"Tell Mr. Adams that I'd be happy to keep working for him."

"Oh, good," June said. "I'm sure he'll be very relieved — just one less problem to worry about right now. And, Charlotte, one more thing. We were wondering if you might, by chance, be able to come in tomorrow as well as on Friday. Just this week," she hastened to add. "The police have been crawling all over the place, and it's a mess. One of the detectives has assured Gordon that they will be finished before tomorrow, though. Justin and Emma will be coming home, and what with people dropping by and all, he wanted the place to look decent."

"Tomorrow won't be a problem," Charlotte told her.

June's sigh of relief whispered through the phone line. "That's great," she said. "I'll meet you there in the morning at nine and give you a house key."

114

Charlotte could tell from June's tone that she was ready to end the conversation, and though she hesitated, she just couldn't let her, not without knowing exactly what had happened to Mimi. "Ah, June, could I ask you something?"

"Sure," June answered.

"What happened? The newspaper said Mimi had died of undetermined causes. Just what does that mean?"

"Oh, Charlotte, it was just awful. I knew that Mimi wasn't feeling well during the meeting, and I knew that, more than likely, Gordon was working late, so I called around seven that evening to check on her. She-she sounded just terrible," June said tearfully. "If-if only I'd done something then, she might still be alive." Several moments passed before she could talk again. "Gordon didn't get home until really late," she continued. "When he went to bed he noticed something wasn't quite right about her breathing. When he tried to wake her and couldn't, he panicked and called 911. They rushed her to the hospital, but by then she was already in a coma. She-she never d-did regain consciousness, and-and she died Tuesday morning, just before noon."

June began to cry softly. "The ER doctor

suspected that she'd been poisoned. She d-died of-of poisoning," she sobbed.

"Poisoning!" Charlotte repeated in shocked disbelief. "As in food poisoning, like salmonella or botulism?"

"Yes, p-poisoning, of all things. But they're not sure what kind. She-she could have been poisoned on purpose. And now poor Gordon can't even have her funeral until the coroner does an autopsy." She paused again, then, with a deep sigh, said, "I almost forgot. The police wanted a list of everyone who was at the HHS meeting on Monday, so I gave them one." She cleared her throat. "I'm sorry — I hate to tell you this — but I had to give them your name too. So don't be surprised if you get questioned. Like I said, I'm sorry."

"No need to apologize. I would have been surprised if they hadn't wanted to talk to me." No sooner were the words out of her mouth than Charlotte heard a sharp rap on her front door.

"Ah, June, there's someone at the door. I have to go now, but I'll see you in the morning. Nine o'clock."

"Yes, of course. See you tomorrow."

Charlotte hung up the phone and walked over to the window. Pulling the curtain back, she peeked out, her gaze scanning the driveway. Even with the pouring rain, she could tell that the car parked there was one she didn't recognize.

Another sharp rap sounded at the door, and she sighed. "Okay, okay," she muttered. "Just keep your shirt on." She went to the door. "Yes," she called out, "who is it?"

"It's Judith, Aunt Charley."

Charlotte frowned. Had her niece bought a new car? No one in the family had mentioned it. "Just a second, hon." She unlocked the dead bolt and opened the door. "You didn't tell me that you bought . . ." Charlotte's voice trailed away. Standing beside her niece was a man whom she had never seen before. "A new car," she finished her sentence.

Judith flashed her a smile. "I didn't. The car belongs to Brian." She motioned toward the man. "Auntie, this is Brian Lee. Brian is my new partner."

Charlotte nodded at the younger man. She knew for a fact that Brian Lee wasn't exactly "new." According to Madeline, Brian had been Judith's partner for at least three months or so, and also according to Madeline, he was a handsome devil.

Madeline had been right about him being handsome, Charlotte decided. But then Madeline was a huge Tom Cruise fan, and Brian Lee could win hands down in a Tom Cruise look-alike contest.

Madeline had been right about the devil part as well, Charlotte suspected. It was Brian's eyes, she decided, jade in color and jaded by life — old, world-weary eyes that belied his age. And there was only one reason why Judith would show up with him now.

Charlotte tilted her head to look directly up at him. "I would say it's nice to meet you, Brian," she said matter-of-factly, "but I've got a feeling that this isn't a social call."

Chapter 7

"No, ma'am, this isn't a social call," Brian Lee said. "This is official police business. Can we come in? We'd like to ask you some questions."

Charlotte nodded. "Just leave the umbrellas on the porch and wipe your feet." She pointed at the welcome mat outside the door.

Once Brian and Judith had obediently propped their dripping umbrellas against the wall of the porch and wiped their feet on the rug, Charlotte motioned for them to come inside. "Can I get you something to drink?" she offered, as she closed the door behind them. "Coffee or iced tea?"

"Nothing for me," Brian said.

Judith shook her head. "Me neither, Auntie," she said, as she seated herself on the sofa.

Brian sat down beside Judith, so Charlotte chose the chair opposite the sofa.

Brian leaned forward and rested his forearms on his thighs. "We understand that you worked for Mary Lou Adams on Monday."

Charlotte nodded.

"What time did you leave?"

"My hours are from nine to three-thirty, but I stayed until around four-thirty on Monday because of the HHS meeting."

"Tell us about the meeting."

Charlotte shrugged. "Like what?"

"Like, for instance, the food and drinks. Who provided it, what was served, and who served it?"

"Fudge brownies, wine, and coffee," Charlotte told him. "Different members provided different items, and I served it all. But if you're thinking that the poison was in any of those things, then everyone there would have been sick."

Brian narrowed his eyes. "No one has said anything about poison. Why would you think Mrs. Adams was poisoned?"

His tone was insolent with a suspicious edge, and Charlotte saw red. Two could play that game. "Because that's what I was *told*," she retorted, her tone just as insolent as his had been. She glared at him. "For your information, young man, I just got off the phone with June Bryant, and she *told* me that she had already been questioned

120

and that you all suspected that Mimi had been poisoned."

Judith held up both hands, palms out. "Whoa — hey, just take it easy, Auntie. No one here is accusing you of anything. There was no way for us to know that you had talked with Mrs. Bryant." She dropped her hands back into her lap, then twisted around to another position.

The nervous fidgets. Any time Judith began fidgeting was a sure sign that she was nervous.

"And speaking of Mrs. Bryant," Judith continued, "according to her there was a bit of conflict going on in the group. What can you tell us about that?"

"Was she poisoned or not?" Charlotte asked, ignoring Judith's question.

"Yes, she was, Auntie, but we're still not sure if it was an accident or on purpose. Now, what can you tell us about the conflict going on at the HHS meeting?"

"What did June tell you?"

Brian spoke up. "We'd rather hear your version, ma'am."

"Well, there's not much to tell. Like I said, I was serving, so I wasn't privy to everything that was said."

"Please, ma'am, just tell us what you do know."

Charlotte heaved an impatient sigh. "There was some disagreement over which charity would benefit from the HHS fall plant sale. But that kind of thing happens in any organization," she hastened to add and then shrugged. "Mimi's side lost. But that's certainly not enough motive for anyone to kill her."

Several silent seconds ticked by, and when Charlotte didn't offer any further information, Judith groaned. "I told you to let me do the questioning," she told Brian. After a tense moment between Judith and her partner, Brian finally nodded his concession. Judith nodded back, then faced Charlotte. "Did you notice anything unusual about Mrs. Adams, Auntie? Did she seem ill or anything while you were there?"

"She did complain about having a headache and being thirsty. And later, once everyone had left, she went straight to bed."

Judith pursed her lips, then said, "Do you remember about what time she began complaining about the headache?"

Charlotte shrugged. "Maybe . . . Hmm, let me see now. The meeting started around two, and she began complaining about a headache during the refreshment break. I'd say that was probably around a quarter of three or so."

Judith nodded. "Good. That's exactly what we needed to know. Now, Auntie, earlier you said there was some contention in the group, a disagreement. Do you know the names of the women who disagreed with Mrs. Adams's side?"

When Charlotte didn't answer immediately, Judith released an exasperated sigh. "Aunt Charlotte, please. I know all about your confidentiality, no-gossip policy, or whatever you call it, but this is important. If you know their names . . ."

Charlotte glared at her niece for a moment. One of her cardinal rules was never to discuss her clients with anyone. She had three women who worked for her full-time and one part-time employee, and each had been apprised of Charlotte's rule when they had hired on. Any infraction was grounds for immediate dismissal.

"Aunt Charlotte! Please."

"Oh, okay." She rattled off the names. "Rita Landers, Karen Douglas, and Doreen Mires. There, are you satisfied?"

"Not quite yet," Brian interjected. "How long have you worked for the Adams family?"

"Monday was the third time I had cleaned for them," Charlotte answered.

"In that time, did you know of or get the

feeling that anyone else had a grudge against Mrs. Adams?"

"Not exactly."

"What do you mean by 'exactly'?" Judith asked.

Though she'd rather eat worms than repeat something a client had told her, Charlotte went on to explain about the feud between Mimi and her neighbor Sally Lawson. "But mind you," she said when she'd finished, "that was just Mimi's version, and there are always two sides to every story."

"Okay, okay," Judith said. "Let's get back to the food and drink. Do you remember who brought what?"

Charlotte grimaced but nodded. "I believe June Bryant brought the brownies that day, and either Rita Landers or Karen Douglas furnished the wine."

"Either?" Judith asked.

"I'm not sure which one. I just remember Mimi saying that one of them — and she didn't remember which one — was supposed to furnish the wine that day."

"And what about the coffee?" Brian asked.

Charlotte glared at him. "What about it?" she repeated. "I'll have you know that I made the coffee, and for your information,

124

I opened a fresh bag that day."

"Okay, Auntie, just take it easy. Like I said before, no one here is accusing you of anything. Let's talk about the wine. Had any of the bottles been opened or were all of them new?"

Charlotte shrugged. "There were a couple of bottles that had been opened, bottles left over from the Friday meeting. The rest were new."

Charlotte paused, suddenly torn by indecision as to whether she should mention the special bottle of wine that Rita had brought with her. "I don't know how important this is," she finally said, "but Rita Landers bought Mimi a special bottle, a particular brand that was supposed to be Mimi's favorite. Rita said it was a peace offering, an apology from all three women for the disagreement they'd had at the previous meeting."

Judith sat forward. "Could you point out the so-called special bottle?"

Charlotte shook her head. "No, after the meeting was over, Rita took what was left home with her."

Brian narrowed his eyes. "Didn't you just say that it was a gift?"

"No, that's not what I said. I said it was a peace offering." Then Charlotte explained about the meeting and how Rita, Karen, and Doreen had ganged up on Mimi to push through their own agenda. "Mimi was upset, and Rita said that Mimi would probably just throw out what was left in the bottle anyway, so she took it home with her."

At that moment, Judith's beeper went off, and once she checked it, she made a quick phone call. "We've got to go," she told Brian, as she hung up the phone. To Charlotte she said, "We'll talk some more later, Auntie, but thanks for the information, and if you think of anything else, give me a call."

Within minutes, Judith and Brian were out the door. As Charlotte stood on the porch and watched them drive away, it suddenly occurred to her that no one had mentioned the fact that Mimi had eaten lunch with Gordon on the day in question. Didn't it stand to reason that something she ate during lunch had been poisoned?

Making a mental note to call Judith later, Charlotte went back inside the house.

It was still raining when Charlotte arrived at the Adamses' house on Thursday morning. Since there was no sign of June waiting for her, Charlotte sat with the van idling for several minutes, as she listened to the weather forecast on the radio. A tropical storm was building southwest of New Orleans in the Gulf of Mexico. Conditions were such that it was possible that the storm could become a hurricane.

Charlotte killed the engine and stared through the windshield at the rain. If she remembered right, she was low on batteries and bottled water, and she needed to check her supply of canned goods as well, just in case the storm did turn into a hurricane, and just in case it headed for New Orleans.

She glanced at the porch again, then checked her watch. She was a few minutes early, but not *that* early. So what now? she wondered. She could just sit in the van and wait or she could brave the rain, unload her supplies, and wait on the porch.

"No time like the present," she murmured. Pulling the hood of her raincoat over her head, she climbed out of the van, hurried around to the back, and unloaded her supply carrier and vacuum cleaner.

She set the vacuum cleaner down on the porch near the front door, and just as she bent over to put the supply carrier beside the vacuum cleaner, the door swung open and June stepped out onto the porch. At the sight of Charlotte, June jumped and squealed with fright.

"It's just me, June." Charlotte pushed the hood of her raincoat off her head and stood up.

"Oh, good grief, Charlotte! You scared the daylights out of me."

"Sorry," Charlotte said. "I didn't see anyone when I drove up and decided to wait on the porch. It simply didn't occur to me that you might already be inside waiting."

"I got here early to check things out," June said, her tone snippy. "And I thought I would hang around while you cleaned. It's not that I don't trust you but," she hastened to add, "it's just that someone might call or come by, and I promised Gordon I would see to things for him. And speaking of trust . . ." She reached into her pants pocket and pulled out a key and a piece of paper. "This is the key to the front door. Just don't lose it."

June placed the key in Charlotte's hand, and from the look on June's face, Charlotte felt as if she'd just been handed the key to the Fort Knox gold bullion depository.

"And I've written down the alarm code for you." June handed Charlotte the piece of paper. "For heaven's sake, don't lose that either." Then, with one last meaningful look, June turned and walked back inside the house.

It's not that I don't trust you but . . . Just don't lose it. Charlotte felt her temper flare as she glared at June's retreating back. In all her years of running Maid-for-a-Day, she'd never had a customer question her trustworthiness nor had she ever lost a key or misplaced the numbers for an alarm code that had been entrusted to her, and she truly resented the insinuations.

Drawing in a deep breath and counting to ten, Charlotte slipped the piece of paper into her pants pocket and pulled out a key ring. Once she'd hooked the key onto the ring, she dropped the key ring back into her pants pocket. Later, she'd tape the paper with the alarm code into her appointment book. Feeling a bit more in control, she picked up the vacuum cleaner and went inside.

June was waiting for her near the dining room entrance. Now what? Charlotte wondered, as she shut the door. Maybe if she ignored June . . . With a brief grimace that Charlotte hoped passed for a smile, she walked past June and headed straight for the kitchen.

So much for ignoring her, Charlotte thought, when she heard footsteps behind her. So what else was on her mind? she wondered. Whatever it was, Charlotte was pretty sure it didn't have anything to do with the key.

They were almost to the kitchen when June asked, "Have you talked to the police yet?"

Charlotte entered the kitchen, her gaze taking inventory of the mess as she set down the supply carrier and the vacuum. "Yes, I have," she answered, momentarily distracted by the sink full of dirty dishes and the food-splattered stovetop. "I talked to the detectives right after our phone call yesterday."

Charlotte had a good idea of what was coming, so hoping that June would take the hint and leave her alone, she walked over to the dishwasher, opened it, and began filling it with the dirty dishes stacked in the sink.

June didn't take the hint, and to Charlotte's annoyance, she followed her across the kitchen. Stopping at the cabinet, June leaned against the countertop near the sink and crossed her arms. "What did you tell them — I mean, what kinds of questions did they ask you?"

Charlotte felt like saying, *none of your business,* and she felt her temper flare again. She had work to do and wasn't in the mood for yet another interrogation after enduring the one from Judith and Brian, especially not from June. In hopes of discouraging June from further questions, she simply shrugged and said, "Just the obvious questions. Probably the same ones they asked you."

"Well, I hope you told them about that little stunt that Rita, Karen, and Doreen pulled. And about that awful Sally Lawson too. You did know about her, didn't you?"

"Not a lot," Charlotte hedged. "Only what Mimi told me, something about some dead trees."

June's face contorted and tears leaked from her eyes. "Well, you can bet that I told them. I gave them an earful. I told them all about Rita and about Sally too. Guess those two hussies are happy now."

At the sight of June's tears, Charlotte frowned. Maybe she'd been wrong about June. Maybe her offensive manner and probing questions were just her way of working through her grief for her friend.

June, evidently misinterpreting Charlotte's frown, nodded and said, "Yeah, they both finally got what they wanted. Rita finally got her revenge, and Sally won't have to worry about her stupid pool being shaded any more. I don't know how they did it —" She sniffed. "But I'd be willing to bet that one of them — either Rita or Sally — is to blame. They were both so jealous of Mimi that they couldn't see straight." She shook her head. "Poor Mimi. She didn't deserve to die like that."

Charlotte knew she should attempt to comfort June in some way, but the truth was, she really didn't like the woman very much.

Do unto others . . . Charlotte suddenly felt like hanging her head in shame. After all, it was pretty obvious that the woman was truly grief stricken over losing her best friend. *Do right and you'll feel right.* The words of her pastor pricked at her conscience.

Charlotte forced herself to reach out and pat June on the back. "I truly am sorry for your loss," she said.

June stiffened for a moment; then, she made a vague gesture with her hand. "It's not me so much," she said, "but my heart breaks for Emma and Justin. And Gordon too, of course," she added in a choked voice. She brushed away the tears with her fingers, sniffed, and then squared her shoulders. "Which reminds me, the kids — Emma and Justin — got in late last night. They're still asleep upstairs."

Charlotte nodded. At least now she had an explanation for the mess in the kitchen.

"I thought I might make them some breakfast when they wake up."

A sudden thought occurred to Charlotte, and she frowned. "Is Mr. Adams here too?"

June shook her head. "No, he left early around seven or so, but I'm sure he'll be back a little later on." She pushed herself away from the cabinet. "Guess I'd better stop gabbing and let you get to work now. I'll be in the library if you need me. I've still got several calls to make to some out-of-town acquaintances whom Gordon wanted notified."

Charlotte had cleaned the kitchen, and while the dishes washed, she'd dusted the parlor and dining room. She was back in the kitchen unloading the dishwasher when Emma and Justin Adams wandered in through the doorway.

Except for Emma's hair being blond — and Charlotte suspected it was bleached — she was almost the spitting image of her mother. Justin's hair was also blond, also bleached, she suspected, but the shape of his face and his eye color were completely different, so Charlotte decided that he must favor his father. Both were dressed in oversized T-shirts and lounging pants, probably the same clothes they'd slept in, Charlotte figured.

"Who are you?" Emma asked.

"Charlotte, Charlotte LaRue. I clean house for your parents. And you must be Emma, and —" She glanced over at Justin. "You must be Justin."

The girl nodded. "Oh, yeah, I remember now. Mom mentioned that she'd hired a new maid."

"I'm truly sorry for your loss," Charlotte said softly.

"Th-thank you." Tears welled in Emma's eyes, and she stumbled over to the table and slumped down into a chair. She scrubbed at her face with the heels of her palms and her shoulders shook with silent sobs. "I-I still can't be-believe sh-she's d-dead," she cried.

Justin rushed to his sister's side. "Aw, come on, Em." He knelt down beside her and put his arm around her shoulders.

June suddenly appeared in the doorway. "What's going on in here?" She took one look at Justin and Emma, sighed, pressed

134

her lips together in a sign of pique, and then marched over to the table. "Now, Emma, you're going to have to get hold of yourself. Your father is counting on you."

Emma jerked her head around to glare at June. "In case you haven't noticed, my father isn't here at the moment. And even if he were, *he* would understand."

Justin gave his sister one last squeeze, then stood up. "Em can cry if she wants to," he told June. When June's only response was to tighten her lips even more, Justin shifted his gaze to Charlotte. "Is there anything here to eat? I mean, I know you're not a cook, but I just thought . . ." His voice trailed away in embarrassment.

Charlotte smiled at him. "It's okay, hon, I know what you meant. I'll check —"

"I had planned to fix breakfast," June interrupted. To Justin she said, "Your father asked me to look after you two until he gets home."

Justin shrugged. "You don't have to do that. Cereal is okay. There's probably some in the pantry. Mom always kept some for when we come home."

"Nonsense," June said sternly. "Growing boys and girls need a good hearty breakfast." She walked purposefully to the refrigerator and took out a carton of eggs, a package of bacon, and butter.

Emma cleared her throat. "We're not exactly boys and girls any longer," she said. "And we can take care of ourselves."

June slammed a container of orange juice onto the counter, then faced Emma. "It was just a figure of speech, Emma."

"Well, excuse me," Emma shot back.

June and Emma glared at each other, but after several tense moments, June was the first to break the deadlock. With a put-upon sigh, she turned her back to Emma, opened the cabinet, and took out a small bowl. She cracked an egg and dumped it into the bowl, then reached for another egg. "I'm making breakfast," she announced, her no-nonsense tone indicating that it was not up for debate.

Charlotte had just put away the last glass from the dishwasher, and out of the corner of her eye she saw Justin wink at his sister. With a smirk, Emma rolled her eyes.

Time to get out of the kitchen, Charlotte decided. Besides, two women working in the kitchen were one too many, especially when one of them was June. Maybe now would be a good time to clean the bedrooms. "I'll be cleaning upstairs if anyone needs me," she said, as she closed the dishwasher door.

"By the way, where is Dad this morning?" Emma asked June, as Charlotte walked briskly toward the doorway. "You'd think that for once, especially today, he could stay home," she added.

"Now, Emma, your father is an important man. He . . ."

June's voice faded as Charlotte climbed the stairs, and she wondered what kind of excuse June was making for Gordon.

Charlotte's heart ached for Emma and Justin. In her opinion, no excuse was good enough for their father being absent when they needed him. From personal experience, she knew how devastating it was to lose a parent — she'd lost both of hers in a fatal airplane crash. For her, there had been no one she could turn to and no time to grieve. Instead, she'd been left with the total responsibility of caring for her sister, Madeline, then only fifteen, as well as Hank, who had been a toddler at the time.

Emma and Justin deserved to grieve, and they deserved more from their father. Gordon was the one who should have been there lending comfort, not his wife's best friend and certainly not the maid, a complete stranger whom neither of his children had ever met. It was no wonder that Emma seemed so resentful of June. But being resentful was no excuse for bad manners. After all, June was just trying to help.

Once upstairs, Charlotte decided that she should probably clean Justin's and Emma's rooms first. After a quick inspection of both rooms, she found that neither was really that dirty, just cluttered.

She had cleaned Justin's room and had just finished scrubbing the shower in Emma's bathroom when the girl stuck her head through the doorway.

"Hey, Charlotte," she said. "Just in case my father calls, Justin and I are going out for a while." She heaved her suitcase up on the bed, unzipped it, and began rummaging through it.

Charlotte scooped up her cleaning supplies and said, "If you have any clothes that need washing, I'll be happy to do that for you."

"Oh, wow, thanks, Charlotte." Emma began pulling different items out of the suitcase. "Actually just about everything I have is dirty."

Maybe the girl's manners were better than she'd thought, Charlotte decided. As for her attitude toward June . . .

Mind your own business. With a sigh, Charlotte placed the cleaning supplies into her supply carrier and set it outside in the hallway. Once she'd gathered up Emma's dirty clothes, she left the room and headed downstairs.

As she passed through the kitchen on her way to the laundry room, she noticed that June was still sitting at the table finishing up a cup of coffee and staring out the window into the backyard. There were dirty dishes still half full of eggs, bacon, and toast on the table, and a greasy frying pan had been left on the stovetop. A partial loaf of bread, the carton of eggs, and a tub of butter, along with a container of orange juice, were still sitting on the cabinet.

Charlotte grimaced but kept walking. A fat lot of good it had done her to clean the kitchen, she grumbled silently, as she went into the laundry room. After dropping the clothes on the floor, she turned on the washing machine and added detergent. Now she'd have to clean it all over again. And, from the looks of things, a lot of good it had done June to insist on cooking breakfast. Next time maybe June would listen, and Charlotte vowed that next time she'd be sure to clean the kitchen last, especially if June was around.

"Charlotte —"

Charlotte jumped at the unexpected sound of June's voice just behind her. With the washing machine filling with water, she hadn't heard her approach.

"Sorry," June said. "I didn't mean to startle you. I just wanted to tell you that I'll be in the library if anyone calls or comes by. And the kids will be out for a while. They're meeting some friends for lunch."

Charlotte simply nodded and didn't bother to tell June that Emma had already told her the same thing.

Charlotte finished loading the washing machine, then went into the kitchen. Still miffed about having to clean it up again, she began clearing off the table. Just as she loaded the last dirty dish into the dishwasher, she heard Emma and Justin on the stairs.

"June, we're leaving now," she heard Justin call out, and within seconds, they entered the kitchen.

"See you later, Charlotte," Emma said as she and her brother walked through on their way out the back door. "And thanks again for doing my clothes," she called over her shoulder.

"You're welcome," Charlotte responded, giving the girl a maternal smile.

The back door slammed, and Charlotte began the task of cleaning the stovetop once more.

★ ★ ★

The kitchen was finally sparkling clean . . . again. Charlotte stood by the sink and was casting an eagle eye over the room to make sure she'd done everything when she heard a rattling noise at the back door. Charlotte went stone still. When she heard the door open and then close, she frowned. It was too early for Emma and Justin to have returned already. Maybe they forgot something.

Then Charlotte heard footsteps . . . deliberate, heavy footsteps that could only belong to a man, and warning bells went off in her head.

Chapter 8

The minute the tall man strolled into the kitchen, there was no denying that he had to be Gordon Adams. The resemblance between the man and Justin was just too amazing for him to be anyone else.

The man nodded at Charlotte, then stuck out his hand. "You must be Charlotte," he said, his voice deep and mellow.

Charlotte released her pent-up breath, forced a smile, and shook his hand. "Yes-yes, I am, and you must be Gordon Adams. I'm truly sorry about Mimi. She was a nice lady."

"Thank you, and thanks for agreeing to come in today." He released her hand and glanced toward the hallway door. "So, where is everyone?" His forehead wrinkled with a frown.

"Justin and Emma went out," Charlotte said. "I believe they were meeting some friends for lunch."

Gordon nodded. "Good. I've been really

worried about them, especially Emma. I was afraid I'd find them just moping around the house." He paused a moment, then said, "Is June still here?"

Charlotte nodded. "I think she's in the library."

At that moment, June strolled into the room. "Did I hear someone mention my name?" She abruptly stopped just inside the doorway. "Why, Gordon, what are you doing home so early? I didn't expect you until lunchtime."

"I heard that the police were looking for me, and I thought I'd better be here in case they showed up."

"The police?"

Gordon nodded. "Have they been here yet?"

"Why, no — no, they haven't. But why on earth would they be looking for you now?"

Gordon didn't answer immediately, and Charlotte suddenly felt like a fifth wheel, just standing and staring at the two of them. The last thing she wanted was to appear to be eavesdropping. But after only a brief battle between her curiosity and her common sense, her curiosity won out, so she turned her back to both Gordon and June, and began scrubbing the sink . . . again.

Behind her, she heard the scrape of a chair. Then Gordon said, "Is there any coffee left?"

June's shoes clicked against the floor as she came farther into the room. "Not much," June told him. "It's old, though, but I'm sure Charlotte won't mind making up a fresh pot, will you, Charlotte?" she asked.

Not a please or a thank-you, or kiss my foot. Forcing a smile, Charlotte turned her head and said, "No, not at all." Grudgingly, she rinsed and dried her hands, then began to prepare the coffeepot.

"Now, what's this about the police?" June asked Gordon.

"My lawyer called," Gordon explained. "He said that the coroner finally finished the autopsy on Mimi, and they've released her body to the mortuary. It was poison alright, a poison called hyoscyamine. Seems it's found in a plant called jimsonweed, whatever the hell that is. But that's not the worst. Chris — he's my lawyer — tells me that I can expect a visit from the police again. He says that, more than likely, they'll consider me their main suspect."

"Why, that's outrageous!" June cried. "That's the most absurd thing I've ever heard of."

"Yeah, well, Chris says it isn't that uncommon. He says that in a homicide, the spouse is always a suspect."

"Common or not, I still say it's outrageous. But, Gordon, this Chris, is he a good attorney — I mean, you know — a good *criminal* attorney? Not that I'm insinuating you're a criminal," she added hastily, "only that you really need the very best there is for something like this."

"No, Chris is a corporate attorney, but he's part of a big firm and has an associate who specializes in criminal law. Daniel something or another is his name."

Charlotte's hand froze in midair as she reached to switch on the coffeepot. *Daniel?* Surely he wasn't talking about her nephew, *her* Daniel.

There you go again, jumping to conclusions.

Charlotte grimaced and switched on the coffeepot. There were probably lots of attorneys named Daniel.

Behind Charlotte, June made a sympathetic noise, a hum that dipped to a lower octave, then lifted to a higher octave. "I'm sure everything will be just fine," she reassured Gordon.

"Yeah, well, I hope so," he said. "Since they've released Mimi's body, I've decided to hold the funeral on Saturday afternoon.

145

I have an appointment after lunch today with the funeral director to go over the plans for the service."

Charlotte figured she'd heard all she was going to hear about what the police were doing. She still had work to do upstairs, and since the coffeepot was gurgling, she quietly left the room.

Just as Charlotte neared the doorway leading into the hall, she heard June say, "You really shouldn't go to the funeral home by yourself. Why don't I go with you? But first I'm going to make sure you eat a good lunch. I'd planned on cooking a roast. That way, you and the kids will have some leftovers this evening."

Charlotte rolled her eyes. Another mess in the kitchen.

It was almost three-thirty that afternoon when Charlotte began to pack her cleaning supplies so she could leave. Everyone was still gone, and the house was quiet.

The police never had showed up. Gordon had been mainly concerned that they would show up when Emma and Justin were there, but since the kids were gone, Gordon and June had decided to go on to the funeral home after they'd eaten lunch.

Charlotte had just wedged the last of her supplies, a bottle of lemon oil, into the supply carrier when the bang, bang, bang of the door knocker echoed throughout the house.

"Now what?" she complained. As she marched out of the kitchen and down the hallway, she figured it would be just her luck for the police to show up while she was still there.

Charlotte half expected to find Brian Lee and Judith standing on the porch. She threw the dead bolt. At the thought of her niece, she suddenly remembered that she never had called her to tell her about Mimi's lunch with Gordon.

She pulled the door open. When she saw the middle-aged, attractive blond-haired woman standing in the doorway instead, she smiled at the woman and asked, "May I help you?"

"You must be Charlotte, from Maid-for-a-Day."

"Yes, I am," Charlotte responded, wondering how this stranger knew who she was.

"I'm Sally Lawson, the next-door neighbor." She motioned toward the right side of the house.

Sally Lawson, the tree killer. According to

June, she was possibly Mimi's murderer as well.

Charlotte's smile faded.

Sally Lawson bent down, and for the first time, Charlotte noticed that there was a picnic basket at her feet. When Sally picked up the basket and held it out to Charlotte, a wonderful aroma of freshly baked bread drifted up from the basket. "This is some food for Gordon and the kids," Sally said. "Just a little something for their dinner tonight."

Mimi had been poisoned . . . more than likely by something she'd eaten or drank.

Don't be silly. The woman would be really stupid to poison the whole family. And, besides, why would she do such a thing to begin with?

Charlotte swallowed hard and took the basket. "That's really nice of you," she said.

Sally shrugged away the compliment. "It's the least I could do. Is Gordon here, or the kids? I'd like to express my condolences."

Charlotte shook her head. "No, they're not in at the moment — sorry — but I'm sure they'll be grateful for such a thoughtful gesture."

"Maybe I should leave a note then," Sally said. "If I could just borrow some paper and a pen, then I wouldn't have to disturb you again."

"Of course," Charlotte told her. "Just follow me."

Once in the kitchen, Charlotte set the basket on top of the cabinet and handed Sally Lawson the notepad and pen that were kept by the telephone.

"Is there anything in here that needs refrigeration?" Charlotte asked.

Sally nodded. "Yes, everything but the bread. And by the way, none of the containers need to be returned. They're all disposable."

The refrigerator was full, and it took Charlotte several minutes to rearrange the contents in order to accommodate the food that Sally had brought. While Charlotte rearranged the food, Sally sat at the table and scribbled a note.

Even after Sally had finished the note, she continued to sit at the table and watch as Charlotte transferred the dishes of food from the basket into the refrigerator.

"You know I really admired Mimi," Sally said. "She was so generous with her time and money, always heading up some type of charity event. And such a beautiful woman — always dressed to the nines and every hair in place." She slowly shook her head. "I still can't believe she's gone. And I still haven't figured out why the police came around to question me. We were neighbors, but it's not as if Mimi and I were the best of friends or anything. And with those high shrubs between our two houses, I sure can't tell what's going on over here." She paused thoughtfully.

Charlotte closed the refrigerator door. "My understanding is that the police are questioning everyone even remotely connected to the Adamses," Charlotte told her.

"I suppose so," Sally murmured. "And don't get me wrong. I wouldn't have minded being friends with her, especially with us living right next door to each other."

Sally paused briefly again, and Charlotte waited patiently when she didn't make a move to leave. From the look on Sally's face, Charlotte could tell she still had more she wanted to say.

Finally, with a sigh, Sally went on. "I tried for a while — to be friends, that is — but Mimi was always a bit standoffish."

As Sally spoke, Charlotte studied her. She seemed genuinely distressed, and contrary to what Mimi had led her to believe, Sally seemed like a nice lady, at least on the surface anyway. Yes, she decided, a nice lady, but perhaps a lonely lady as well. Why else would she be confiding in a maid, a complete stranger?

Though Charlotte wasn't sure exactly how to respond to Sally, she still felt like she needed to respond in some way. "Well, like you said," she finally commented, "Mimi was involved in a lot of charity events. Maybe she just didn't have a lot of time to make friends."

Sally shrugged. "I guess, and you're sweet to say so, but I really think she simply didn't like me for some reason." She shrugged again. "At first I thought she was jealous of my past friendship with Gordon. He and I go back a long way. Our families were friends. Of course, when he married Mimi, our friendship more or less ended. But I also wondered if it had something to do with the fact that I didn't join her garden club."

A sad little smile pulled at Sally's lips. "But why on earth would I want to join a garden club? It's like I told her, I don't know beans about flowers and plants — no pun intended. And I honestly don't think she did either. I never could understand how she could head up a garden club.

"It really is ironic if you think about it,"

Sally continued. "Mimi has all of these lovely plants inside and outside, yet she didn't seem to know much about them at all. The previous owners of the house planted most of the plants, especially the ones outside. But between you and me, I always suspected that her gardener was the real expert. I don't mean to speak ill of the dead or anything, but she couldn't even get a silly tree to grow. Why, just in the past year alone she planted two in the same spot and both of them died. If you ask me, I think she overwatered the silly things — drowned them." Sally paused and stared with unseeing eyes into space.

Two sides to every story. After hearing Mimi's complaints about Sally, Charlotte had wondered about Sally's side, and now that she'd heard Sally's side of the issue, Charlotte was thoroughly confused. Sally's version didn't even vaguely resemble what Mimi had told her. So which version was the truth?

"You know," Sally said, interrupting Charlotte's thoughts, "this is the first time I've been in this house since Mimi and Gordon moved in." She glanced around the room. "This really is a beautiful old home, and Mimi had impeccable taste."

Sally suddenly frowned when her gaze

took in Charlotte's supply carrier and vacuum cleaner sitting near the cabinet. "Oh, my goodness, I'll bet you were leaving, and here I am rattling on and on." She stood and handed the notepad and pen to Charlotte. "Thanks for listening, though." She motioned toward the picnic basket. "I hope Gordon and the kids can use the food. I just felt like I needed to do something to help them out, for old times sake."

Sally's mouth suddenly twisted into a disapproving grimace. "Of course, I'm sure June Bryant has been more than eager to see that Gordon and his kids are well taken care of." She let out a put-upon sigh. Then, as if realizing how what she'd said must have sounded, she quickly added, "Of course, June was one of Mimi's best friends, so naturally she'd want to do all she can." She gave Charlotte a quick fake smile. "Like I said before, I just wanted to express my condolences."

When Charlotte packed up her van to leave the Adamses' house, the rain had finally let up and the sun was out. But the resulting heat and humidity were brutal. The moment Charlotte opened the van door, a rush of pent-up heat assaulted her, and as she settled into the driver's seat, she rolled down all of the windows and switched the air-conditioner on high. Even with the windows down and the air-conditioner blowing, the inside of the van was still like an oven.

As Charlotte drove home, she kept reliving the conversation she'd had with Sally Lawson. First there had been Sally's remarks about Mimi's lack of gardening abilities, then the snide inference about June. But if Sally and Mimi weren't that friendly and, as Sally had pointed out, the high shrubs obstructed her view of the Adamses' house, then how did Sally seem to know so much about Mimi's lack of gardening skills?

June had said that both Rita and Sally were jealous of Mimi, but after listening to Sally, it appeared that Sally was really more jealous of June's friendship with Mimi than anything else. After all, Sally had said she'd wanted to be friends with Mimi, and evidently Mimi had rejected her attempts at friendship. Or was there something else going on, something to do with Gordon? Maybe, as Sally had pointed out, Mimi was jealous of Sally and Gordon's past friendship.

Charlotte shook her head. It was just

plain too hot to even think straight, and in spite of the air conditioner running full blast, the van was still stifling.

By the time Charlotte turned onto Milan, she was drenched in sweat. As she approached her driveway, her heart sank when she caught sight of the red Dodge Neon parked in front of her house.

"Nooooo," she groaned. For a split second, she was tempted to not even stop, tempted to just keep on driving. "Why me?" she complained, as she pulled into the driveway. "And why today of all days?"

Chapter 9

Charlotte loved her sister. She really did. Any other time, she would have been delighted with a visit from Madeline. She grimaced as she applied the brakes. Well, not exactly delighted. Maybe pleased was a more appropriate word, she decided. But not today.

Now be nice, Charlotte.

"Okay, okay," she grumbled, as she turned into her driveway. To give Madeline credit, she had come a long way over the past few months, and the change in her had been for the better. Though Madeline and her new daughter-in-law, Nadia, had gotten off to a rocky beginning, they'd well made up for it since.

Slowly but surely, mostly due to Nadia's little son, Davy, Charlotte suspected, Madeline had been learning to give instead of take, to be more selfless instead of selfish. Madeline simply adored her new little step-grandson and was eagerly anticipating the little granddaughter due to be born at the end of September.

But despite the change in Madeline, Charlotte still couldn't bring herself to completely trust her sister's turnaround. "Old habits die hard," she murmured, as she switched off the engine. Once trust had been betrayed, it was almost impossible to give it again, and Madeline had betrayed Charlotte's trust one too many times in the past.

Charlotte climbed out of the van and trudged up the steps to her front door. Though she hated thinking the worst, usually the only time that Maddie came by for a visit was when she wanted something. So what did she want this time? Charlotte wondered.

"Where on earth have you been?" Madeline asked the minute Charlotte stepped inside the front door. Without giving Charlotte time to answer, Madeline plowed right on ahead. "I've been waiting for over an hour," she complained. "Good thing you keep that extra key under that silly ceramic frog in the flower bed, or else I'd have already had a heat stroke. Why, on the way over here I heard on the radio that the heat index was one hundred one degrees this afternoon."

Madeline, looking cool and relaxed with a glass of iced tea in her hand, was lounging on the sofa, and Charlotte, still damp and sticky with sweat, found it hard to be sympathetic.

"Nice to see you too, Maddie," she drawled. "For the record, I've been working." As she slipped out of her shoes and stepped into her moccasins, out of habit she glanced over to the window. When it registered that Sweety Boy and his cage were missing, she rounded on Madeline. "What have you done with Sweety Boy?"

"Now, Charlotte, don't get upset. He's just fine. Besides, you know that bird doesn't like me. Why, he was squawking and thrashing about in his cage like a wild thing. I tried covering the cage, but he still didn't stop, so I moved him back there in the bedroom." She motioned toward the bedrooms.

"How long ago was that?"

"About a half an hour or so."

"And have you checked on him since?"

"No." Madeline shrugged as if Charlotte's concerns were no big deal. "Seeing me would probably just agitate him all over again. Besides, I figured he'd be okay once he was by himself back there."

Charlotte held her tongue and silently

counted to ten, then did an about-face and marched off toward the bedroom. Even before she opened the door, though, she could hear the little parakeet's pitiful squawks. At least the cage wasn't rattling, which meant he'd stopped his battering-ram mode.

Charlotte entered the bedroom and closed the door behind her. "It's okay, Sweety," she crooned, as she walked to the cage and knelt down beside it. "There, there, now. Sweety Boy's a pretty boy." Almost the second that she lifted the corner of the cover, he grew quiet.

On the floor of the cage were several loose feathers, he must have lost from thrashing around. But other than looking a bit ruffled, the little bird didn't appear to be any the worse for wear.

Charlotte stuck her finger in between the wires, and he immediately sidled over along the perch for her to rub the back of his head. "Yeah, there, there, that's my good little bird."

Once she was finally reassured that he was okay, she stood up. With one last look at the little parakeet and a sigh, she turned and trudged back to the living room.

"Was there something you wanted in particular, Maddie?" she asked, as she entered the room. "Or did you just drop by to terrorize my bird?"

"Well, gee, thanks a lot, Charlotte. And aren't we in a good mood."

Charlotte shook her head. "Sorry. I shouldn't have said that. It's just that I'm hot and I'm tired. It's been a long day — a long week, for that matter." Charlotte frowned as a thought suddenly occurred to her. "Speaking of a long day, why aren't you at work?" She narrowed her eyes. "Please tell me that you didn't get fired."

Madeline rolled her eyes. "No, Charlotte. I didn't get fired. For your information, I took half a day off. I figured I deserved it after all of the overtime I've been putting in lately. Now, if you're through interrogating me, why don't you just sit down, put your feet up, and relax, and I'll get you a glass of tea."

"Sounds heavenly," Charlotte told her, but even as she said the words, she couldn't help being suspicious of Madeline's motives. As Madeline rose, Charlotte collapsed onto the sofa.

"By the way," Madeline said, pausing near the door leading to the kitchen, "where is Louis off to these days?" She motioned toward a stack of mail on the small table near the front door. "That's quite a pile of mail over there that he's accumulated."

Louis Thibodeaux was a retired New Orleans police detective who rented the other half of Charlotte's double. Before he'd retired from the NOPD, he'd approached Charlotte about renting from her. He'd said he needed a place to stay, just until he finished building his retirement home on the North Shore. At the time, she'd had her doubts about the arrangement working.

Another of her clients had been murdered, and she and Louis had clashed big time during the investigation. Since Louis was her niece's partner at the time, she'd given in and rented to him. But once he'd finished building his house, he'd changed his mind about moving and decided to stay in New Orleans instead. When he'd asked if he could keep renting from her for a while longer until he found a house to buy in the city, she'd had even more doubts. By that time, though, her doubts were mostly due to her own growing personal feelings for him.

To her surprise, the arrangement had worked out, especially since he had been working for J.T.M. Security and had to travel a lot. And, unlike a former tenant she'd had, Louis was reliable and prompt with his rental payments each month.

"Louis is in New York, Miss Nosy Rosie," Charlotte told her sister. "And I honestly don't know when he's coming home. And why are you going through my mail anyway?"

Madeline shrugged. "I got bored waiting for you," she said. "But too bad about him being gone so much. With all of the crime in the city, it has to be a comfort to know that an ex-cop is your neighbor." She waggled her eyebrows. "And such a cute one at that, especially if you're the type who likes older men," she added with a giggle. "Of course you're older too, aren't you?"

Charlotte rolled her eyes. "Thanks a lot. Just what I needed, to be reminded of how old I am. That's okay, though. Your time's coming, missy. Just remember, you're only a few years behind me. Now — where's that tea you said you were getting for me?"

Madeline laughed. "Okay, okay, but you're not getting any younger," she teased, "and eligible men your age don't grow on trees. At least not the good ones," she added.

"Enough already! The tea, Maddie!"

"Okay, okay, I'm going."

"And next time, don't be going through my stuff."

With a saucy grin, Madeline turned and disappeared through the doorway.

Charlotte groaned from exhaustion, propped her feet up on the coffee table, then leaned her head back against the sofa. It was bad enough that she had to endure teasing from Judith about Louis, but now Madeline was doing it too. "Like mother, like daughter," she muttered. And once they got started with their teasing, they didn't seem to know when to quit. Time for a change of subject, she decided.

"So what's up, Maddie?" Charlotte called out, settling farther down into the sofa.

"Be there in a minute," Madeline answered. When she returned with the promised glass of tea, she handed it to Charlotte, then plopped down beside her. After a moment, she finally said, "It's Nadia. I'm worried about her."

"How come?" Charlotte took a long drink of the tea.

"For one thing she's still working. As you well know," Madeline added pointedly.

"Now, Maddie —"

"Don't 'now, Maddie' me. All of that stooping and scrubbing and stuff can't be that good for her or for the baby. She's got dark circles around her eyes, Charlotte, and she can't even sit still a minute without nodding off to sleep. Why on earth she insisted on continuing to work is beyond me. It surely can't be the money. My son's an attorney, for crying out loud. He makes plenty to support them."

Charlotte sighed. "It's not the money, Maddie. It's just that Nadia is still a bit insecure plus she has a lot of pride. The last thing she wants is for anyone to think that she married Daniel for his money."

"Why, who on earth would believe such a thing, and even if they did, who cares? It's nobody's business and —" Madeline suddenly stopped in midsentence. "Oh, no," she whispered. "It's because of me, isn't it? Because of all those awful things I said when Daniel first told us they had run off and gotten married."

"That's part of it," Charlotte acknowledged. "But, like I said, Nadia has her pride."

Madeline waved a dismissing hand. "Pride, smide — that's just plain silly. And dangerous," she added. "Besides, what's that old saying? Something about pride coming before a fall?"

"So what's your point, Maddie?"

"The point is that the girl needs to stop working. I want you to fire her."

Charlotte heaved a sigh. "Now you know good and well that I can't do that." She shook her head emphatically. "I won't do it."

"You could too do it, if you wanted to. You're just being stubborn."

"No, I'm not 'just being stubborn,' not this time," Charlotte snapped. "Read my lips, Maddie. Nadia is a grown woman, perfectly capable of running her own life without any interference from me. Or you," she stressed.

"Okay, okay. No need to get your panties all in a wad. And don't look at me like that."

"That's a disgusting phrase."

"Yeah, well, sorry, but Charlotte, if you won't fire her, at least talk to her. Please? She'll listen to you."

As if I don't have enough to do already, Charlotte thought to herself. "I do plan to talk to her," she finally conceded grudgingly. "But not to insist that she stop working," she quickly added. "Only to let her know that when she's ready to stop, I have someone who's agreed to take her place."

"Well, why the devil didn't you say so in the first place?"

"Because, it's none of your business, Maddie. Get it? None-of-your-business."

On Friday morning Charlotte awakened to thunder and the sound of pounding rain. "Not again," she groaned, as she rolled out of bed.

The moment that her feet hit the floor, a sudden thought struck her. She'd missed the weather forecast last night and she hadn't bothered to stop at the store on her way home to stock up on hurricane supplies.

Madeline had hung around until dinnertime, and since neither one of them had felt like cooking, Charlotte had suggested that they order pizza. It had been nearly seven when Madeline had finally gone home. By then, Charlotte had been simply too tired to worry about the weather or anything else.

In the kitchen, Charlotte turned on the coffeepot; then, after a brief detour to uncover Sweety Boy's cage, she headed for the shower. By the time she'd showered and dressed, the coffee had brewed. With hopes of catching the weather forecast before it was time to go to work, she decided to drink her first cup in front of the television.

According to the weather forecasters, the tropical storm was finally on the move again, heading east-northeast. The storm was showing definite signs of strengthening, and the experts were predicting that it would obtain a category three hurricane status before it made landfall. The projected path put it coming ashore around Mobile, Alabama, sometime early Saturday morning, but since New Orleans would be on the west side of the huge system until it moved farther east, the city would receive a soaking just the same from the outer bands of rain.

With a sigh of relief laced with a dash of sympathy for the people living in Mobile, Charlotte switched off the TV and took her empty coffee cup to the kitchen. If the forecasters were right and the storm did hit Mobile, New Orleans would once again dodge the bullet.

For as long as Charlotte could remember, there had been dire predictions that a direct hit by a hurricane could wipe out New Orleans. The city was below sea level and located in a giant bowl that was surrounded by Lake Pontchartrain, the Mississippi River, and farther to the southeast, the Gulf of Mexico. The only real protection that the city had against flooding was its huge pumping system. In a normal downpour, the pumps worked just fine, but everyone knew that there was no way the pumps would be able to keep up with the amount of water that a direct hit from a major hurricane could produce.

But this wasn't a major hurricane — not yet. All the same, Charlotte decided that she still needed to stock up on supplies, just in case. Maybe she'd have time to pick up a few things after work, if there was anything left in the stores by then.

Though the streets weren't flooded yet, they were already beginning to hold water, and the drive to the Adamses' house was slow and tedious.

At the Adamses' front door, Charlotte hesitated before using the key that June had given her. Should she knock first or simply let herself in? For all she knew, no one was at home. But if she knocked and Emma and Justin were home, were still sleeping . . . Charlotte inserted the key into the keyhole, twisted it, and opened the door. No use waking up the kids.

Sure enough, the house was quiet, without a sign of anyone stirring around. Charlotte locked the door, disarmed the security system, and headed for the kitchen. Whether they were asleep or already up and out somewhere, she was sure she'd find out sooner or later. She'd begin cleaning downstairs first, she decided, and maybe by the time she was ready to vacuum, she'd know if they were home or not.

Except for vacuuming and mopping, Charlotte had finished in the kitchen and was polishing the dining room table when she heard a noise at the front door. Just as she poked her head around the doorway, the front door swung open, and June Bryant stepped inside.

Now why on earth would June have a key, especially if both of the Adams children were home? Then again, maybe they weren't home after all.

Charlotte stepped into the wide hallway just as June turned around. June's hand flew to her chest and she froze. "Oh, Charlotte!" She took a deep breath. "You startled me."

Charlotte felt like rolling her eyes. After all, surely the silly woman had noticed that her van was parked out front. She forced a smile instead. "Well, you kind of surprised me too," she said. "I wasn't expecting anyone."

June held up a key. "Gordon asked me to

check on the kids and clean out Mimi's closet."

At least now she knew that the kids were home, but personally, Charlotte felt it was a bit odd that Mimi's husband had even thought about having her closet cleaned out, especially so soon after her death. Most men wouldn't. *Be nice, Charlotte.* Then again, maybe Gordon Adams was different. Maybe all of the reminders of his wife were just too painful.

"He could at least wait until we bury her!"

The outraged voice of Emma Adams caught both Charlotte and June off guard, and they spun around in the direction of the staircase.

Emma, her eyes narrowed and glaring at June, descended the remaining steps of the staircase with angry deliberation. "No one is touching my mother's things. *No one!*" she shouted. "And I've already told you that Justin and I don't need *anybody* checking up on us. We're both perfectly capable of taking care of ourselves."

"Now, Emma —" June held up a placating hand. "Your dad means well, and I'm just trying to help."

"That's a lot of bull, and you know it," Emma shot back. "If he meant well, then *he'd* be here with us," she argued.

June planted her fists on her hips and glared at Emma. "I think you've said just about enough, young lady. I've tried to be nice to you, tried to consider that you're grieving, but you're not the only one hurting, you know. Fred and I have been friends with your parents for a long time, and your father trusts us. Whether you like it or not, I intend to do what your father asked me to do."

"We'll just see about that!" Emma yelled. And with one last hateful glare at June, she whirled around and stomped back up the stairs.

"Emma! You come back here," June demanded.

Emma totally ignored June, and at that moment, Justin, looking as if he were still half asleep, appeared at the top of the staircase just as his sister flounced past him. "Hey, Em," he called out, "what's all the yelling about?"

"Ask June," Emma snapped. "She seems to know everything." Then, like a shot, Emma took off down the hallway and slammed her bedroom door so hard that the front hall chandelier rattled.

Charlotte's heart went out to the girl. She was hurting and hurting badly. June's presence and phony sympathy weren't helping one iota.

Unsure of what, if anything, she should say, Charlotte decided that June probably wouldn't welcome any comments from her and wouldn't be interested in her opinions either. "I'll be cleaning in the dining room if you need anything," she told June instead.

It was just after lunch, and Charlotte was dusting the front parlor when Gordon Adams came home.

"Hello," he called out. "Anybody home? Charlotte?"

"In the parlor," she answered, and a moment later, he appeared at the doorway.

"Where is everyone?" he asked her.

"You just missed Justin. He left about ten minutes ago. He said something about buying a suit."

Gordon nodded. "Good. I told him to get a new one for his mother's funeral. And speaking of the funeral, I don't know if June has asked you yet, but I was wondering if I could impose on you again. Would you be available to help out afterward here at the house? I would really appreciate it if you could."

Charlotte hesitated, trying to think if she

had made any plans for Saturday afternoon.

"If it's the money," Gordon said, "I'll pay you well."

She shook her head. "No, no, it's not the money. I was just trying to remember if I had anything else going on. I'm pretty sure I don't, though, so I'll be glad to help."

"Thanks, that's a load off my mind." He suddenly frowned. "Is Emma still locked up in her room?"

Gordon's question caught Charlotte off guard, and she frowned. Had Emma called her father? Or had June? "Afraid so," she finally answered. "Poor thing. She's really hurting right now."

He nodded. "I know she is, but that's no excuse for being rude to June. And what about June? Is she still here? Not that I'd blame her if she weren't," he added.

Charlotte nodded. "I believe she's up in the master bedroom. She's, ah . . . she's packing up Mimi's clothes."

As if the very mention of June's name had conjured her up, she suddenly appeared behind Gordon.

"I've finished packing up the clothes," June said. Gordon turned to face her. "And I'm sorry you had to come home. As if you didn't already have enough on your mind," she added. "Believe me, I didn't want to have to call you, but I didn't know what else to do after Emma pitched her little tantrum. Why, she wouldn't even come down for lunch."

Little tantrum? The woman was an idiot, Charlotte decided.

"I'm sorry about that, June," Gordon said. "Emma owes you an apology, and I'll talk to her."

"Speaking of lunch, have you had yours yet?" June asked.

Gordon nodded. "I had a bite earlier."

June placed her hand on Gordon's forearm. "You look exhausted. After you talk to Emma, you should really try to get some rest. Tomorrow is going to be a long, hard day for everyone. And I don't want you worrying about dinner tonight. I'll take care of that for you. I always cook more than Fred and I can eat anyway."

The conversation between June and Gordon stayed with Charlotte during the rest of her time at the Adamses' house. She also wondered about June's husband and her son, wondered what they must think about her absence and her generosity toward the Adams family. Of course, her son had been shipped off to military school, if

174

she remembered right. But what about her husband? Did he even know or care that June had completely taken over Gordon and his children? He might, she finally decided. He might care if he knew how June had been acting all afternoon.

But it wasn't just June's fawning, ingratiating attitude toward Gordon or that she kowtowed to his every wish that was so strange. It was one thing to be helpful, but June carried things to the extreme. What aggravated Charlotte the most was the way June had followed her around all afternoon, giving her orders. She'd reminded Charlotte of Bitsy Duhe, except that Bitsy was much nicer, and Charlotte had had just about all she could stomach.

Using the excuse that she had an appointment, Charlotte decided to leave a few minutes earlier than she was supposed to. It was either leave or say something to June Bryant that she was sure to regret later.

It was still pouring rain when Charlotte pulled the van into the parking lot beside the beauty shop. She was early for her appointment and in no hurry to get drenched.

She shifted into park but left the van running. The thump-thump rhythm of the windshield wipers broken only by the swishing sound made by passing cars through the flooded street was hypnotizing as she stared out at the gloomy weather with unseeing eyes. She would have liked nothing better than to go home and crawl into bed, to forget everything and everybody just for a little while. At times like this she often wished that the good Lord had included a tiny button on the side of her head that she could push to turn off her thoughts.

Charlotte recognized the feeling for what it was and readily admitted to herself that she was depressed. Being tired had a lot to do with it, and the gray, rainy day didn't help, but she knew that those were just excuses for what was really bothering her. If she were honest with herself, she'd admit that Mimi's murder had more of an effect on her than she'd thought it had and was just now catching up to her. But why, she wondered? It wasn't as if she really knew the woman.

Charlotte sighed deeply, then reached down and turned off the engine. Maybe a haircut and a little pampering would make her feel better.

An hour later, Charlotte, sporting a new

haircut covered by a rain hat, made a mad dash through the rain back to the van.

Being pampered by her beautician had made her feel somewhat better. But not even a new haircut could dim the fact that yet another of her clients had been murdered or that any one of a number of people she'd come in contact with over the last few days could be Mimi's killer.

Charlotte drove the van slowly through the flooded parking lot. She had finally figured out what was really bothering her, though. If she kept losing clients, she wouldn't have to worry about Hank nagging her to retire. At the rate she was going, it wouldn't be long before no one would want to hire her for fear of being murdered.

By the time Charlotte got home, showered, and changed clothes, she still had a few minutes before it was time to leave again for her dinner date with Hank and Carol, just enough time to satisfy her curiosity about something that Gordon had mentioned the day before.

In the living room, she had two matching bookcases, both filled with her favorite books. Most of the books were ones she couldn't bear to part with — her keepers — and some were even autographed by the authors. In addition to the books, there was an up-to-date set of encyclopedias.

Once Charlotte had located the *J* volume, she pulled it out and took it over to the sofa. She switched on the lamp, then sat down and thumbed through the book until she found jimsonweed.

Along with the short text about the plant, there was a small color picture of the plant. As Charlotte stared at the picture, a strange, cold dread filled her being.

Chapter 10

Charlotte drummed her fingers against the page of the encyclopedia. There was no doubt about it. The same weed-looking plants that Mimi had used to replace her dead tree were jimsonweed.

Mimi . . . poison . . . jimsonweed . . . Sally Lawson . . . the dead trees . . .

In spite of Sally Lawson's so-called version of her relationship with Mimi, had there been a feud between Sally and Mimi after all? Had Sally lied?

Charlotte glared at the color picture of the deadly weed. Even if Sally had lied, surely a silly feud over a couple of dead trees wasn't enough motive to commit murder.

But what if there were more to the feud than just the trees. What if Sally were the one having an affair with Gordon instead of Rita? What if Sally had decided she wanted more than just an affair?

Charlotte frowned. After motive, there

had to be opportunity, so *how* would Sally have poisoned Mimi? Charlotte's frown deepened. What was it that June had said? Something about Mimi never locking her back door when she was home. What if Sally had sneaked into Mimi's kitchen during one of the HHS meetings and . . .

"Yeah, right!" Charlotte shook her head in denial. Even if Sally had sneaked into Mimi's kitchen without getting caught, there was no way she could have poisoned her, not without poisoning the rest of the HHS members as well. Was there?

Charlotte could feel the beginning of a headache. She abruptly slapped the encyclopedia closed and turned her head from one side to the other, then forward and back, to release the tension in her neck and ward off the headache. Time to go to dinner.

Prytania Street was almost covered with water and still the blowing rain kept coming down. As Charlotte drove ever so slowly down the street, her mind still raced with possibilities about Mimi's murder. Someone had poisoned Mimi. But who? Who would do such a thing? Gordon? What reason could he have, unless, as Mimi had suspected, he was having an affair? But even if he were having an affair and wanted to be rid of Mimi, why not simply divorce her?

"Money," Charlotte whispered. *The love of money is the root of all evil.* And for someone like Gordon, a divorce could prove to be expensive. Charlotte sighed. Yes, a divorce could cost Gordon, but according to Bitsy, he had more money than he could spend in a lifetime.

So, if Gordon didn't do it, then who did? Though Sally didn't exactly have opportunity, Charlotte couldn't completely dismiss her. But there were others as well: Rita Landers, Karen Douglas, Doreen Mires, and possibly even June. No, not June, she decided. June had no motive, at least none that was apparent.

Charlotte figured that out of the bunch, Rita Landers was the best choice. Revenge was always a viable motive, and there was no question that Rita had it in for Mimi.

Charlotte frowned, trying to remember what Mimi had said about Rita. Then it came to her. Something about Rita getting back at Mimi for her so-called affair with Rita's husband, Don. Even Mimi herself had believed that Rita was out for revenge.

Of course, maybe she shouldn't completely dismiss Karen Douglas or Doreen

Mires, especially Doreen.

Please-please don't hold what happened against George — not because of me . . . Charlotte could still hear Doreen pleading with Mimi. Doreen had known that Gordon had fired Rita's husband because Rita had maligned Mimi. It stood to reason that she would be fearful of the same punishment.

Charlotte slowed the van for a pedestrian crossing the street. Once the pedestrian was safely on the other side, she continued down the street.

Even if Doreen had wanted to poison Mimi, Charlotte couldn't, for the life of her, figure out how she could have done it or even how any of the others could have done it. And as long as she was going over the list, why not include Mimi's gardener as well?

Charlotte winced. *Now you're really getting ridiculous.* What earthly motive could the gardener have, or, for that matter, what real motive could any of them have?

Just stop it! Stop it right now!

Charlotte had always considered herself both blessed and cursed with the gift of imagination, and at times like tonight, she leaned heavily toward it being a curse.

Up ahead, she caught sight of the restaurant. "Thank goodness," she whispered. Eating dinner with Hank and Carol was just the distraction she needed to stop thinking about the whole mess for a while. Besides, if she didn't stop thinking about it, she wouldn't be able to eat a bite. If she didn't eat, Hank would wonder why.

Just thinking about the grilling that Hank would give her if he found out that yet another of her clients had been murdered made her cringe. Thank goodness she hadn't told him. Being interrogated by her son was the last thing she needed.

Suddenly, a horrible thought struck Charlotte. What if Hank already knew? What if Judith had told him? Charlotte loved her niece like a daughter and, in fact, had helped raise her, but she also knew that Judith had a big mouth at times, especially when it came to family matters.

Charlotte sighed. If Judith had blabbed to Hank, then the damage was done, and there wasn't much she could do about it. For now, she'd just have to play it by ear.

Charlotte had hoped to find a parking spot close to the restaurant. August Moon was one of her favorite places for Chinese food, but parking could sometimes be a problem. But parking anywhere in New

Orleans was usually a problem. And the rain just made things worse.

"With this awful weather, you'd think everyone would stay home," she grumbled.

You didn't stay home.

"Yeah, yeah." Charlotte glanced at the dashboard clock. "Great! Just great!" Thanks to the rain she was late.

Charlotte gripped the steering wheel tighter. She'd drive around the block one more time, she decided, and if she didn't find somewhere to park this time, then she'd have no choice but to go farther up Prytania.

You should have let Hank pick you up like he offered.

"Should've, would've, could've," she muttered. "And hindsight's a wonderful thing."

With still no luck after the second time around the block, she drove farther up Prytania. Halfway up the block, she finally found an empty parking space.

Once she parked, she grabbed her purse and umbrella. No doubt about it, though, umbrella or not, she was going to get wet. She pulled her purse strap over her shoulder and tucked the purse beneath her armpit.

"Could be worse," she whispered,

keeping an eagle eye on the flow of traffic in the side-view mirror. The pumps could break and everything could flood, or the silly storm could decide to head for New Orleans instead of Mobile. After all, the weather forecasters weren't infallible. They had been wrong with their predictions before.

Charlotte finally spied a break in traffic. In one awkward move, she wrenched open the door, stuck the umbrella outside, and released the spring. When it popped open, she hit the door lock, clamored out of the van, and slammed the door. Once she rounded the front of the van, she eyed the two-foot span of water that had collected in the gutter. Either she could wade through the water and spend the rest of the evening with wet feet or she could jump across it.

Make up your mind, Charlotte, before you get soaked.

With a quick prayer that she wouldn't fall and break her neck, she jumped to the sidewalk. Juggling the umbrella and her purse, she fished out several quarters, but just as she was about to shove them into the parking meter, she remembered that paying to park wasn't required after six p.m.

For the most part, the overhang of the buildings, along with her umbrella, protected her from the blowing rain and kept her upper body dry. By the time she reached the restaurant, though, the bottoms of her slacks and her shoes were wet, despite her earlier acrobatics to avoid the water.

Hank was waiting for her just inside the entrance. She smiled at him as he opened the door for her.

At times, it was still hard to believe that her son was a grown man. It seemed like only yesterday that she was a frightened young woman, alone in the world, and that Hank was just a precious toddler. Thanks to the nasty conflict in Vietnam that had taken his father's life, there had been many times she'd wondered how she was going to raise Hank by herself.

But they had both survived those early years, and her little boy had turned into a handsome and successful man, one any mother could be proud of.

Even so, he didn't look his age. In spite of his demanding medical practice and rigorous surgical schedule, he made time to keep himself physically fit. Tall and lean, with sandy-colored hair and piercing blue eyes, he was the spitting image of his father, a man he'd never known except through Charlotte's memories and a few pictures she'd kept.

"I was beginning to get worried about you," he told her, as he leaned down and kissed her on the cheek. "You should have let us pick you up."

"My thoughts exactly, hon." She shivered in the cooler air of the restaurant. "Sorry I'm late. I guess I should have called, but," she motioned toward the door, "I didn't count on such nasty weather." She craned her neck and glanced around the restaurant. "Where's Carol?"

"In the restroom. Our table is over there by the window." He pointed toward the side window. Within moments after she was seated, a waiter appeared to take their drink order. "Iced tea, Mom?" When Charlotte nodded, Hank told the waiter, "Three iced teas."

"Oh, look," Charlotte exclaimed, "isn't that a new one?" She pointed at the wall opposite their table. Besides the wonderful food at August Moon, one of the things she loved about the place was the décor, especially the luminous, framed pictures on the walls. Each picture was different and each scene was constantly changing within the frame. The one she'd pointed at was a waterfall scene, a moving picture within a frame, only better.

Hank shrugged. "Could be new."

Charlotte continued to stare at the waterfall. "If I ever find out where to buy those things, I'm going to get me one."

"Get what?" Carol Jones asked, as she approached the table. A slim woman, Carol was a little taller than Charlotte and had warm, brown eyes and dark, shoulder-length hair. She was a nurse Hank had met through one of his associates. From the first time he'd introduced her, Charlotte had immediately liked her. But Carol wasn't just another woman with a pretty face. Unlike some of the women Hank had dated, she was also sensible, the kind of practical nature that Charlotte admired. And, unlike Hank's ex-wife, Mindy, Carol loved children, another trait that had endeared her to Charlotte.

Both Charlotte and Hank stood. Hank pulled out Carol's chair, and Charlotte leaned over and gave her a quick hug. "I'd like to get one of those moving pictures," Charlotte explained, motioning to the one she'd been admiring.

"Those are nice, aren't they?" Carol responded. "My personal favorite is the one over there of the ocean. That one actually has sound effects."

"Yeah, I like that one too," Charlotte said, and as she seated herself again with Hank's assistance, she noticed the dress Carol was wearing, a classic silk chemise. "You look lovely, hon," Charlotte told her. "Royal blue is definitely your color."

Carol smiled as she sat in the chair to Charlotte's right. "Thanks. You'll never guess where I got it." When Charlotte shrugged, Carol cupped her hand over her mouth, leaned toward Charlotte, and whispered, "Don't tell Hank, but I found it at the Junior League thrift shop."

Hank shot her an exasperated look. "I heard that," he said, as he settled back into his chair. "How many times have I told you —"

Carol shook her finger at him, and with narrowed eyes, she said, "Don't even go there." She turned to Charlotte. "He gets all uptight about me buying secondhand clothes, but I honestly don't see what the big deal is. I think of it as recycling, and a lot of those clothes, especially the ones at the Junior League, have hardly been worn at all." She shrugged. "Besides, there's a good chance that even those that are supposedly brand new in the department stores have been tried on by someone. In a sense, they're secondhand too."

Charlotte glanced over at Hank and fought to keep from grinning. "She does have a point, son."

Hank rolled his eyes. "Women! If I live to be a hundred, I'll never understand them. I've told her time and time again that if she wants to go shopping, she can charge it to me. I even gave her a charge card — which she's never used, I might add. She's more stubborn than you are about taking money from me. But all that's going to change after we're married —"

"Married!" Charlotte cried. "Did I hear you say married?"

Hank grinned and winked at Carol. "Yes, Mother, you heard right." He motioned at Carol. "Show her, honey."

Beaming, Carol held out her left hand. On her ring finger was a sparkling solitaire diamond ring. Charlotte was no expert on diamonds, but the pear-shaped diamond that was set on a wide band of what appeared to be either white gold or platinum had to be at least three carats.

"That's part of the reason we wanted you to join us for dinner tonight," Carol told her. "We're hoping that you approve."

Charlotte's throat grew tight, and to her horror, her eyes filled with tears. When

Carol's face fell in disappointment, Charlotte shook her head. "No, hon —" She picked up her napkin and blotted her eyes. "Tears of joy," she tried to explain in a choked voice. She cleared her throat, grabbed Carol's hand, and squeezed it. "Of course I approve. Nothing would make me happier." She turned to Hank, and with her other hand she cupped his cheek. "Congratulations, son. It's about time."

"Don't blame me," he shot back. "I asked her six months ago and she turned me down flat."

Carol shook her head. "That's not true, Charlotte. Don't listen to him. I —"

The waiter arrived with the iced tea, and Carol waited until he left before continuing. "I didn't turn him down — not exactly. What I told him was that I just needed a little more time to get a few things taken care of first."

Charlotte was well aware of the "few things" that Carol had to take care of. Fiercely independent, Carol had spent the past five years paying off a debt that she'd incurred from a previous relationship. She'd been engaged to a man who not only turned out to have a gambling problem but who was a con man as well. He'd duped

Carol into borrowing money to invest in one of his so-called business ventures; then he'd lost it all at the casino. Rather than claim bankruptcy or risk a bad credit rating, Carol had set out to pay back every penny of the loan by living as frugally as possible and holding down two jobs.

Charlotte knew for a fact that Hank had offered to finish paying off the loan for her, but Carol had refused. Since Carol had finally accepted Hank's marriage proposal, Charlotte figured that she must have at long last paid off the debt all by herself.

Charlotte squeezed Carol's hand. "Well, I, for one, am certainly glad that you finally agreed. Maybe now I'll get a grandchild before I'm too old and decrepit to enjoy one."

"Whoa, hold on, Mom — one step at a time. Wedding first."

"I take it you've set a date then?"

Carol nodded. "We figured the first or second Saturday in October. By then Nadia will have had the baby, and we'll have a few weeks to work out our schedules and make all of the arrangements. We're shooting for something small and intimate — just family and a few close friends. Besides," Carol said, a blush on her face, "I thought it would be kind of neat to have the wedding near your birthday. Kind of like an extra present for you."

Charlotte was truly touched. "I can't think of anything nicer than to get a daughter-in-law for my birthday."

At that moment, their waiter approached the table. "Are you folks ready to order or do you need a little more time?"

"Mom? Carol?" Hank asked.

"I already know what I want," Charlotte told him.

"Me too," Carol chimed in.

They placed their orders, and throughout most of the meal, conversation centered on the wedding plans.

"One thing, Charlotte," Carol said, as the waiter handed Hank the dinner check. "I was wondering if you would have time to meet for lunch one day. I'd like to get your opinion on some of the details, and eventually I'd like you to go with me when I talk to the caterer to pick out the food for the reception."

Charlotte laughed. "After next Wednesday, I should have plenty of time on my hands for a while." At Carol's puzzled look, Charlotte explained, "One of my clients has decided to move to the North

Shore, so I'll have Wednesdays and Thursdays off now."

"Oh, I'm so sorry, Charlotte, but I'm sure that once word gets around, you'll have no trouble getting another Wednesday client."

Hank glanced up, and his expression grew serious. "Personally, I think it sounds great. In fact, it sounds like a prime opportunity for you to begin cutting back on your clients and letting those women who work for you take more of the load. Cutting back will make it easier for you to retire."

Charlotte sighed. "Hon, I know you mean well, but please don't start that up again. As for the women who work for me, they're already booked solid and have more than they can handle as it is. And another thing, I did try cutting back for a few weeks. I keep telling you, though, that I'm not ready to retire — not yet. For one, I'm not old enough to retire. And even if I were old enough, I'm not willing or financially able to just yet. I really need to work at least a few more years. Besides," she quickly added, "I'd be bored silly."

"I've told you that the money is no problem. As for being bored, once we have a baby, you'll have plenty of time to spoil him rotten."

"Her!" Charlotte and Carol said in unison, then burst into laughter.

"Whichever," Hank said, as he rolled his eyes and shook his head. Then he added, "But seriously, Mom, promise me you will at least think about it before you go looking for a new client. Please," he added softly.

Charlotte lowered her eyes and stared at the white tablecloth. She could have pointed out that she'd never had to "go looking for a new client," but tonight of all nights, she didn't want to argue. "Okay," she finally answered, mostly to appease him. "I'll think about it."

On the way home that night, as she'd promised, Charlotte did think about what Hank had said about cutting back and about retiring . . . again. She thought about it for all of about two minutes before completely dismissing the idea.

Bless his heart, Hank meant well, and she was sure that his offer of financial assistance was genuine, but she just couldn't do it. One day she might have to depend on him, but she was hoping that day was a long way off. For now, she couldn't see herself having to depend on him or anybody else while she was still able-bodied and healthy. Besides, she'd been paying her own way for too many years, and she liked not having to answer to anyone but herself. And though she knew better, knew that he truly loved and respected her, ever since he'd become a doctor, she'd always wondered if he wasn't just a wee bit embarrassed that his mother still worked as a maid.

By the time Charlotte reached Milan Street, the rain was slacking off. At some point tomorrow, she decided, she'd go ahead and give Bitsy a call to let her know that she had a Wednesday opening for a new client.

As Charlotte turned the van into her driveway, the rain had slowed to a misty drizzle. "It figures," she muttered, as she parked, switched off the engine, gathered her purse, and slid out of the van. Now that it didn't matter if she got wet or not, the rain had let up.

As she climbed up the steps leading to the front porch, she noticed that Louis's car was parked in the other driveway. There was also a light burning in the front window of his half of the double, which meant he was back in town and still up.

Louis Thibodeaux. How long would he be home this time? she wondered, as she unlocked her door.

When Charlotte entered her living room, Sweety Boy greeted her with squawks and whistles. "Sorry, boy," she told him, "but I'm not letting you loose — not tonight." Charlotte slipped out of her wet shoes and stepped into her moccasins. "It's too late, and I'm too tired to fool with you." All she could think about at the moment was getting into her pajamas and simply relaxing. Maybe she'd let the little fellow loose for a few minutes first thing in the morning.

Charlotte glanced over at her answering machine, and when she saw that there were no messages, she sighed with relief.

She bent down and picked up her still damp shoes. Maybe she'd read a bit . . . if she could stay awake long enough.

Always on the lookout for a good mystery, she'd discovered a series of books by an author named Lee Child and fallen in love with his Jack Reacher character.

The loud knock on the front door gave Charlotte a start. "Who on earth could that be at this time of night?" she complained. According to the cuckoo clock, it was a few minutes past ten o'clock. She turned and glared at the door.

197

Chapter 11

"Charlotte, it's just me," a gruff voice called out.

With a frown, Charlotte unlocked the door. "Good grief, Louis, you scared the daylights out of me."

He was barefooted and dressed in faded jeans and a Saints T-shirt that had seen better days. Madeline was right about Louis. For a man his age, he was attractive in a rugged sort of way, a stocky man with gray hair, a receding hairline, and a nice flat stomach.

"Sorry," he said. "I know it's getting late, but I need to talk to you. Can I come in for a minute?"

"Wait just a second," Charlotte told him. "Let me cover up Sweety Boy." Though Louis had been her tenant for over a year now, the little bird still went crazy every time he and Louis were in the same room. One time he had thrashed about the cage so wildly that Charlotte had feared he would injure himself.

Charlotte hurried over to the parakeet's cage and quickly covered it. Sweety Boy's bizarre reaction to Louis might have made sense if Louis resembled the bird's previous owner, but he didn't. The little parakeet's previous owner had been a tall, skinny man with a mean disposition. The shyster had not only skipped out owing Charlotte money, but he'd left the little bird to starve.

Charlotte motioned at Louis. "You can come in now, but why don't we go back to the kitchen to talk?"

Louis sighed, but he followed Charlotte anyway. "That is one spoiled bird, Charlotte. You cater to him too much."

Another time, Charlotte might have argued with him, but tonight she was simply too tired. Besides, Sweety Boy was a defenseless little bird and she was just protecting him. For reasons she'd yet to figure out, he only reacted violently whenever Louis or Madeline was around. If she didn't know better, she'd swear that the parakeet could sense her own topsy-turvy emotions concerning both Louis and her sister.

In the kitchen, Charlotte faced Louis. "Have a seat." She motioned toward the kitchen table.

He shook his head. "I'd better not. I've still got to pack."

Charlotte frowned. "But didn't you just get home?"

"Yeah, but only for the night. I've got an early flight out in the morning."

Disappointment was sharp and swift, and though she would never admit it out loud to anyone, especially to Louis, she had missed knowing he was right next door. "That's a pretty short turnaround," she pointed out.

"Yeah, well, I wasn't too happy about it myself."

"So — what was it you needed?"

"Two things," he answered. "First of all, as I said, I have to pack. I'll be leaving early in the morning, and I'll probably be gone for at least a couple of weeks this time. I keep meaning to have my mail stopped but —" He shrugged. "Would you mind?"

"No, I don't mind collecting it for you," she said. *Again,* she wanted to add but didn't. Louis was always forgetting to have his mail or newspaper stopped, and she'd begun to suspect that he did it on purpose, just to have an excuse to call her.

Yeah, right, in your dreams. Suddenly embarrassed by her silly thoughts, she quickly added, "That's no problem, and don't forget to pick up what came for you while you were gone. It's stacked on the table by the door in the living room."

If the truth were known, Louis's forgetfulness was probably just that, forgetfulness, and had nothing to do with her. Certainly nothing personal anyway. After all, except for that one night on her sixtieth birthday when he'd kissed her, he'd never made another move to deepen their strange relationship. One of these days, she figured, she'd just come right out and ask him why, but not tonight, not when she was so tired she could barely think straight.

"I won't forget," he said. "I think I've got a couple of bills in there that are overdue." He paused, then said, "In case I haven't told you so before, I really do appreciate you taking care of this stuff for me."

Suddenly uncomfortable with the way he was looking at her, she decided to change the subject. "You said you needed two things," she reminded him.

He nodded and then held out a small plastic cup. "Could I borrow some sugar?"

Up until that moment, Charlotte hadn't even noticed that he had the cup in his hand, and the embarrassed look on his face was so priceless that she couldn't help but burst out laughing. Unlike her, Louis almost never seemed to get embarrassed over anything.

Louis rolled his eyes. "Yeah, go ahead and laugh. I had plenty of sugar, I'll have you know — at least enough for morning coffee — but Stephen brought Amy by tonight, and the little scamp knocked over the sugar bowl, broke it, and ruined what little sugar I had left. I just need enough for a couple of cups of coffee."

Still laughing, Charlotte took the cup and filled it with sugar from the canister on the kitchen cabinet. As she handed it back to him, she said, "Speaking of sons and grandchildren, I may be having a grandchild myself before too long."

Louis frowned. "Hank?"

Charlotte nodded. "I just found out tonight that Hank and Carol are finally going to get married. That's where I was tonight. They treated me to dinner so they could tell me the news."

Louis's frown deepened and he shook his head. "I swear — call me old-fashioned — but I always thought a couple was supposed to get married first and then have a kid. Nowadays, though, they —"

Charlotte shook her head. "No — you

misunderstood. Hank and Carol *are* getting married first. I just meant that once they're married, they intend to have children, so I might actually live long enough to be a grandma after all."

"Well, that's a relief — about them getting married first, I mean. Maybe there is still some decency left in the world." He stared at her expectantly, then narrowed his eyes. "This is where you say that of course there's some decency left and you tell me how cynical I am."

Again, ordinarily she would have argued with him and often did. For the most part, the two of them were like oil and water and their opinions almost always clashed. "Well, since you already know all that, there's no point repeating it, is there?" she quipped. "Besides, to tell the truth, I'm just too dog-tired to argue with you tonight. It's been a long, eventful day."

"You didn't find another dead body, did you?"

Louis's sarcastic dig conjured up a kaleidoscope of horror images of dead bodies and human bones, images she'd tried to repress. And now Mimi . . . dead . . . poisoned. For a second, Charlotte felt like hauling off and punching him.

"I've only found *one* dead body," she retorted. "And before you say it, the bones don't count. Besides, technically, I didn't find those bones. I just happened to be there when they were discovered. So, no, Mr. Smarty-Pants, I didn't find another dead body. If you must know, I did lose one of my main clients, though." The words just popped out, and when she realized what she'd said, she was mortified.

"Lost as in the client died, or lost as in the client disappeared?"

Charlotte rolled her eyes. *Think, Charlotte. Think.* Given Louis's opinion about her previous involvements, there was no way she wanted to discuss Mimi's murder with him. Then, out of the clear blue, the perfect solution came to mind. "Oh, for Pete's sake," she told him. "Give it a rest. Neither one!" *Liar, liar, pants on fire.* "For your information, lost as in I got fired." It wasn't exactly a lie. "And before you draw any other erroneous conclusions, I got fired because Marian Hebert has decided to move to the North Shore. Now — if you don't mind — like I said, I'm tired and I'd like to go to bed."

A teasing, leering grin pulled at Louis's lips. "Is that an invitation?"

"No, it is not!" She pointed at the door. "Out!"

"Aw, Charlotte, lighten up. I was just kidding . . . well, not kidding entirely, but . . ." His voice trailed away. Then, he shrugged. "Whatever, but seriously, I'm sorry about your client, but you know you won't have any trouble replacing her, so I don't see that there's much of a problem . . ." He gave her a shrewd look. "Not unless Hank started up again about you retiring."

"Yeah, well, he did, and I halfway considered it, but —"

"Let me guess. But no deal, right?"

Charlotte nodded. "And to tell you the truth, it's getting pretty tiresome."

Louis reached out and squeezed her upper arm. "Take it from me. Stick to your guns. Don't retire unless you're good and ready. It's not all it's cracked up to be." With another gentle squeeze, he released her arm. "Now, get some rest, and I'll see you in a week or so."

The man was an enigma, she decided, as she closed the front door behind him a few minutes later, then locked it. She reached up and rubbed the spot on her arm where he'd squeezed. One minute he could make her so angry she could chew nails, and the next minute he . . . *not kidding entirely.*

"Don't even go there," she muttered.

205

"Humph, and men are always complaining about women being teases." As she switched off the living room light, the mechanical bird in the cuckoo clock began chirping out the hour. Charlotte counted eleven cuckoos before he finally stopped. "Way past my bedtime," she grumbled.

On Saturday morning, Charlotte awoke to the sudden roar of her neighbor's lawn mower accompanied by the howls of the Doberman pinscher that lived across the street.

"Oh, for pity's sake," she complained, as she raised her head long enough to glance at the clock on the bedside table. When she saw that it was only seven o'clock, she burrowed back beneath the covers. The rain must have finally stopped, she decided. But even if it had stopped, it had been raining for days and the ground had to be saturated. Surely it was too wet to mow, especially at seven o'clock on a Saturday morning.

Charlotte closed her eyes and breathed deeply and evenly, but it was no use. Between the racket outside and her mind already racing with chores she needed to get done before leaving for work that afternoon, going back to sleep was impossible.

With a groan, Charlotte finally threw the covers back and crawled out of bed. Coffee first, she decided. And if the rain really had stopped, maybe she could take a nice long walk before it got too hot to breathe outside.

On her way to the kitchen, she detoured long enough to uncover Sweety Boy's cage and peek out the front window. The sun was shining. So, what had happened to the hurricane? she wondered.

Charlotte walked over to the coffee table, picked up the remote control, and switched on the television.

In the kitchen, she set up the coffeepot, turned it on, and then headed back to the bedroom to dress. By the time she was dressed, the coffee was ready. Charlotte poured herself a cup, settled in front of the television, and switched the channel to a local station.

According to the newscast, the hurricane had finally made landfall about two a.m. near Mobile, and as she watched the videos of the wind and flood damage that the storm had left in its wake, her heart ached for the people living in and around the southern Alabama area. She clicked off the television, bowed her head, said a prayer for the survivors, and added a prayer of thanks for New Orleans being spared once again.

Half an hour later, drenched with sweat from her walk but invigorated, Charlotte entered her house. The blinking light of the answering machine caught her eye.

With a puzzled frown and wondering who would be calling her so early, she stepped over to the machine. The number display indicated that there had been two calls.

Charlotte's insides tightened as her imagination took wing and all kinds of possibilities filled her head. Two calls within an hour and before eight o'clock on a Saturday morning had to mean trouble. Had there been a family emergency of some sort? Was someone hurt or . . .

She shook her head. "Stop it," she whispered. "Stop borrowing trouble and stop imagining the worst. It's probably nothing important." She took a deep breath. "Only one way to know for sure, though. Just do it." Sending up a quick prayer, Charlotte reached and hit the PLAY button.

The machine beeped; then, "Ms. LaRue, this is Sandra Wellington. I'm looking for a maid. Now, I know that you have a maid service with other people working for you, but I understand that you personally have an opening. I would only need you to come in once a week. If you're interested, please give me a call."

Charlotte stared at the machine with stunned disbelief as the woman rattled off her phone number. Again the machine beeped, and the second message played.

"Ms. LaRue, this is Abigail Thornton. I'm looking for a maid. You came highly recommended, and I was told that you might possibly have an opening. Two mornings a week should be sufficient. If *you* are available, I'd like to talk with you about working for me. My number is . . ."

Charlotte backed up a few steps, and shaking her head in amazement, she collapsed onto the sofa. "And here I've been worrying about losing clients," she murmured.

But how on earth had either of the women even known that she had an opening to begin with? If she had made that call to Bitsy like she'd intended, she could understand how they might have known. But she hadn't.

Charlotte pushed herself off of the sofa and walked over to the desk. With pen in hand, she replayed the messages and jotted down each woman's name and phone number. Then she stared at the names and numbers.

Abigail Thornton wanted her to work two mornings a week, but the only two mornings she had available were Wednesdays and Thursdays, and it was highly doubtful that Ms. Thornton wanted her to work two mornings straight in a row. On the other hand, Sandra Wellington wanted a maid only one day a week, and if per chance Ms. Wellington would be satisfied with Wednesday being that day, it would fit nicely into her schedule.

Charlotte added a star by Sandra Wellington's name. Of course, she'd give Abigail Thornton a call anyway, just to see if she would be interested in having one of her employees do the cleaning.

. . . *Promise me you will at least think about it before you go looking for a new client. Please.* Hank's plea swirled through her head, and Charlotte thoughtfully tapped the pen against the notepad on top of the desk. If she didn't take either client, she'd have both Wednesdays and Thursdays off during the week; then, if and when Hank and Carol have a baby, she'd be free to . . . *If and when.*

God forbid that something should

happen, but what if something did happen? What if, for some reason, Carol couldn't get pregnant?

Charlotte's throat grew tight. Hank would be heartbroken, especially after his experience with his ex-wife. Charlotte could still picture her son's beaming face when he told her that he was finally going to be a father. Then, another picture came to mind . . . her son, tears streaming down his cheeks, his voice choking, as he told her that Mindy had aborted his baby.

Charlotte shook her head as if doing so would shake away the image of her son's tormented face. Thank God, Mindy was out of the picture now. Hank had immediately divorced her. And, finally, after so many years of being angry and bitter, he had opened up again, all because he had found Carol.

Carol. Even if she did get pregnant right away, it would be nine months before she would have the baby.

Nothing says you can't quit work any time you want to.

Charlotte suddenly smacked her forehead with the heel of her hand. "Of course, dummy. You *can* always quit." She reached for the phone and dialed Sandra Wellington's number.

Mimi's funeral was being held at two o'clock that afternoon. Traditionally, close friends and relatives of the deceased usually would gather at the family's home after the services. Charlotte had agreed to be at the Adamses' house by two-thirty to straighten up a bit, make coffee, and have the food that June had ordered from the caterer set up before everyone arrived.

Charlotte had just placed the last of the food on the dining room table when she heard a commotion at the back door. Leaving the platter of sandwiches on the table, she returned to the kitchen just as Gordon, Emma, and Justin entered.

Gordon was wearing a dark gray suit, and Justin, a dark navy one. Both looked very distinguished, but the long black dress that Emma had chosen to wear only accented her pale face and brought out the dark circles beneath her eyes. Charlotte hated thinking such a thing, but the poor girl looked like something dredged up from an old vampire movie.

In spite of her ill-chosen clothes, though, the young woman's swollen eyes and the grief-stricken look on her face tugged at Charlotte's heart.

Emma spared a brief glance Charlotte's

way, then told her father, "I'm going to my room."

"I'd rather you wouldn't," he said. "Not just yet. People will be coming by soon, and —"

Emma shook her head and her eyes filled with tears. "No, please, Daddy, I don't want to see anyone. I don't know half those people, and besides, they're not coming to see me. Please, don't make me stay down here."

The bang, bang, bang of the door knocker echoed throughout the house and Gordon turned to Charlotte. "Would you mind answering the door, please?"

"Sure," Charlotte replied. With a sympathetic smile for Emma, she left the room.

Within minutes after the first group of people arrived, Judith and her partner, Brian Lee, showed up.

Judith glanced over her shoulder at a group of people coming up the walkway. "Just pretend we're part of the crowd," she told Charlotte. "And for goodness sake, don't let on that I'm your niece. We're just here to observe."

"Sure, I understand," Charlotte said, as they stepped into the hallway.

Among the crowd behind Judith and Brian was June, escorted by an older man, who Charlotte assumed was Fred, June's husband. Everyone but June walked toward the parlor. "Aren't those the same two detectives who were asking all the questions?" June asked Charlotte.

Not sure how to answer, Charlotte simply shrugged.

"So what are they doing here?" June asked.

"I think it's standard procedure for the detectives to attend the funeral in a murder case."

June's eyes narrowed. "How do you know that?"

Charlotte swallowed hard at being put on the spot. "I read a lot of mystery books," she explained.

June nodded slowly, her gaze following Judith and Brian as they entered the parlor. Then she fixed her eyes on Charlotte. "Now that's strange. I hadn't noticed it until just now. That woman detective and you could pass for mother and daughter. Are y'all related?"

Charlotte had often been mistaken as Judith's mother, more so than Madeline, and for years it had been a sore point between her and her sister. Since Charlotte didn't want to outright lie, mostly because she'd never been much good at it, she smiled. "I don't have a daughter. Just a son."

Giving Charlotte one last suspicious look, June walked past her and went into the parlor.

When Charlotte turned to greet the next group coming up the steps, she was shocked to see Rita Landers and Sally Lawson.

At first Charlotte didn't immediately recognize Rita. Her hair was styled differently, and it had been bleached from dark brown to blond. Though the style and color were attractive enough, Charlotte personally thought Rita looked better with brown hair.

Both women nodded a greeting at Charlotte, then went into the parlor. Within minutes, June returned to the front door. "Can you believe the nerve of that Rita Landers showing up here?" Her eyes flashed in anger. "Tell you what. Why don't you go check on the food, and I'll finish greeting the guests? Besides, I don't think I can stand to be in the same room as Rita."

With a nod, Charlotte happily took refuge in the kitchen.

Later, as Charlotte was checking the parlor for dirty dishes, she spotted Emma sitting by herself near the front window.

The young woman looked even more miserable than she had earlier, but evidently, whatever Gordon had said to her had been enough to convince her to stay downstairs.

Back in the kitchen, Charlotte unloaded the tray of dirty dishes, then began replenishing a crystal platter with the last of the sandwiches from the caterer's box. The food was disappearing fast, too fast, she thought, as she carried the platter into the dining room and placed it on the table. With one last look at the table, Charlotte turned to go back to the kitchen, but June sidled up beside her before she'd taken two steps.

"The coffee urn is almost empty," June said.

"I'm brewing more," Charlotte told her, "but this —" She motioned toward the tray of sandwiches. "This is the last of the sandwiches."

June shrugged. "Guess I didn't order enough, but too bad. Maybe once the food is gone, all these people will finally leave." She glared at Rita Landers, who had cornered Gordon and was having what appeared to be an intimate conversation with him. "Can you believe the nerve of that woman? After all of the trouble she's caused, and she has the gall to show up here. She was also at the funeral."

June's eyes suddenly grew wide with astonishment. "Well, that just beats all. I didn't realize that Sally Lawson was here too. Why didn't you tell me?"

When Charlotte just stared at her and didn't answer, June shook her head. "Never mind. Poor Mimi — she's probably rolling over in her grave."

Though Charlotte didn't feel it was her place to keep tabs on who showed up and who didn't, for once she agreed with June. Personally, she thought it was a bit tacky for the two women to show up, especially since they both had to know how Mimi had felt about them.

Back in the kitchen, Charlotte checked the coffeepot, and when she saw that it hadn't quite finished brewing, she gathered up the empty caterer boxes and carried them outside to the large garbage receptacle near the back door.

When she reentered the kitchen, three men she didn't recognize had seated themselves around the kitchen table. Each had a cup of coffee, and each had a small plate piled high with what Charlotte feared were the last of the sandwiches that she'd just put out in the dining room.

Each man in turn gave her a cursory

glance, and she could tell from the expressions on their faces that they had dismissed her as only the hired help, someone not worthy of their concern or attention. Then, they ignored her.

"What's this crap I'm hearing about Gordon?" one of the men asked the other two.

"What'cha heard," the man across from him said.

The man lowered his voice. "I heard that the cops think he did it, that he poisoned Mimi."

"Uh uh, no way, man," the second man said.

"I heard the same thing," the third man chimed in.

"So what's the motive?" the second man asked. "Gotta have a motive. And what kind of evidence do they have on him?"

"Oh, he's got motive alright," the third man said. "About two million motives, a life insurance policy he took out on her last year."

The first man shrugged. "So what? If you ask me, that's not much of a motive, especially considering how much he's worth."

"That's where you're wrong," the third man said. "I hear he's been playing the stock market and he's lost a bundle."

"Yeah, well, who hasn't, but you don't see me offing my old lady, do you?"

"No, but you don't have a little honey on the side either."

The second man rolled his eyes. "Oh, yeah, I forgot about that. But that could be just a rumor. Does anyone know who she is?"

"If they do, they're not talking, and if they're smart, they sure as hell won't talk now, not with the cops breathing down Gordon's neck."

"Hmm, very interesting," the first man said. "Could be even more interesting if we knew who she was for sure. Might even be good for a little blackmail."

The other two men guffawed at the first man's little joke, and it was all Charlotte could do to keep from giving them a piece of her mind.

The coffee had finished dripping, so Charlotte welcomed the opportunity to leave the kitchen before she said something she shouldn't. With a disgusted look directed at the men, she picked up the steaming decanter and carried it into the dining room.

Was it true after all? she wondered, as she wove her way through the crowd to the coffee urn. Was Gordon having an affair? Charlotte felt her temper spark. And what about the other things the men had said . . . the two million–dollar insurance policy and his losses in the stock market? Were those things true as well? If so, it was no wonder the police considered him a suspect.

Charlotte stopped next to the coffee urn and glanced around, her gaze resting on each of the women in the room. Which one? she wondered. Which one was Gordon having an affair with?

Chapter 12

Rita Landers was standing near the hallway door. Was she the one? Charlotte wondered. Was she Gordon's "honey"? Mimi had thought so, had even said as much to June, but Charlotte wasn't so sure. For one thing, it didn't make much sense. Why would Gordon have an affair with a woman who had spread such vicious rumors about Mimi, especially when Rita's penchant for gossip was supposedly the reason he had fired her husband to begin with?

Charlotte's gaze roamed the room again until she spotted Sally Lawson standing near the table talking with a woman whom Charlotte didn't recognize. Was she the one? Had there been more to Mimi and Sally's feud than just a couple of dead trees? Had the real reason for their feud been over Gordon?

With a slight shake of her head, Charlotte turned her attention back to the task at hand and poured the coffee into the urn.

She'd poured almost half of it when, out of the corner of her eye, she saw Gordon come through the doorway.

Charlotte's grip on the decanter handle tightened, and for a split second, she pictured herself flinging the rest of the hot beverage right in Gordon's smug, hypocritical face. She'd never actually do it, of course, and she knew she should be ashamed for even thinking of such a thing, but . . .

What goes round comes round. If the gossip is true, then Gordon will get his comeuppance one of these days. He will reap what he's sowed.

Somewhat comforted by the thought, Charlotte poured the rest of the coffee into the urn. When she returned to the kitchen, she was relieved to see that the three men were no longer there.

At the sight of the table, though, her lips thinned with irritation. The men were gone, but they'd left a mess, and they had also left half of the sandwiches uneaten on their plates.

Waste. Charlotte hated waste of any kind, but especially food. There were far too many hungry people in the world for anyone to carelessly waste food.

As Charlotte set the decanter on the cabinet next to the sink, for a second she was tempted to gather the uneaten sandwiches and put them back out on the platters in the dining room. After a moment, though, she changed her mind. Besides, someone might see her, and no matter what her personal opinion of Gordon was, he was still her employer. As such, she had an obligation not to do anything that might cause him embarrassment.

With a grimace, she marched over to the table, and once she scraped all the leftovers onto one plate, she took the plate and dumped the sandwiches into the trash. When she turned to take the plate to the sink, June entered the room.

"We're out of coffee, Charlotte," she said.

Shaking her head, Charlotte walked to the sink and deposited the plate on top of the others that were already soaking in sudsy water. "That's impossible," she told June. "I just finished filling the urn."

"Are you sure?"

Charlotte silently counted to ten to keep her temper in check. "I'm absolutely sure," she finally said.

June shrugged. "Why don't you go ahead and put on another pot to brew anyhow? That way, we'll be sure we won't run out."

That's exactly what Charlotte had intended to do, but it irked her that June seemed to take a strange pleasure in exerting her so-called authority.

Just do your job and ignore her.

Charlotte forced what she hoped looked like a smile and picked up the decanter.

"I'll be back to check on things in a little while," June told her. Then, with a tight smile of her own, June turned and left the room.

Charlotte stared out the window as she rinsed out the decanter under the faucet, then filled it with water. The woman really was a pain, and bossy to boot.

You don't have a little honey on the side either.

Maybe June was Gordon's "honey," she thought. Come to think of it, June was certainly a likely candidate, especially considering the way she'd stepped right in and taken over the entire Adams family since Mimi's death.

Now you're being downright mean and spiteful.

Though Charlotte knew she should listen to her conscience and she should be ashamed of herself for thinking badly about anyone, she simply couldn't ignore the feeling in her gut that had nothing to do with her own resentful feelings toward June. There was just something about the woman, something that went beyond her own personal dislike of June.

Charlotte felt as if a battle were being fought in her head, a battle of good versus evil, of choosing to have a positive outlook on life or choosing a negative outlook. She preferred to believe that there were still generous, selfless people in the world, people who only wanted to help others out of friendship. And there were people like that, she reassured herself. She was sure of it. But there were evil people in the world as well.

So which was June? Was she one of the generous types or did she have an evil, more sinister motive for doing all the things she did?

As Charlotte turned off the faucet and poured the water into the coffee maker, she thought back to the first time she'd met June; more specifically, she recalled the conversation she'd overheard between June and Mimi on that day. June had seemed truly distressed about the situation with her husband, Fred, and she had seemed truly concerned about him.

As for June taking over, even Mimi had acknowledged that June looked after her, made sure she didn't overdo, and hadn't Sally Lawson commented about June's penchant to take over as well? Maybe June had always been a take-charge, caring sort of person. Maybe trying to run things was simply part of June's personality, her way of showing friendship.

But what about Emma?

Charlotte grimaced. That Emma had resented June's so-called help had been more than clear. But Emma was still young, and she'd been grieving. To be fair, the girl might have resented anyone at that particular time.

On Sunday morning, the sun was shining, and already the air was hot and muggy. Since it was Madeline's turn to cook Sunday lunch for the family, Charlotte drove straight to her sister's apartment complex when church services ended.

Charlotte, Madeline, and their children were all that were left of Charlotte's immediate family, and from the time the children were small, it had long been a tradition for everyone to gather at either Charlotte's house or Madeline's apartment for lunch on Sundays after church. Charlotte always looked forward to the event, but today she looked forward to it even more than ever. Today was the day that Hank was going to announce his and Carol's engagement and wedding plans to the family.

When Charlotte knocked on the door, Judith was the one who answered. "Hey, Aunt Charley." She gave Charlotte a hug.

"Hey, yourself." Charlotte stepped through the doorway. "I didn't see you at church this morning. Where were you?"

"After I left the Adamses' house yesterday, I got called out — a double homicide." She shrugged. "I didn't get to bed until early this morning."

Charlotte patted her niece on the back, made a sympathetic sound, and then glanced around the small living room. "Guess I'm the first to arrive, huh? So, where's your mother?"

Judith rolled her eyes. "Would you believe that she has everything ready — cooked, that is — and all she has to do is heat it up when everyone gets here. But during church Davy asked her if she was going to have brownies for dessert, so, the minute she got home, she rushed back to the kitchen to whip up a batch?"

Charlotte laughed. "That little schemer. He knows just how to wrap her around his little finger."

Judith grinned. "You're right about that. She's impossible when it comes to that little boy. She's spoiling him rotten. What a change, huh?"

"Humph, just wait until Davy's little sister decides to make her entrance into the world."

"Speak of the devil, I think I just saw Daniel, Nadia, and Davy drive up." Judith walked over to the window. "Yep, that's them, and right behind them are Hank and Carol."

"Will Billy be able to make it today?" Charlotte asked. "You are still seeing him, aren't you?"

Judith nodded. "Yes, ma'am, I am. And so far, so good."

"So what does he think of your new partner, Brian?"

Judith shrugged. "Billy knows that Brian is no threat to our relationship, and Brian respects the fact that Billy and I are together."

Charlotte nodded her approval. "So, is Billy coming over?"

Judith shook her head. "Not this time. Poor thing, he's been working double shifts now for two weeks, so I told him to just stay home and get some rest." Judith grimaced and lowered her voice. "Besides,

Mother doesn't exactly welcome him with open arms when he does show up."

Charlotte reached out and patted her niece's arm. "Just give your mother a little time, hon. She'll come around eventually."

Madeline had disapproved of Judith's relationship with Billy Wilson from the beginning. Like Judith, Billy was a cop, but as Madeline had so often pointed out to Charlotte, unlike Judith, who was a detective, Billy was just a patrolman. Madeline was of the opinion that Judith could do a lot better for herself.

"Just look how much she's changed her attitude toward Nadia and Davy," Charlotte pointed out.

"I hope you're right, Auntie. If she'd just give Billy half a chance, she'd see what a really great guy he is."

Hank waited until the family sat down for lunch to make his announcement, and the rest of the lunchtime was filled with excited chatter about his and Carol's upcoming wedding.

When it was time for dessert, Madeline brought out an angel food cake stacked with strawberries. Then she brought out a plate of double fudge brownies, which she set in front of Davy.

"For my favorite grandson," Madeline told the little boy.

Grinning from ear to ear, Davy suddenly stood up in his chair and grabbed Madeline around the neck. As he hugged Madeline fiercely, Charlotte felt her throat tighten with emotion. One of these days . . . one of these days, she hoped soon, she'd finally have her own grandchild to spoil.

In deference to her son's presence and because she didn't want to hear a lecture from him, Charlotte chose a small slice of the cake, but just thinking about the brownies made her mouth water.

Later, after the table had been cleared and they were cleaning up in the kitchen, temptation overcame Charlotte's willpower, and she snitched a brownie.

"And how has your blood sugar level been lately," Madeline taunted.

"None of your business," Charlotte retorted.

"Well, you'd better not let Hank see you."

"Don't worry, I won't." Charlotte broke the brownie in half, handed one of the halves back to Madeline, and took a generous bite out of the other half. When the luscious chocolate melted over her tongue, she said, "Hmm, these are absolutely wonderful, Maddie. I think I just died and went to heaven."

Brownies . . . death . . . June . . . the HHS meeting . . .

Startled by the sudden sickening thought, Charlotte stopped chewing. She'd told Judith and Brian Lee about June furnishing the brownies for the Monday HHS meeting, but had she told them about Mimi's complaint that the brownie she'd sampled earlier that morning had been bitter?

Charlotte thought back to the brief interrogation and decided that she had neglected to mention Mimi's complaint. Then again, she'd still been in shock over Mimi's death, and she'd been in a snit over the attitude of Judith's new partner, so there was no telling what else she'd neglected to tell them. Of course, the brownie that Mimi had insisted on Charlotte sampling had tasted just fine — more than just fine — and she hadn't suffered any ill effects from eating it, but . . .

"Charlotte? Are you okay?"

Though Charlotte nodded absently, her mind was suddenly racing, and the small bite of brownie in her mouth felt as if it had suddenly tripled in size.

Charlotte sat down hard in a chair near the kitchen table. Of course. The answer was as plain as the nose on her face, so simple that she couldn't believe it hadn't occurred to her before, and the longer she thought about it, the more clear it became. Why couldn't two batches of brownies have been prepared? One batch for the HHS members and one batch laced with juice or ground up leaves from the jimson-weed.

"Charlotte, for Pete's sake, what's wrong with you?"

It was the alarmed tone in Madeline's voice that finally got Charlotte's attention. She swallowed hard, almost choking on the bite of brownie, then said, "Nothing's wrong, Maddie. I'm fine. Really I am." She handed the rest of the uneaten half of brownie to her sister. "But I think you're right. Hank would have a fit if he saw me eating this."

That afternoon, long after Charlotte had left her sister's apartment, the thought of Mimi's complaint about the bitter brownie haunted her. She probably should have mentioned it to Judith right then and there, but Judith was having such a good time talking to Carol and Hank about the wedding plans that Charlotte hated to ruin the happy occasion. Besides, without any proof other than her say-so, what good would it have done anyway?

Mimi had said that a "friend" had suggested planting the jimsonweed, but she never did name the "friend." The "friend" easily could have been June, though. If it had been June, who suggested that Mimi plant the jimsonweed, even if Mimi had told someone about it, there was no way to prove it now and no way the poisonous plant could be directly linked to June. And there was no way to prove that June had baked two batches of brownies or that she'd laced one of the batches with the jimsonweed. By now, June would have gotten rid of any evidence. Even so, Charlotte decided that maybe she'd give Judith a call later that evening, just to see if the police had come up with any suspects.

Except for Sunday, Charlotte hadn't had a full day off in over a week, and she was bone tired. On Monday morning she had to force herself to get dressed and head out to work.

When Charlotte parked the van in front of the Adamses' house, for a moment she simply stared at the beautiful old place.

Such a shame, she thought. Mimi had put her heart and soul into turning the old house into a home and a showplace, and now . . .

Charlotte sighed. And now Mimi was gone, her life cut short at the hands of a murderer. Yet, as cold and heartless as it seemed, life went on, and sitting there thinking about it all wasn't getting her work done. Besides, there was nothing anyone could do about Mimi's death except find the killer and see that he or she was punished.

Another day, another dollar, she thought, as she climbed out of the van. All the work she'd been doing for the Adams family since Mimi's death had been good for her bank account, but she'd gladly give it all back in a heartbeat if the reason for it had never happened.

Charlotte trudged around to the back of the van and unloaded her supplies. She had tried to call Judith several times before going to bed, but she never was able to reach her. Finally, she'd given up and gone to bed. But she hadn't slept well at all for thinking about June and the brownies, and she'd dreaded the thought of coming face-to-face with June.

There was simply no way she could

prove June had laced the brownies with the poisonous jimsonweed, not unless June confessed, and Charlotte didn't think that was a likely possibility. But there was also the little matter of motive. What possible motive could June have for murdering her best friend?

. . . But you don't have a little honey on the side either.

For the umpteenth time, Charlotte wondered if Gordon's "honey" could be June, and for the umpteenth time she told herself that just because she didn't like June didn't mean that the woman was a murderer and an adulteress.

Charlotte had the house key in her hand and was reaching to unlock the front door when it suddenly swung open. She fully expected to see June standing in the doorway and was surprised when she saw Emma instead.

"Hey, Charlotte."

"Good morning."

Emma craned her head around either side of Charlotte. "You didn't happen to see June, did you?"

No, and I hope I don't was what Charlotte wanted to say, but she simply shook her head.

Emma frowned. "She said she'd be here

before we left to go back to school."

"Maybe she's just running a bit late." Charlotte bent down and picked up her vacuum cleaner and supply carrier.

"Need some help with that stuff?" Emma asked.

Charlotte shook her head again. "No, hon, I'm used to lugging it around, but thanks anyway." She walked past Emma and headed for the kitchen. Behind her, she heard Emma close the door.

In the kitchen, Justin, who was reading the newspaper at the table, glanced up when Charlotte entered.

Charlotte smiled. "Good morning." The boy smiled back. Charlotte set her stuff down by the cabinet. "Emma says you're leaving this morning, going back to school."

Justin nodded. "Yes, ma'am."

Emma entered the room. "I didn't see June," she told her brother. "Think I should call her?"

Justin shrugged. "She'll be here, Em. You know she's always late."

Emma made a face and plopped down in one of the chairs. "Yeah, I know, but I really wanted to talk to her before Dad got here." To Charlotte's surprise, Emma said, "I need to apologize to her for being such a brat about everything."

When the back door opened, then closed, all three turned toward the back hallway. Within seconds, June, carrying a Krispy Kreme donut box in one hand and a plastic grocery bag in the other hand, walked into the kitchen.

"Sorry I'm late," June told them, placing the box and the bag on the countertop. "I wanted y'all to have some donuts and orange juice before you left." She turned and took glasses and plates out of the cabinet.

"June?" Emma approached the older woman, and June turned to face her. "I-I want to apologize," Emma said, her eyes filling with tears. "I've just been awful to you and I want you to know that I'm sorry and that I really do appreciate everything you've done for us this week."

June's face went slack with surprise, and a lone tear slid down her cheek. After a moment, she reached out and pulled the girl into her arms. "Aw, honey, it's okay. I know this has been rough on you, and I understand. I loved your mother too, you know, and I just did what I did because I love you as well."

Charlotte's throat tightened and her own eyes misted over. Feeling like an intruder and feeling horrible because of all the nasty things she'd been thinking about June, she slipped out of the room.

Either she'd let her wicked imagination get the best of her, Charlotte decided, and June was truly sincere, or June was a deceitful fraud, a consummate actress who was evil, through and through.

But which one was she?

Chapter 13

Within an hour after June had arrived with the donuts and orange juice, Gordon showed up to drive Emma and Justin to the airport. June walked outside with them to see them off, and once they drove away, she came back inside the house.

"I'm going to miss those two," she told Charlotte. "I just hope they'll be okay." She sighed and bowed her head, staring at the floor. "It's nice having the kids around," she murmured. "I wanted more children, but Fred didn't. And now, with Johnny away at school . . ." Her voice trailed away. Then, after a moment, she shrugged. "Who knows, I'm not too old yet and maybe it's not too late."

Then, as if suddenly remembering that she'd been talking to the maid, June straightened her shoulders and said, "If anyone calls or if you need me, I'll be in the library for most of the day. Gordon and the kids went through a lot of the cards

239

from the florists yesterday after everyone left, but there are still a few thank-you notes that need writing." June shook her head. "And I've got to figure out what to do with all of those blasted flowers and plants that people sent. There were so many that the walls of the church were lined with them. Way too many to leave at the cemetery." She paused thoughtfully. "I suppose I could see about donating some of them to a hospital or maybe a nursing home."

June's topsy-turvy mood really made Charlotte uncomfortable and wary, and the last thing she wanted was to have to stand there and listen to the woman carry on as if everything were normal.

"Donating them to a hospital or nursing home is probably a good idea," Charlotte finally forced herself to say. "Especially considering how much Mimi loved plants and flowers."

June nodded absently. "Yes, well, I guess I'd better get busy and let you do the same."

So relieved that she could have cried, Charlotte nodded back, and it was lunchtime before she saw June again. Charlotte was seated at the kitchen table eating the chicken salad and crackers that she'd brought from home when June walked into the room.

"Hmm, that looks delicious," June said, eyeing Charlotte's salad. She stepped over to the refrigerator and, after rummaging through it, pulled out what looked like a dish of jambalaya.

"Guess I'll have the jambalaya," June said, placing the dish in the microwave. "I've noticed that you eat a lot of salads," she said. "You don't look like you need to lose weight. Is that why you always bring a salad?"

Charlotte shook her head. "Not really. I'm a borderline diabetic, so I try to watch what I eat."

The microwave beeper sounded, indicating that the jambalaya was ready. To Charlotte's surprise and dismay, June seated herself at the table across from her.

For the first few moments, they both ate in silence, but Charlotte's curiosity finally got the best of her. Why not pump June? Why not just see what she had to say?

Charlotte cleared her throat. "If you'd rather not talk about it, I'll understand," she said, "but I was wondering if the police have come up with any suspects yet?"

Charlotte hadn't felt comfortable asking Judith on Sunday during lunch, but she'd tried to call her later that evening and never reached her. Since Judith's beeper went off just before she left Madeline's, Charlotte figured that her niece was still tied up with a case.

But if June happened to be guilty, Charlotte was sure she would have made it her business to find out all she could about what the police were doing.

June suddenly laughed. "If everyone they've questioned is a suspect, then the suspect list includes all the HHS members, as well as Sally next door, poor Gordon, you, and me." She paused a moment, then shook her head. "I still can't get over how much you and that woman detective favor each other."

Charlotte simply shrugged, and June took a bite of the jambalaya. Once she'd chewed and swallowed, she said, "My personal favorite suspect of the whole bunch is Rita Landers. She made Mimi's life miserable the last year or so with her gossiping. Why, did you know that she accused Mimi of having an affair with Don? He's Rita's husband," she added.

It was the same thing Charlotte had heard being discussed at one of the HHS meetings, but she decided against saying so.

"Humph!" June grunted. "As if anyone would want to have an affair with Don Landers." She shuddered. "The man is as poor as a church mouse and a total sleaze. Besides which, Mimi would never have an affair. She had way too much invested in Gordon."

Later, as Charlotte was polishing the handrail of the staircase, she thought about what June had said. Because of the scene she'd witnessed between June and Emma that morning, and in spite of her revelation about June's brownies, she had to admit that her next favorite suspect would have to be Rita as well. After all, jealousy was a powerful motive, and she'd yet to come up with a real motive for June.

As for Rita, if she was jealous of Mimi because of her own affair with Gordon — and Charlotte still couldn't quite believe that she was — then what better way to hide the affair than for Rita to accuse Mimi of having one with her husband, Don?

It was a sick scenario and a bit far-fetched, but Charlotte even fancied that she had figured out how Rita could have dispensed the poison without poisoning the rest of the HHS members.

The wine was the clue. Charlotte was

sure of it. Rita had used the wine as the vehicle to get close enough to administer the poison. Though Charlotte hadn't been in the kitchen when the women had uncorked the bottle and she didn't know who had actually poured the wine, she'd be willing to bet that Rita had done the honors. If Rita had poured the wine, she could have easily slipped the poison into just Mimi's glass without anyone being the wiser.

Rita certainly seemed to have motive and opportunity, but of course now there was no proof. Rita had made sure of that when she'd sneaked back in the kitchen and washed the wine glasses. And come to think of it, washing the wine glasses was pretty suspicious.

Charlotte paused, admiring the sheen of the old wooden banister. Then suddenly she frowned. So why had Rita come back and taken the leftover wine after the meeting was over? If she'd only laced Mimi's glass, then why bother taking the bottle?

"Must be something wrong with my theory," she murmured, as she finished polishing the banister, then moved on to the tables in the main hall. Maybe she should try to call Judith again and see what she could find out. Then again, maybe not.

Judith might be a blabbermouth when it came to family matters, but she could be pretty closemouthed about police matters when she wanted to be. Charlotte paused. Maybe it was a good thing after all that she hadn't been able to get in touch with Judith. For one thing, Judith would want to know why she was so curious, and then she'd have to endure another of her niece's lectures about getting involved, and one of her niece's lectures was the last thing she needed right now.

Charlotte sighed and capped the bottle of lemon oil. Thinking about it all was giving her a headache. Either that or the smell of the polish.

Bitsy Duhe, Charlotte's Tuesday client, lived on the same street as the vampire novelist Anne Rice used to. Bitsy's house was a very old raised-cottage-style Greek Revival and was surrounded by huge azalea bushes.

Charlotte had begun working for Bitsy after the death of Bitsy's husband, a former mayor of New Orleans. Before his death, Bitsy and he had led an active social life. Since his death, though, Bitsy had nothing but time on her hands. Her only relatives, a son and two granddaughters, lived some distance away, so the elderly lady spent most of her days either gossiping on the telephone or adding to her enormous collection of kitchen gadgets.

As usual, Bitsy was already outside standing on the front gallery when Charlotte drove up. And as usual, the spry, birdlike elderly lady was dressed in one of her many midcalf flowered dresses.

Bitsy waved as Charlotte parked her van behind an unfamiliar truck in front of the house. Wondering whom the truck belonged to, Charlotte smiled and waved back. As she unloaded her supply carrier from the back of the van, a tall, dark-haired man, who Charlotte guessed was in his mid- to late thirties, came out of the house.

When Charlotte reached the porch, Bitsy introduced the man. "Charlotte, this is Patrick McDonnell. Mr. McDonnell is giving me an estimate on renovating my kitchen."

Charlotte nodded a brief greeting to Patrick McDonnell. To Bitsy she said, "I guess I didn't realize you were considering a renovation."

"I wasn't until I came across an article in an old magazine about Julia Child's kitchen."

Charlotte frowned. "I don't understand."

Bitsy sighed impatiently. "You know. Julia Child, the cooking expert."

"Yes, ma'am, I know who Julia Child is, but —"

"Well, then, pay attention, Charlotte. Back in November 2001, Julia donated her kitchen to the Smithsonian National Museum, and I thought, why not?"

"Why not what?" Charlotte asked, her frown deepening. Sometimes, following Bitsy's nonstop dialogue was like being lost in a maze.

"For goodness sake, what I meant was why not make over my kitchen like hers? Now, wouldn't that be a hoot?" Bitsy waved a dismissive hand. "Anyway, I asked Jenny — remember, she's my granddaughter who lives in New York — well, I asked her to drive down to DC and go to the Smithsonian. I wanted her to see if she could get pictures of Julia's kitchen, or a copy of a blueprint of it, so I could re-create it."

Bitsy paused thoughtfully. "One of the biggest problems, though, will be finding one of those old Garland Commercial Ranges like Julia used, you know, the kind they built back in the early fifties. I believe the article said that the model number was one hundred eighty-two, but —"

To Charlotte's relief, Patrick McDonnell cleared his throat and interrupted Bitsy's endless chatter. "Mrs. Duhe, I'm afraid I have bad news."

"Bad news? Oh, dear, what now?"

Charlotte didn't wait around to hear what Patrick had to say. With Bitsy preoccupied, Charlotte seized the opportunity to slip inside the house.

On the days that Charlotte worked for Bitsy, the only reprieve she got from the old lady's endless chatter was when Bitsy was on the phone or had a doctor's appointment. Otherwise, she followed Charlotte around jabbering on and on about the latest gossip she'd heard from her cronies.

Charlotte began cleaning in the kitchen, and as she loaded the dishwasher, she prayed that Patrick McDonnell would have lots to talk about, enough to keep Bitsy out of her hair for a little while, anyway.

After loading the dishwasher, Charlotte wiped down the stove, but Bitsy's new venture stayed on her mind. For months, Bitsy had been complaining that her son was trying to persuade her to sell the house and move into an assisted-living facility. Charlotte grimaced. Something like this newest harebrained idea of hers just might be the final straw for her son. It might make him even more determined to move her into a "home."

An hour later Bitsy finally came inside. Charlotte was changing the sheets in the master bedroom. When the older lady tracked her down, Charlotte could see from the petulant expression on her face that something was wrong and that Bitsy was very unhappy.

"He says that my kitchen isn't quite big enough to be an authentic replica," Bitsy said.

Someone should really say something to the old lady to discourage her, Charlotte thought, as she wrestled the fitted sheet onto the mattress. It was bad enough that Bitsy collected every kind of kitchen gadget imaginable, but this latest obsession was totally off the wall.

Though there was a lot that Charlotte wanted to say to the old lady, and she was sorely tempted, she held her tongue, as she spread the top sheet over the bed. Knowing Bitsy, she probably wouldn't listen to reason anyway.

Bitsy was staring up at the ceiling. "I suppose I could have someone come in and enlarge it, but that would mean a lot of construction work — tearing down walls and such."

Charlotte couldn't stand it a moment longer. She threw a blanket on the bed, and once she smoothed it down, she turned to Bitsy and said, "Are you sure you want to go to all of that expense and trouble? I can't help but believe it would cost you an arm and a leg."

Bitsy's head snapped around, and she glared at Charlotte. "It's not the cost that concerns me. I have plenty of money. It's the mess and all of those strangers — the workmen — coming in and out."

"What about Bradley?" Charlotte persisted. "What's he going to think about such a project?"

Charlotte's question brought Bitsy up short, and her eyes clouded with uncertainty.

In a kinder voice, Charlotte said, "You've told me time and again that he's just been looking for an excuse to force you to sell the house, and I'm afraid this might aggravate the situation even more."

Bitsy nodded slowly. "As much as I hate to admit it, you're probably right," she conceded. "Maybe I should think about it a while longer."

Charlotte nodded as she threw the chenille comforter on top of the bed and tugged it into place.

"By the way," Bitsy said, "Did Sandra Wellington call you?"

Charlotte froze. "How did you know?"

"That must mean that she did." When Charlotte nodded, Bitsy grinned. "Good," she said. "She's really a lovely woman, but a terrible housekeeper, or so I hear."

"B-but how did you know about —"

Bitsy waved her hand. "Oh, for Pete's sake, Margo Jones told me, and I saw Sandra at the Garden District Book Shop the other day."

"Now I'm really confused. What does Margo Jones have to do with anything?"

"Margo's daughter is buying Marian Hebert's house." She shrugged. "I put two and two together and —" She shrugged again. "I knew Sandra was looking for someone to clean for her."

All Charlotte could do was shake her head. "You're amazing, absolutely amazing."

Bitsy grinned again. "Why, thank you."

"No," Charlotte said. "Thank *you*. I appreciate your recommendation."

Bitsy nodded. "Any time, any time at all." Her grin suddenly faded. "Speaking of your clients, I heard that someone poisoned Mimi Adams. Does that mean you're going to have a couple of more days free? The only reason I'm asking," she rushed on, "is because I also told Abigail Thornton that you might have an opening."

Charlotte hesitated before answering Bitsy. She truly didn't like discussing her clients or her business with anyone. But after all, the old lady's recommendation had netted her a new client. "Yes, I did receive a call from her too," she finally said. "But for the time being, I've agreed to continue working for Gordon Adams, so I don't really have another opening right now."

"Oh, my." Bitsy shook her head. "My, my, my. If you're going to keep working for Gordon without Mimi around, I'd better fill you in on him."

The temptation to listen to what Bitsy had to say about Gordon was strong, but Charlotte resisted. After all, more than likely, anything that Bitsy told her was pure gossip.

In hopes of discouraging further talk on the subject, Charlotte gathered up the dirty sheets. "I really need to put these in to wash," she said. Then, with a quick apologetic smile for Bitsy, she headed for the laundry room.

Unfortunately, Bitsy wasn't easily discouraged, nor was she one to be ignored. Just as Charlotte had expected and dreaded, Bitsy followed her every step, tagging along like a little puppy, all the way to the laundry room.

"He's a handsome devil, that Gordon," Bitsy continued, as if there had never been an interruption. "Don't you think so?" Not waiting for an answer, she said, "But, as my momma used to say, handsome is as handsome does. Or maybe that was pretty is as pretty does?" She frowned. "Never mind about that — anyway, Gordon was considered quite a catch for Mimi. Now don't get me wrong. Mimi had money too, but she didn't have the pedigree to go with all of her money, if you know what I mean."

Charlotte knew exactly what Bitsy meant all too well. Evidently, Mimi's family had new money, as opposed to having old money, the kind that a family passed along from one generation to the next. And in New Orleans, having new money instead of old money made all the difference when it came to a family's social standing.

"But that Mimi was smart," Bitsy chattered away. "She outsmarted them all and snagged Gordon right out from under more than one hopeful debutante's nose. And, believe me, there were a bunch of them trying to get their hooks into Gordon. Like I said, though, Mimi was smart. When she got him, she made sure she got pregnant right away, a surefire way of keeping him." Bitsy giggled. "Had everyone counting the months until Justin was born."

They had reached the laundry room, and Charlotte nodded, mostly to be polite, as she piled the clothes on top of the dryer, then turned on the washing machine. Again, temptation reared its ugly head, and she had to bite her tongue to keep from asking for the names of the unhappy debutantes. She was just itching to know if Sally Lawson was among the ones whom Gordon had rejected in favor of Mimi.

Reminding herself to tend to her own business, Charlotte measured out the detergent, dumped it into the machine, and waited for the machine to fill with water.

"Rumor has it," Bitsy went on, "that Gordon —"

The loud ringing of the telephone interrupted her, and though Bitsy was clearly irritated by the interruption, and even

Charlotte was a bit irritated herself, there was no way Bitsy would ever ignore a phone call.

The old lady hurried off to answer the phone but still managed to call out over her shoulder, "I'd be careful around Gordon, if I were you. He seems like a nice enough man, but I hear that he can be meaner than a snake and just as lethal."

Bitsy never did get around to telling Charlotte what she had meant about Gordon being "meaner than a snake and just as lethal." Bitsy's phone call was from her son. By the time she finished talking to Bradley, the old lady was much too upset to bother with further gossip about Gordon Adams.

Later, that afternoon, physically and mentally exhausted, Charlotte loaded the supply carrier and vacuum cleaner back into the van. She felt as if she'd been tiptoeing through a minefield ever since Bradley's phone call. And she was depressed.

Bitsy had been in rare form after her conversation with her son, especially once she'd learned that he was flying in from California for a visit the following weekend. Any other time, Bitsy would have

255

been overjoyed by a visit from him. But not this time. Bitsy was convinced that the only reason Bradley was coming was to force her to move to an assisted-living facility.

After the phone call, Bitsy had been like a woman possessed. She'd followed Charlotte around, double-checking everything that Charlotte did. Nothing seemed to suit her, and nothing Charlotte had said had dissuaded the old lady of her fears. And Charlotte had said a lot, a lot more than she'd intended to say and a lot more than she should have said.

By the end of the day, Bitsy had worked herself up into a royal tizzy and had been so upset that she'd all but begged Charlotte to work on Saturday.

As Charlotte slammed the van door shut, she could still hear Bitsy's squeaky, pathetic voice. *I know you don't usually work on Saturdays, but I'd just feel better knowing someone I trusted was there — you know — someone who could vouch for me. Bradley would listen to you. I just know he would.*

Though there were times it was nearly impossible, Charlotte had always tried to make it her policy to separate business from her personal life. The last thing she wanted was to get embroiled in yet another client's family situation, especially Bitsy's. In the end, though, she hadn't had the heart to refuse the old lady, and, calling herself all kinds of a fool, she'd reluctantly agreed to work the extra day.

"At least you still have Thursday off," Charlotte muttered to herself as she climbed into the driver's seat of the van and pulled the door shut. She fastened her seat belt, cranked the van, and checked her side-view mirror. But during the short drive home, she was already adding the chores that she'd planned to do on Saturday to her mental list of chores she needed to get done on Thursday.

One of her so-called chores was to meet Carol for lunch to discuss some of the wedding arrangements. Charlotte smiled as she turned onto Milan Street. That was one task that she was looking forward to with great pleasure.

Trying to dodge the potholes, Charlotte felt a warm glow of contentment flow through her as the van bumped along the narrow street. Bitsy's problems soon faded, and just thinking about Carol and Hank's upcoming wedding lifted her spirits.

On the radio, the oldies-but-goodies station was playing "I Can See Clearly Now," an old Johnny Nash tune, and Charlotte found herself humming along. Indeed, her son's happiness was exactly the rainbow she had been praying for, and his relationship with Carol had to mean that the pain of his relationship with his ex-wife, Mindy, was finally gone.

When Charlotte arrived at Marian Hebert's house on Wednesday, the movers were already parked out front, and the hallway was filled with packing boxes waiting to be loaded. After greeting Marian and saying hello to Aaron and B.J., Charlotte began cleaning in the kitchen.

Half an hour later, Marian, flanked by her two sons, entered the kitchen. "Charlotte, we're leaving now," she said. "The movers only have a few more boxes to load, and I want to be across the lake at the other house before they get there."

Charlotte was wiping out the insides of the upper kitchen cabinets, but she stopped, pulled off her rubber gloves, and climbed down from the stepladder. Leaving the gloves on the countertop, she walked over to where Marian and the boys were standing.

Her throat tight with emotion, Charlotte said, "You know I only wish the very best for you, but I'll miss you. All of you," she added, her eyes resting on each of the boys. "You guys be good for your mom, now, and help her." She held open her arms in an invitation for a hug, and Aaron, the youngest of the boys, stepped into her embrace first.

"Bye, Charlotte," he said, hugging her around the waist. "I wish you were coming too."

Charlotte's throat grew even tighter, but she smiled down at the little boy. "Maybe I'll come for a visit one of these days."

Aaron looked up at her, his eyes brightened, and then he stepped back.

B.J., almost as tall as Charlotte, stepped forward, and much to Charlotte's surprise, the teenager embraced her as well. "Bye, Charlotte," he said. "And thanks for everything."

"You're welcome." Charlotte gave the teenager an extra squeeze around his shoulder. With a teasing grin, she added, "And don't you be sneaking out after hours over there on the North Shore. I hear they have some tough curfew laws."

B.J.'s cheeks reddened. "Yes, ma'am — I mean no, ma'am." He grimaced. "I won't."

"I'm just teasing you, hon. I know you won't," Charlotte murmured.

"Okay, boys, it's time to load up,"

Marian told them. "And don't —"

Aaron suddenly punched his brother on the arm. "Race ya," Aaron challenged.

"No!" Marian told him sternly. "No racing or running in the house."

Though both boys grumbled, Charlotte was pleased to see that, unlike just a few months earlier, now they listened to their mother and actually obeyed her.

"I'm impressed," she told Marian, as she watched them march down the hallway.

"Me too," Marian whispered, watching them as well. Then she snickered. "I suspect they're just showing off for you. But, actually, they have improved tremendously, considering how they used to act." She turned to Charlotte. "Thanks again for everything, Charlotte. We'll never forget you."

Charlotte swallowed the lump in her throat. "Just be careful and be happy," she said. Reaching out, she gave Marian a brief but heartfelt hug.

Marian returned the hug, then said, "And by the way, that was a great idea you had."

Charlotte frowned. "Idea?"

Marian nodded. "About paying us a visit."

"Well, you never can tell. I might just do that."

"Please do," Marian said. "You will always be welcome. And if you ever need a recommendation or a new house, just let me know." Then, with a tiny wave and a smile, Marian turned and hurried off down the hallway. "I've already locked the door," she called out over her shoulder. "Just pull it closed when you leave."

After Marian and the boys left, it was another hour before the moving men finally loaded the last of the furniture and boxes into the van.

Charlotte stood on the porch until the moving van pulled away from the curb, and then she went back inside the house. Strange, she thought, as she walked through the now vacant house. Strange how a house could be so full of life one moment and so empty the next. And all because of the people who lived there.

A shiver ran up her spine as she thought about returning to the Adamses' house, the house where Mimi Adams had been murdered, a house that was now empty of the one soul who had made it so vibrant and alive.

Chapter
14

As agreed, on Thursday, Charlotte and Carol met at Joey K's Restaurant on Magazine. In between bites of grilled chicken salad, they made a good-sized dent in the list of things that had to be decided.

The most urgent item was securing a place for the wedding and the reception. Both Carol and Hank wanted a small wedding at the church, one that would include just family and a few of their closest friends. But the reception was another matter. They each had numerous business acquaintances and felt the need to include them in the reception.

"The facilities at the church are nice enough," Charlotte told Carol. "But, in my opinion, and considering the number of guests you want to invite to the reception, the recreation room at the church they use for receptions is way too small."

"You're right, of course," Carol agreed.

"How about that hotel that Daniel and

Nadia used for their reception?" Charlotte suggested.

Carol chewed thoughtfully on the bite of salad she'd just taken. She swallowed, then nodded. "I'll have to check and see what dates it's available on such short notice."

Feeling stuffed to the gills, Charlotte and Carol parted ways, but as Charlotte climbed into her van to leave, she still had Nadia on her mind.

She'd meant to talk to Nadia on Sunday to let her know that Janet Davis had finally agreed to temporarily take over the clients whom Nadia serviced, just until Charlotte could find a permanent replacement. But with all of the excitement about Carol and Hank's upcoming wedding and her disturbing revelation about June's brownies, she'd completely forgotten. With Nadia's baby due in the latter part of September, though, time was getting short.

Charlotte reached into her purse, pulled out her notebook and pen, then jotted down a memo to herself to call Nadia when she got home. Below the memo, she added glucose tablets. She paused and tapped the point of the pen against the notepad.

She really should go ahead and put an ad in the paper for more full-time help while she was at it. Up until now she'd been procrastinating, hoping that Janet would agree to work full-time in Nadia's place instead of part-time. She'd even offered Janet a small raise, but Janet had stuck to her guns, and now Charlotte really had no choice but to begin interviewing for another full-time employee.

As Charlotte drove to the Adamses' house on Friday morning, she wondered if, once again, June would be waiting for her. She hoped not. She was tired of being at June's beck and call and tired of worrying and wondering if June had murdered Mimi.

She parked the van, unloaded her cleaning supplies, then, taking a chance that no one was home, let herself inside the house and turned off the security alarm.

Once inside, though, she couldn't get past the feeling that she wasn't alone. Charlotte couldn't begin to count the number of times that she had been alone in clients' homes, and she'd never given it more than a passing thought. So why am I getting jumpy now? she wondered.

Standing very still, she tilted her head, listening for the slightest sound that would indicate someone else might be in the house. Nothing. Nothing but the ticking of the case clock in the parlor, and after a moment, an overwhelming relief washed through her. But following fast on the heels of relief came an unexpected wave of apprehension.

For goodness sake, just lock the door and get busy.

Charlotte turned and threw the deadbolt; then, telling herself she was over-reacting about nothing, she picked up the supply carrier and vacuum cleaner and headed for the kitchen first. But when she stepped inside the room, she could hardly believe her eyes.

The kitchen was spotless, not a dirty dish in sight. Charlotte set down the supply carrier and vacuum cleaner, then walked over to the dishwasher. She un-latched it and opened it to find that it was full of clean dishes.

"Aha," she murmured. Now she knew. Gordon was a neat freak . . . or was he? Charlotte pulled out the bottom rack and frowned. Every slot was filled with a plate. Charlotte counted eight of them as she stacked them on top of the cabinet — way too many for one lone man to use for just the evening meal for the four days since Monday. Still puzzled, but with an oh-well shrug, Charlotte began putting away the clean dishes.

Who knows? she thought. He could have had guests during the week. Charlotte shook her head. Not likely. For one thing, she couldn't picture Gordon planning a dinner party. For another thing, given his social background, he would realize that people would talk if he did something like that so soon after burying Mimi. People of Gordon's social status still adhered to the older traditions of a proper mourning period.

Within minutes, Charlotte had put away all of the dishes, and since no one was home, she decided to start cleaning upstairs and work her way down. She was sure there had to be at least one load of dirty laundry just waiting for her in the master bedroom. Gordon might be a neat freak in the kitchen, but he probably didn't know the first thing about doing his own laundry.

There were some dirty clothes in the hamper, but not as many as she had thought there would be. And the bed in the master bedroom had been left unmade.

"Finally," she murmured. There was finally proof that *someone* had been there since she'd last cleaned on Monday. For a moment, Charlotte stood and stared at the unmade bed. One side of the king-size bed had clearly been slept on whereas the other side was undisturbed. How sad, she thought, as she stripped the sheets off the bed. Here was a man in the prime of his life, a man who'd had a wife, a family, and a beautiful home. Now he was all alone.

All alone except for his "honey."

Ignoring the aggravating little voice in her head, Charlotte gathered up the bed linens as well as the clothes in the hamper, and carried the bundle down to the laundry room. There, she dropped the dirty things on the floor, then turned on the washing machine and added detergent. While she waited for the washing machine to fill with water, she sorted through the clothes. There were a couple of knit shirts and a pair of jeans, but the rest were towels, washcloths, and Gordon's underwear.

She laid aside the shirts and jeans and loaded the rest with the bed linens into the machine.

By the time Charlotte took her lunch break, she had almost finished cleaning the entire house. All she had left was to fold the first load of wash, put the shirts and jeans in the dryer, and vacuum and mop.

As she munched on the mandarin chicken salad she'd brought, she wrestled with her conscience. She'd be through cleaning way before three-thirty. Charging Gordon for a full day's work seemed a bit dishonest. Maybe she should talk to him about it, possibly even suggest that he could get by with having her come in two half days a week instead of full days. Of course, she could make it clear that she would be available for full days when and if he needed her.

By the time she'd finished her salad, she'd made up her mind to wait a few days before saying anything. The weekend was coming up, and there was no telling what kind of mess she might be faced with on Monday.

After Charlotte's lunch break, she headed for the laundry room. Once she transferred the clothes from the dryer into the laundry basket, she checked the tag on the knit shirts to make sure they wouldn't shrink, then dropped the shirts, along with the jeans, into the dryer and turned it on. The last time she'd done the laundry, she'd folded the clothes on top of the washer and dryer, but this time, since no one was home, she decided it would be easier to fold the items on the kitchen table.

She was standing at the kitchen table and had almost finished folding the items in the basket when she came across a pair of nylon panties.

With a frown, she held up the panties. They were white and trimmed with elasticized lace around the leg openings and the waist. "Where on earth did these come from?" she murmured. She didn't remember seeing them when she'd transferred the clothes from the washer to the dryer, which meant they must have been left in the dryer from a previous load. From experience she knew that even with the use of dryer sheets or fabric softener, static electricity created by nylon could sometimes still make items cling to the tub of the dryer. But even if that were the case, whom did the panties belong to?

She supposed that they could have belonged to Mimi, but that was doubtful. June had cleaned out all of Mimi's clothes, and if nothing else, June was thorough.

"And not Emma either," she whispered. She'd washed Emma's clothes, and all of Emma's panties were the hip-hugger style. Besides, the nylon panties were about two sizes too big for Emma, and Emma's panties were made of cotton.

Charlotte folded the panties, then finished folding the rest of the items, but the mystery of the panties bothered her long after she'd put away the clothes. For one thing, she didn't know what to do with them. What she finally decided was to put them in one of the empty dresser drawers that had once held Mimi's lingerie.

Downstairs, Charlotte had just turned on the vacuum cleaner when she felt the cell phone in her apron pocket vibrating against her stomach as it rang. With a frustrated sigh, she switched off the vacuum and answered the call.

"Maid-for-a-Day, Charlotte speaking."

"Charlotte, Bitsy Duhe here."

Charlotte crossed her fingers. Maybe Bitsy had changed her mind about wanting her to work on Saturday, after all. "Hi, Bitsy," she said. "What can I do for you?"

"Just checking to make sure you didn't forget about working tomorrow."

Charlotte grimaced and uncrossed her fingers. "No, I didn't forget," she said. "I'll be there at eight."

"Well, I have to tell you, I'm as nervous as a long-tailed cat around a rocking chair. That son of mine would never come all this way unless he had something on his mind, and I'm pretty sure I know exactly what that something is."

Please, not again, Charlotte thought. Dreading yet another monologue of complaints from the old lady, she decided to try a different tack with her. "Did you ask him why he was coming?"

There was a long silence before Bitsy finally answered. "Well, no, no I didn't. But what other reason would he have?"

Charlotte truly wanted to believe the best about people, and most of the time she tried to give everyone the benefit of the doubt before passing judgment. "Maybe Bradley is homesick or maybe he simply misses you," she suggested. "It's been a while since he came home, hasn't it?"

"Yes it has, and I'd like to believe that," Bitsy said, her squeaky voice full of longing. "I really would, but knowing my son, it's not likely."

"Don't borrow trouble, Bitsy. Try thinking positive," Charlotte encouraged, and after once again reassuring the old lady that she would be there bright and early on Saturday morning, she ended the conversation and switched off the phone.

Charlotte sighed and dropped the phone back into her apron pocket. All she could do now was hope and pray that, for Bitsy's sake, Bradley was simply homesick, and not for the first time did she wish that she hadn't given in to Bitsy's pleas and agreed to work the extra day for her.

She shook her head. "Enough already," she murmured. Tomorrow, along with the problems it might bring, would come all too soon. Charlotte turned the vacuum back on. It was today, the here and now, that concerned her, though.

As Charlotte vacuumed, once again she experienced the odd feeling she'd had when she first arrived — that she wasn't completely alone, that there was another presence there too, a restless, malevolent presence that was watching her. Again she tried to ignore the feeling, tried to tell herself she was being silly, but the feeling wouldn't go away.

Mimi's ghost? Charlotte shook her head as if the action alone would dispel the unsettling thought. She'd never really completely made up her mind about whether she truly believed that ghosts existed, but she did believe that there were evil spirits in the world.

Charlotte shivered. "Just stop it," she told herself. All the doors and windows were locked. She had checked to make sure. But telling herself that no one else was there and believing it were two different things. What if someone was already in the house when she got there? After all, the old house was huge, and there were all

272

kinds of hiding places. Besides which, locked doors and windows wouldn't keep ghosts or evil spirits out.

"Oh, for crying out loud!" She jerked the vacuum cleaner around. "Enough's enough." Yet, in spite of herself, she couldn't resist the urge to glance over her shoulder.

Of course, when she looked, there was nothing there, and she would have felt foolish except that the eerie feeling still persisted.

"Too much imagination and one too many horror movies," she muttered, her words lost in the roar of the vacuum cleaner. And too many childhood tales about restless spirits haunting old houses where people had met untimely deaths at the hand of a murderer. It sometimes seemed that almost every old building in New Orleans boasted of a ghost at one time or another. Best thing, she figured, was to finish up as soon as possible and get the heck out of there.

Charlotte had almost finished vacuuming the double parlor. She figured that mopping the kitchen and dining room would only take another fifteen minutes or so, and by the time she finished, the clothes in the dryer would be dry. Once she put those away, she could leave.

A few minutes later, she was finally done in the parlor. She shut off the vacuum, unplugged it, and then began winding up the cord. Once the cord was secure, though, she suddenly froze. The weird feeling was back again and she could swear that she'd heard something.

But had she really heard something other than the clock ticking or was her imagination playing tricks on her again?

"Charlotte?"

At the sound of her name, fear seized Charlotte with a vengeance. With a startled shriek, she whirled around, ready to do battle with whatever demon was there.

Chapter
15

"June!" Charlotte cried, as she clutched her fist to her chest. Beneath her fist her heart pounded furiously. "My goodness," she gasped. "You scared the daylights out of me."

"Sorry about that, but I was sure you heard me come in."

Charlotte shook her head. "Not with the vacuum going." As her heart finally slowed down, Charlotte dropped her hand. "Is there something you wanted?" she asked. Or did you just come by to terrorize me? she added silently.

June flashed her a brief smile that was as fake as a three-dollar bill. "No, just making sure that everything here is okay. And just checking to see if you needed anything."

Charlotte figured that, more than likely, June had come by just to make sure she was working and not just lollygagging around eating bon-bons and watching the soaps on television.

"Everything's fine," Charlotte told her. "I'm almost finished. All I have left is to mop and put away a few clothes that are in the dryer, but you're more than welcome to inspect what I've already done."

Talking about the clothes brought to mind the dilemma about the panties. Should she mention them? Or should she just mind her own business and keep her mouth shut? Though Charlotte was pretty sure she already knew what June's answer would be, she couldn't resist the temptation to ask anyway, just to see what kind of reaction June would have.

"There is one thing," Charlotte added. "I found a pair of panties in the dryer, and I wasn't exactly sure where to put them."

June simply stared at her for what seemed like endless moments. When she finally did speak, her tone was brisk and sharp. "I'm sure Emma probably left them. Just put them in her room."

Charlotte shook her head. "They're not the type she wears, and besides, they're too big for Emma."

"Too big? Oh, well then, they're probably some of Mimi's that I missed when I was clearing out her things. What did you do with them?"

"I put them in one of the empty dresser

drawers in the master bedroom," Charlotte answered.

June groaned. "Oh, good grief. Why didn't you just throw them in the garbage?"

Charlotte paused. Why so testy? she wondered. Not knowing how else to respond, she shrugged and said, "I didn't think it was my place to throw them away."

"Well, I'm telling you to do it. Okay?"

"No problem. I just didn't —"

"Tell you what," June interrupted. "On second thought, it's been a long week, and I know you must be tired. Why don't I take care of the panties and the clothes in the dryer for you? As for the mopping, you can do that on Monday. A couple of days won't make a difference. That way, you can go ahead and leave — get a head start on the weekend."

It was on the tip of Charlotte's tongue to point out that Gordon, not June, was her client, but she decided that doing so would probably only antagonize June. So, in an attempt at being a bit more tactful, she simply said, "Are you sure that would be okay with Gordon?"

June's lips thinned with irritation. "Yes, I'm sure," she snapped. Then, as if realizing how impatient she'd sounded, she quickly flashed Charlotte another of her fake smiles. "Besides, Gordon would probably tell you the same thing if he were here."

"Well, if you're sure, then it won't take me but a minute to get my stuff together."

Charlotte gathered her supplies in record time, and once she had loaded the vacuum cleaner and supply carrier into the van, she walked back inside the house to tell June she was leaving.

Charlotte rounded the bottom of the staircase just as June was coming down the stairs, and just in time to see a flash of white before June stuffed something into her pants pocket.

Had to be the panties, Charlotte figured. But why would June put them in her pocket unless . . .

It suddenly hit her like a ton of bricks — unless the panties belonged to June. No wonder June had offered to take care of the panties and the clothes. As far as Charlotte could see, there was only one viable reason that she could think of as to why June's panties would be there in the first place.

Charlotte grimaced. She'd once overheard a group of women talking about how women who dallied in extramarital affairs always carried an extra pair of panties in their purse. Personally, she thought the whole idea was not only immoral but disgusting as well.

You could be mistaken, though. You could be jumping to conclusions.

What other reason could there be? she argued silently.

Maybe she just stuck them in her pocket until she could put them in the kitchen trash can.

Yeah, right, she thought, as her insides began to churn with righteous indignation on Mimi's behalf. In Charlotte's opinion, the only thing worse than having an affair with a married man was having an affair with your best friend's husband.

"My goodness, Charlotte, I thought for sure that you'd already left."

The sound of June's voice jerked Charlotte out of her reverie.

"Was there something else you needed?" June said, as she descended the last few steps of the staircase.

It was all Charlotte could do to keep a civil tongue in her mouth. "I'm leaving," she said. "I just came back inside to let you know that."

"Well, have a good weekend, and I'll see you bright and early Monday morning."

Not if I see you first, Charlotte felt like

saying. Not trusting herself to respond, Charlotte nodded curtly, executed an about-face, then walked swiftly to the door.

Outside the sun was shining, and, for a change, the temperature was almost pleasant, but inside her van, Charlotte was too upset to notice the beautiful afternoon as she drove slowly up Prytania.

Lecture or no lecture, she should really try to call Judith again.

Leave it alone. Just mind your own business — stay out of it.

"Easier said than done," she argued with the aggravating inner voice of her conscience, as she turned onto Milan Street. Besides, what could it hurt just to mention her suspicions about June having an affair with Gordon? And while she was at it, she could also mention her theory about the brownies. At least the affair was a motive of sorts for murder. People had been known to kill over a lot less.

And what if you're just imagining things again?

"But what if I'm not?" she muttered.

Facts and evidence. That's all that Judith is interested in. Otherwise, it's just gossip and hearsay, and she'll just think you're turning into an old busybody.

Charlotte pulled the van into her driveway, and once she'd switched off the engine, she sat staring straight ahead, yet not really seeing the outside wall of the storage room. Facts, she thought. Judith would want facts or hard evidence.

She drummed her fingers against the steering wheel. So what were the facts? And what evidence did she have?

Fact one: Mimi had said that a "friend" had told her about the jimsonweed. So what evidence did she have that June was that "friend"?

None, none at all.

Charlotte sighed. Mimi probably had lots of friends, and with the exception of Rita, Karen, and Doreen, she probably considered most of the HHS members her friends.

Fact two: There had been rumors that Gordon was having an affair, and because of the panties and the way that June had more or less taken over the entire Adams family, she'd assumed that he was having an affair with June. As for the evidence . . .

Face it, there is no evidence, only your half-baked theories and conjectures.

Charlotte groaned and shook her head. "You *are* nothing but an old busybody," she grumbled. She jerked open the van door, grabbed her purse, climbed out, and then slammed the door hard just for good measure.

Just as Charlotte entered the house and closed and locked the front door, she heard a car pull into the driveway outside. Curious, she peeked through the window just in time to see Louis climb out of his blue Ford Taurus.

The sight of Louis sent a tiny unexpected jolt through her. Maybe the old adage was true after all, she thought. Maybe absence did make the heart grow fonder.

As Louis walked around the front of the car to the passenger side, Charlotte tried to examine her feelings more closely. It was true that she had missed him, but why had she missed him?

Her eyes followed him as he opened the passenger door, and only when a woman stepped out of the car did Charlotte suddenly realize that Louis hadn't come home alone.

But who was the woman? Immediately dismissing the possibility that Louis could have a lady friend, Charlotte figured that, more than likely, the woman was a sister whom Louis had neglected to mention or maybe even a cousin.

Whoever she was, even at a distance, it was hard to miss the woman's full head of flaming red hair or her trim, almost emaciated figure. From what Charlotte could see, she guessed that the woman was her own age or younger. Probably younger, Charlotte thought, eyeing the snug-fitting jeans and the body-hugging tank top that the woman was wearing.

Louis had his hand on the woman's back, and as he escorted her around the front of the car, he glanced toward the window where Charlotte was standing. Before Charlotte could decide whether he could see her standing there watching him, the woman stopped and turned to face Louis. She tilted her head upward and said something to him. Then, she clasped either side of his face with her hands, pulled his head down, and kissed him full on the mouth.

Charlotte felt as if someone had just punched her in the stomach as she watched the seemingly endless kiss. By no stretch of the imagination could the woman's kiss be called a sisterly peck, nor was it the kind that cousins would exchange.

Swimming through a fog of feelings and

regrets, Charlotte backed away from the window. In a daze and ignoring Sweety Boy's noisy attempts to get her attention, she automatically slipped off her shoes, stepped into her moccasins, and stumbled over to the sofa.

In Charlotte's mind's eye, she could still see the woman kissing Louis, but the vision disappeared when her ears picked up the sound of footsteps on the front porch. The door to Louis's half of the double opened, then closed. A few minutes later, the door opened and closed again. There were more footsteps on the porch, then the sharp rap of knuckles on wood at her own front door.

Charlotte knew within her bones that the visitor was Louis, but the last thing she wanted at the moment was to have to face him. Before she could do that, she had to get a grip on her emotions, had to come to terms with the fact that she'd fooled around and waited too long to make up her mind about her feelings for him. And now it was too late. From the looks of things, he'd found someone else.

Charlotte glanced over uneasily at the front door. Maybe if she just ignored him, he would go away.

But he didn't go away, and the knocking

grew louder and more insistent. Then . . . "Charlotte, open up. I know you're in there."

For lack of a better excuse, she swallowed hard, then called out, "I'm busy right now."

"That's a bunch of bull, and we both know it. Open the door."

Blood suddenly pounded in her temples and the heat of embarrassment stung her cheeks. He *had* seen her at the window, and knowing Louis, he felt he had to explain.

"I know where you hide the extra key," Louis taunted, in a singsong voice. "Either you open up or I'll use it."

Charlotte didn't want to hear his explanations. Doing so would be admitting that there had been something between them.

"I'm warning you," Louis called out.

Don't be such a coward. Just do it and get it over with. With a sigh of resignation, Charlotte gathered her dignity, pushed herself off the sofa, and marched to the door. Taking a deep breath, she threw the dead bolt. When she opened the door, she kept one hand on the doorknob and placed her other hand on the door frame to make it clear that she didn't intend to invite him inside. "What do you want, Louis?"

"I want to —" He shook his head. "No — not want — I *need* to talk to you, to explain."

Charlotte gave a one-shouldered shrug. "So talk."

"Can't I come inside?"

Charlotte shook her head. "Like I said, I'm busy."

"Yeah, right. Sure you are." He gave an exasperated shake of his head. When she still didn't budge, he sighed. "Never mind then. Look, Charlotte, not everything is always as it appears. And don't even try to pretend that you don't know what I'm talking about."

Charlotte gripped the doorknob even tighter. "What you do or don't do is none of my business," she retorted.

Louis narrowed his eyes and studied her a moment. "Are you sure about that?"

"I'm sure." *Liar, liar, pants on fire.*

As if he'd heard her thoughts, he said, "You and I both know you're lying."

"So, what's your point, Louis?"

He briefly squeezed his eyes shut and grimaced. With another long-suffering sigh, he opened them and said, "My point is that I'd like to explain who my guest is." He quickly added, "And don't you dare say that I don't owe you an explanation. If for no other reason, you are my landlady. And I thought you were my friend — my good friend," he continued. "Be that as it may, I felt I needed to explain, especially since my guest will be staying for a while, just until she gets her own place." His mouth twisted into a lopsided grin. "Besides, Judith would have my hide if I brought another woman in and didn't explain it."

When Charlotte simply stared at him and didn't respond to his attempt at humor, his expression grew tight with strain.

"She's my ex-wife, Charlotte. She's Stephen's mother."

Chapter 16

Charlotte's knees went weak. Stephen's mother . . . the woman who had abandoned her son and her husband because she couldn't cope with the troubled boy or her husband's long hours as a police detective. Louis's ex-wife . . . the woman who had left him, left him to raise their troubled teenage son all by himself.

"I looked her up while I was in San Francisco," Louis said. "I thought she should know about Stephen, how well he's doing. And I thought she should know that she's a grandmother. I — I thought it might make a difference. Well, actually, it was Stephen's idea."

Charlotte's insides churned with confusion. *Make a difference?* Make a difference how? She shook her head. "I don't understand."

"I know you don't, but if you'll just let me come inside, I'll try to explain."

Charlotte swallowed hard. "Like I said

before, you don't owe me an explanation, Louis."

"I may not 'owe' you one, but it's important to me that you understand. Please," he pleaded.

It was the "please" that finally convinced her. Louis wasn't the type of man to beg. Charlotte released her hold on the door frame. "Wait here a minute." She walked over to Sweety Boy's cage. "Sorry, Sweety," she murmured, as she slipped the cover over it. "Now you be a good little bird," she chided, as she turned and walked back to the front door. "You can come in now," she told Louis.

Once inside, he asked, "Would a cup of coffee be too much trouble?"

Charlotte closed the door and locked it. "I suppose I could use a cup myself."

Louis followed her back to the kitchen, then seated himself at the table. While Charlotte prepared the coffee, she could feel the heat of his gaze following her every move. Only when she switched on the coffeepot and joined him at the table did Louis finally begin to talk.

"Her name is Joyce," he said. "I've known for some time now that she was living in San Francisco. And so did Stephen. Like I said, when he found out that I was going there this last trip, he asked me to look her up, just to check on her. I don't guess I'll ever understand it, but even after all she did, all she put us through, he still cares about her."

"That's because she's his mother," Charlotte whispered.

"Yeah, well, some women don't deserve to be mothers, but that's a whole other discussion. Anyway, I found her address and showed up on her doorstep." His expression turned grim. "Her address was a halfway house. She'd been living there for the past six months, ever since she got out of jail."

"Jail," Charlotte whispered. "Why on earth was she in jail?"

Louis shifted in his chair and stared out the window. " 'Cause she's an alcoholic, Charlotte. The only way the judge would release her was if she agreed to live at the halfway house for six months. Before that, she'd been living a hand-to-mouth existence on the streets."

Clearly embarrassed, he glanced over at the coffeepot. "Looks like the coffee's ready." He pushed himself out of the chair, went over to the cabinet, then took down two mugs from the cabinet. After he poured the coffee, he brought the mugs back to the table.

Once Louis settled back in his chair, he added sugar to his coffee, took a sip, then wrapped both hands around the mug and stared out the window again. After a moment, he said, "She's also dying. Cirrhosis of the liver — too many years of a poor diet and too many years of drinking herself into oblivion."

"But she looks healthy enough." The moment Charlotte said it, she immediately realized she'd just admitted she'd been spying on Louis, and the look on his face told her as much.

A ghost of a smile pulled at Louis's lips. "Yeah, well, one thing about Joyce, she always was an artist of sorts when it came to makeup." Then, Louis sobered. "Heaven help me, I couldn't leave her, Charlotte." He shook his head. "I just couldn't leave her there to die among strangers."

An aching sensation tightened Charlotte's throat, and before she even realized that she'd done it, she reached out and placed her hand on Louis's forearm. "Of course you couldn't," she told him.

Louis covered her hand with his and stared into her eyes. His own eyes were full of torment. "Good or bad, she's the mother of my son and she's Amy's grandmother. For his sake and for Amy, I-I —"

"You did the right thing, Louis."

"I guess," he whispered, "but —"

"No buts," she told him. "Just the other day I was reminded of what my pastor once said. He said, 'Do right and you'll feel right.'" She paused, then asked, "How long? How long does she have?"

"Not long. Maybe six months — probably less."

"Is there anything I can do to help?"

Louis shook his head. "No, but thanks for offering, especially under the circumstances."

Long after Louis left, Charlotte sat on her sofa, nursing a second cup of coffee and staring into space. She couldn't stop thinking about his situation, and she couldn't help comparing Louis to the Gordon Adamses of the world. For all of Gordon Adams's money and all of his suave good looks and social background, in her opinion, he wasn't fit to lick the boots of a man like Louis. That Louis was willing to do what he was doing spoke volumes about the type of man he was.

But, then, hadn't she known all along that beneath that know-it-all, chauvinistic shell beat the heart of a good man, a dependable, responsible man of principle? As far as she was concerned, a man like Gordon Adams had nothing more than a thumping gizzard for a heart.

Later that night, before she climbed into bed, Charlotte added Joyce Thibodeaux to the list of people whom she prayed for each day.

On Saturday morning, for a change, Bitsy wasn't waiting for Charlotte when she drove up to her house. A man whom she assumed had to be Bradley Duhe was waiting for her instead. Well, not exactly waiting, she thought, as she parked the van. It looked more like he was pacing.

Charlotte climbed out of the van and gathered her supply carrier and vacuum cleaner. Before she got very far, though, Bradley called out, "Hold up and I'll help you carry that stuff inside." Before she had a chance to respond, he bounded down the steps and jogged over to her. "Here —" He took the vacuum cleaner out of her grasp. "I'll take that in."

Up close Bradley Duhe was every bit as good-looking as he was in the many pictures Charlotte had seen scattered throughout Bitsy's home. He was more than likely in his late fifties or early sixties and stood a good head taller than her own five-feet-three. He was a big man without appearing to be fat and had a head full of salt-and-pepper hair that was a bit on the long side, just brushing the collar of his shirt.

"Momma's inside cooking breakfast," he explained, as they climbed the steps to the porch. When they reached the porch, he set the vacuum cleaner down and turned to face her. "I was waiting out here hoping for a chance to talk to you a minute without her around."

Sudden dread filled Charlotte. Why on earth would he want to talk to her? And about what?"

"I'm afraid she's got some harebrained idea that I've come to force her to sell the house, that I want to stick her in a nursing home."

Charlotte nodded. As far as she could see, there was no use in beating around the bush. "She has mentioned that a few times," Charlotte told him.

Bradley rolled his eyes. "Where on earth does she come up with this stuff? All I've been trying to do is get her to talk about it so I'll know what she wants, if and when the time comes — just talk about it and nothing else." He shook his head in exasperation. "I love my mother, but I swear, she can worry the horns off a billy goat."

Charlotte snickered. Poor Bradley, he didn't know the half of it. And poor Bitsy, all this time worrying about what had turned out to be a misunderstanding.

"She really thinks highly of you," Bradley said. "And she respects you and your opinions. I was hoping that you might give me some insight as to how to handle her."

Feeling uncomfortable with the compliment, Charlotte swallowed hard and sent up a quick prayer for forgiveness for all the times that she'd passed judgment on Bitsy and for the unkind thoughts she'd had about her.

"She's just afraid of losing her independence," she finally said. "It's a natural fear the older a person gets. We all *know* we're getting older and we *know* we can't do all the things we used to do, but knowing it up here —" She tapped the side of her head with her forefinger. "And coming to grips with it here —" She placed her hand over her heart. "Are two different things."

Bradley crossed his arms and stared down at the porch floor. "Yeah, I know you're right about all of that, and I'm dreading the day when she can't take care of herself." He raised his head and looked at Charlotte. "But how in the devil do I convince her that I'm not out to do her in?"

Since Charlotte had thought long and hard about the day she might have to give up her own independence, she had a ready answer. "Just tell her that, straight out, then explain that you only want what's best for her. And keep telling her. Ask her what *she* wants — in other words, let *her* plan ahead. Let her plan how she wants things handled once she can no longer take care of herself." She shrugged. "Otherwise, the only thing you can do is keep reassuring her that she's handling things just fine."

"Except for the 'reassuring' part, that's what I thought I'd been doing."

Charlotte smiled sympathetically. "That 'reassuring' part is the most important part of all. We all like to feel that we have the approval and respect of the people we love."

After a moment of thought, Bradley slowly nodded. "Yeah, I guess so," he said. Another moment passed, then he sighed. "Thanks, Charlotte. And for the record, my mother was right."

Charlotte raised her eyebrows. "Right?"

He nodded. "She told me you were a wise lady."

Again, shame and embarrassment warred within, causing Charlotte's cheeks to grow warm. From now on she'd have to make more of a concentrated effort to be less judgmental and a whole lot less impatient, she vowed.

Bradley cleared his throat. "Just one more thing before we go inside. I know it's short notice, and I apologize for that, but would you be free for dinner tonight?"

A nasty little imp inside urged Charlotte to accept Bradley's dinner invitation just to spite Louis, to show him that he wasn't the only man interested in her.

Pride goes before destruction and a haughty spirit before a fall.

When the verse from Proverbs popped into her mind, she immediately squashed the little imp. She'd learned a long time ago that nothing good ever came from spiteful behavior. Besides, her on-again, off-again "relationship" with Louis wasn't entirely his fault, and Louis had enough on his mind right now without her rubbing salt into his wounds and acting like a jealous ninny. Of course, that was assuming that he really cared about her in a relationship way.

Charlotte smiled kindly at Bradley. "I don't think —"

"You'd be doing me a huge favor," Bradley interrupted. He reached up and pinched the bridge of his nose, then dropped his hand and sighed. "You see, I suspect my mother is trying to play matchmaker. I told her that I'd take her out to a nice restaurant to eat tonight, and now she wants to invite another woman to join us — a daughter of one of her friends." He shrugged. "I just thought if another woman was along . . ." His voice trailed away.

Charlotte felt her face grow hot for even thinking that Bradley was interested in her. She laughed to cover up her embarrassment. "Sorry, but I'm afraid you're on your own. I —"

"Aw, come on, Charlotte. Be a sport. I-I'll pay you."

Embarrassment quickly yielded to indignation. The very idea that he thought he could *pay* her to go to dinner. Besides, regardless of Bitsy's compliments, the thought of spending an entire evening having to listen to her endless chatter was enough to make Charlotte want to pull her hair out by the roots.

Charlotte slowly counted to ten before she answered. "Look," she told him, "if you don't want this other woman to tag along, why not just say so? Why not convince your mother that you wanted this dinner to be a special thing just between the two of you, a mother-son thing?"

Bradley hung his head. "You're right, of course — again. And please accept my apology. I didn't mean to insult you."

Suddenly, the front door swung open and Bitsy appeared. The old lady's face was flushed and her eyes snapped with excitement. "Oh, Charlotte, I'm so glad you're here. You'll never guess what I just heard. I just got a call from Margo Jones and she said that the police have arrested Mimi Adams's murderer."

Chapter 17

Shock rippled through Charlotte. "Say that again."

Bitsy rolled her eyes. "I said that Margo called to tell me that the police have arrested Mimi Adams's murderer."

"Did she say *whom* they arrested?"

"Well, no — no she didn't." Bitsy suddenly grinned. "But I told Margo that if anyone could find out, it was you, what with your niece being a detective and all."

For the moment, Charlotte ignored Bitsy's inference to Judith. "How does your friend *know* that someone was arrested?"

"She heard it from Sandra Wellington, and Sandra's friend Jane works as a police dispatcher."

"Who's Mimi Adams?" Bradley asked his mother. When she didn't answer, he turned to Charlotte. "Your niece is a police detective?"

Both Charlotte and Bitsy ignored him.

"So will you do it?" Bitsy asked, her eyes glittering with anticipation. "Will you call Judith?"

Now what? Charlotte wondered. Of course she would call Judith, just as soon as she got a moment to herself. But she couldn't tell Bitsy that. There was no way she was going to get sucked into Bitsy's rumor mill. Charlotte shook her head. "I can't do that."

"Well, why in blue blazes can't you?" Bitsy demanded.

Charlotte heaved a sigh. "For one thing, Judith probably wouldn't tell me." It was a half lie at best, but it was all Charlotte could come up with at the moment. "The police are funny about that kind of thing," she added, which was the truth. Then, Charlotte thought of another reason, and though she hesitated before saying it, she decided that it was time someone said it. "And another thing," she added, "we don't really know if it's true or not."

Bitsy stiffened and her eyes flashed indignantly. "Well of course it's true. That's not the kind of thing that Sandra would lie about. And why would she lie to begin with? My goodness, Charlotte, don't be so paranoid."

Charlotte shrugged and slowly shook her

head. "I'm sorry, but I just can't," she lied.

Bradley made a production of clearing his throat. "A-hem, excuse me, but would one of you please tell me what's going on here?"

Clearly miffed at Charlotte, Bitsy glared at her son. "Oh, put a sock in it, Bradley." With that, she whirled around and stomped back inside the house.

His mouth hanging open, Bradley turned to Charlotte. "What's got into her? What did I do now?"

Charlotte felt sorry for Bradley and took pity on him. "It's not what you did. It's what I did, or, to be exact, it's what I won't do." She laughed. "Your mother does like to have her own way."

Bradley rolled his eyes. "Don't I know it. So, will *you* tell me what this is all about?"

Charlotte nodded. "A woman whom both your mother and I know was murdered a few days ago," she explained. "And —"

"Bradley!" Bitsy yelled from inside the house. "Your breakfast is getting cold."

Frustrated, Bradley made a growling noise, and Charlotte smiled sympathetically. "Go ahead. I'll be inside in a minute. I need to get something out of the van."

With a slightly dazed look and a shake of

his head, Bradley picked up the vacuum cleaner and went inside. The moment he closed the front door, Charlotte whipped out her cell phone and dialed Judith. A few moments later, she let out her own frustrated growl when she got Judith's voice mail.

Deciding against leaving a message, Charlotte switched off the phone. Either Judith had her phone turned off or she wasn't answering on purpose, which probably meant that she was busy.

Charlotte dropped the phone back into her apron pocket and, bracing herself for what she figured was going to be a long day, picked up the supply carrier and went inside the house.

By the time Charlotte left Bitsy's that afternoon, she still didn't know if the rumor Bitsy had heard was true or not. Bitsy had been on the phone, on and off, most of the day, but none of her connections had produced the name of the person who had supposedly been arrested for Mimi Adams's murder.

All afternoon while Charlotte was cleaning, she'd been making a mental list of the suspects and had narrowed the list down to two, possibly three people —

Gordon, Rita, and maybe June — whom the police could have arrested, but, like Bitsy, the not knowing was driving her crazy.

On the drive home, she was sorely tempted to swing by the police station, just on the off chance that she might catch Judith there. But after thinking about it, she decided that doing so probably wasn't such a good idea, and besides, she didn't want to cause any trouble for Judith.

When Charlotte pulled into her driveway, she noticed that Louis's Taurus was gone. But as she walked up the steps to the porch, she saw a brief flicker of movement at the window on Louis's side of the double. Louis wasn't home, but evidently Joyce was there.

Charlotte had just inserted her key into the lock when Louis's front door opened and Joyce stepped out onto the porch.

The mental image of Joyce that Charlotte had carried with her from the previous day paled in comparison to the thin woman now standing on the porch. It was like seeing a completely different woman, an extremely ill woman.

Up close there was a telltale yellowish tinge to Joyce's skin and to the whites of her eyes. Again, Joyce was wearing a tank top, but with shorts instead of jeans, and along her shoulders spider-like blood vessels were visible.

"You must be Charlotte," Joyce said, managing a small, nervous smile.

Charlotte nodded and managed a smile of her own. "And you must be Joyce. Would you like to come inside?"

Joyce shook her head. "Oh, no, I'd better not, but thanks. I've been watching for you to come home and hoping for a chance to talk to you without Louis around." She paused a moment, as if embarrassed. "I'm not sure how he would feel about me talking to you, so please don't say anything."

Charlotte frowned. "Why on earth would Louis care if you talked to me?"

Joyce gave a one-shouldered shrug. "I'm not sure. That's just the impression I got, and I don't want to do anything to aggravate him. You won't say anything, will you?"

Charlotte shook her head. "No, I won't."

"Good. The reason I wanted to talk to you is to thank you. Louis told me how you encouraged him to contact Stephen," she explained, "and how that it was because of you that they're on such good terms now after being estranged for so long."

Charlotte wasn't sure what she'd expected, but she hadn't expected gratitude from Joyce.

"As you probably know," Joyce continued, "I haven't been much of a mother to Stephen or much of a wife to Louis, but I've always loved my son and only wanted the best for him. And for Louis, too. At the time I left, believe me, that was the best for both of them. But now, thanks to you, he and Louis can be a family again." Once more she paused. Then, as if gathering her courage, she said, "I also wanted you to know that I won't be causing you any trouble. Louis is gone a lot, and he said you wouldn't mind me staying for a while."

"No, of course I don't mind," Charlotte reassured her. "And it's really none of my business anyway."

"Well, then, thanks again." With a brief nod, Joyce turned and went back inside, and Charlotte was left standing on the porch by herself.

For several moments Charlotte continued standing there, staring at the closed door to Louis's half of the double. *Trouble?* What kind of trouble could Joyce cause? Then, with a shake of her head, she turned, unlocked her door, and went inside.

"Missed you, missed you," Sweety Boy chirped the moment she entered. Then he began squawking and dancing back and forth along his perch, a ploy to get her attention.

"Hey, Boy," she called out. "I missed you too. Just give me a minute and I'll let you out for a while."

Charlotte pulled off her tennis shoes, and as she slipped into her moccasins, bits and pieces of her brief conversation with Joyce kept playing through her mind. But one particular phrase kept coming back to her over and over.

I haven't been much of a mother to Stephen or much of a wife to Louis.

" 'Much of a wife to Louis,' " she murmured, mulling over the words and wondering why they bothered her. Then, suddenly, she knew why. The way Joyce had said it implied that she was still married to Louis, that she was still his wife.

Charlotte's insides churned, as she made her way to the kitchen. Had Louis ever actually *said* he was divorced?

Charlotte racked her brain, as she fixed the coffeepot, and tried to recall just exactly what he had said about his and Joyce's relationship. If she remembered right, he'd said that Joyce had left him and

Stephen when Stephen was about twelve, that she'd just packed a bag and walked out.

The next thing I knew I was being served divorce papers.

As Louis's words came back to her, she remembered something else he'd said just yesterday: "She's my ex-wife."

Relief washed through Charlotte. But relief quickly gave way to doubt and confusion. Just because divorce papers had been served didn't necessarily mean that he'd signed them or that he and Joyce had actually gone through with the divorce. And just because he'd called her his "ex-wife" didn't necessarily make it true.

Still disturbed by it all, Charlotte glanced at the coffeepot and saw that the coffee was ready. She had just finished pouring herself a cup when the phone rang.

With a sigh, she hurried into the living room and snatched up the receiver. "Maid-for-a-Day, Charlotte speaking."

"Charlotte, have you heard anything else yet?"

Just the sound of Bitsy's voice made Charlotte want to groan out loud. She took a deep breath and prayed for patience. "No, Bitsy," she said firmly. "Nothing yet."

"Well, you will be sure to let me know when you do hear something, won't you?"

Charlotte didn't want to outright lie to the old lady. She already had told enough lies to confess to for one day, so instead of answering Bitsy, she tried changing the subject. "How are things with you and Bradley? Are y'all working out your misunderstandings?"

"Humph! That son of mine is just as stubborn as his father ever thought about being. Why, would you believe he didn't like my idea about remodeling the kitchen, didn't like it one bit — said it was a waste of money?" Bitsy snickered. "But I'm still working on him."

As usual, Bitsy had her own agenda and had completely misunderstood the question. "Well, maybe you ought to reconsider," Charlotte told her. "Remember, all those strangers in and out and all of that noise and mess could really be nerve-wracking."

"Yes, well . . . I suppose you do have a point."

"Just promise me you'll think about it," Charlotte said. "And I'll see you on Tuesday," she added. Without waiting for a response, Charlotte then said, "Bye now," and quickly hung up the receiver.

Glaring at the phone, she made a silent vow that first thing Monday morning she was phoning BellSouth and having caller I.D. added. At least that way she would know when Bitsy was calling, and she could let the answering machine take Bitsy's calls.

Charlotte continued staring at the phone. As long as she was there, she might as well try to call Judith again. She tapped out Judith's cell phone number, and after the third ring, her call was answered.

"Judith Monroe here."

"Oh, Judith, finally. Can you talk a minute?"

"Oh, hey, Aunt Charley. Yeah, sure, but I only have a minute. What's up?"

Charlotte twisted the phone cord around her finger. "Well, I hate to bother you with this, but rumor has it that the police have made an arrest in the Mimi Adams murder. Ah, I was just wondering, is it true? Have you arrested Mimi's murderer?"

Chapter 18

There was a long pause over the phone line, then Judith said, "Now, Auntie, you know I'm not supposed to discuss an ongoing investigation. And since when did you begin listening to rumors anyway?"

Charlotte ignored Judith's question for the time being. "Well, if it's still ongoing," she said, "that must mean you haven't arrested anyone yet."

"Where did you hear this so-called rumor?"

Charlotte had to smile at Judith's maneuver to avoid confirming or denying her assumption. "Do you want the actual source of the rumor?" she asked. "Or just the person who told me?"

"This is getting us nowhere fast, and I'm pretty busy right now. How about we talk later?"

"Will you and Billy be able to come to lunch tomorrow after church?"

"I hope so, but I can't make any promises."

"Well, you take care of yourself now."

"You too, Auntie. Talk to you later."

Charlotte hung up the receiver and walked over to Sweety Boy's cage. "Well a lot of good that did," she told the little bird. She reached to unlatch the cage door, and when Sweety Boy sidled up to the opening, Charlotte smiled. "Yeah, yeah, and a lot you care, huh, Boy?" She opened the door, stuck her forefinger inside, and the little parakeet hopped on her finger. Once she eased him out of the cage, he immediately took flight. After several swoops around the living room, he landed on the cuckoo clock, his favorite out-of-cage perch.

With a slight shake of her head, Charlotte headed for the kitchen. She'd long suspected that Sweety Boy actually thought that the bird in the cuckoo clock was real. And though it hadn't happened yet, she'd often wondered how the little parakeet would react if he happened to be perched on the clock when the cuckoo bird popped out.

Once in the kitchen, Charlotte opened the freezer and stared at its contents. If she remembered right, she'd bought a nice big roast a couple of weeks ago. Charlotte spied the edge of the package containing the roast hiding behind a bag of chicken tenders. She dug out the roast and placed it below in the refrigerator to thaw out overnight. A roast with potatoes and carrots was something she could cook ahead of time before church on Sunday and then heat up for lunch.

Charlotte spent the next hour gathering receipts and logging them into her monthly accounts. She'd just finished and was ready to put Sweety Boy back inside his cage when the phone rang. Charlotte narrowed her eyes and tapped her pen against the desk. Probably Bitsy again, she figured. With a sigh, she picked up the receiver. "Maid-for-a-Day, Charlotte speaking."

"Hello, Aunt Chardy."

"Well, hello yourself, Davy. How's my favorite little guy doing? Are you being a good little boy for your momma?"

"I good boy and I love you. Bye."

"Ah-Davy, wait — Aunt Charley loves you too, hon," she told him.

Charlotte could hear Nadia in the background telling Davy to hand her the phone. "Sorry about that," Nadia said, after a moment. "But Davy insisted that he needed to talk to his Aunt Chardy."

Charlotte laughed. "Well, I'm glad he

did. I've been meaning to call you anyway to let you know that Janet has agreed to work for you when you have the baby. So, how are you feeling? Madeline said you haven't been well lately."

"Fat and pregnant," Nadia responded. "That's how I'm feeling, and for a change, my mother-in-law is right. The last couple of weeks have been pretty hard. And that's the other reason I called. I went for my checkup yesterday and my doctor wants me to get as much bed rest as possible. Do you think Janet would mind taking over my clients a little sooner than planned?"

"Whether she minds or not, don't you worry about it for one second. I'll manage. You just take care of yourself and that little baby. Now, is there anything else I can do? What about Davy? Do you need some help with him?"

"Thanks, Charlotte, but no. Between Madeline and Daniel, we've got it covered, I think. But I'm afraid we'll have to miss church and lunch tomorrow, so don't plan on us being there."

"Well, that's a shame, but I certainly understand. Tell you what, why don't I bring lunch to you tomorrow?"

"Aw, Charlotte, that's really sweet of you, but Madeline has already offered to bring something by."

"Hmm, how about this, then? Let me bring something anyway and you can have it for dinner tomorrow night or save it for your lunch or dinner on Monday."

"Thanks, Charlotte."

On Sunday after church, Judith was the first to arrive at Charlotte's for lunch, and from the moment her niece stepped through the doorway, the temptation to ask her again if indeed someone had been arrested for Mimi's murder was eating Charlotte alive.

All in good time, she kept telling herself, as Judith followed her back to the kitchen. Judith would tell her when and if she was good and ready.

"Guess it's going to be just Hank, Carol, and me today," Judith said, as Charlotte checked on the roast heating in the oven. "Nadia's doctor put her to bed, and Mom's busy helping out with their lunch and with Davy."

"Yes, I know," Charlotte responded. "I talked to Nadia yesterday afternoon. But what about Billy? Is he coming?"

Judith made a face. "He said he'd try to stop by, but for us not to wait on him. I really doubt he'll make it."

"Hmm, that's too bad," Charlotte murmured, as she opened the refrigerator and took out ingredients for a salad.

"Aunt Charley? About that rumor you heard — the one about Mary Lou Adams's murderer being arrested. This isn't exactly public knowledge yet, but I just thought you'd like to know that we did arrest someone."

Charlotte froze, then firmly closed the refrigerator and turned to face Judith. "Who?" she whispered.

"Actually we've arrested two people, a couple by the name of Mires — Doreen and George Mires."

Charlotte frowned. Of all the people she'd considered as suspects, she'd never truly considered Doreen. "What happened? What made you think they were guilty?"

Judith shrugged. "There were several things that just didn't add up, but the most damning evidence was a freshly dug spot in their backyard. The Mireses claimed that they were putting in a new flower bed, but our boys found traces of jimsonweed. We figured they were trying to get rid of it to cover up the fact that they had it to begin with."

Charlotte's frown deepened. "But Mimi

had jimsonweed growing in her backyard too," Charlotte pointed out. "Any one of a number of people could have taken enough of it to poison her . . . couldn't they?"

All along, Charlotte had thought June had to be the "friend" who had suggested that Mimi plant the jimsonweed, not Doreen. And she'd been sure that whomever that "friend" was had to be the murderer. So why would Doreen even suggest planting the jimsonweed when she already had some? The only reason Charlotte could come up with was that Doreen was trying to use Mimi's jimsonweed as a decoy.

"Yes, I suppose they could have," Judith said, "but after interrogating Rita Landers and Karen Douglas, we learned that Doreen had been the one who had uncorked and poured the wine that Rita had brought for Mrs. Adams, the Mauro 1998. With her pouring the wine, it would have been easy enough to slip something in Mrs. Adams's glass."

Charlotte stared at Judith with unseeing eyes. She'd been almost certain that Rita had poured the wine. But if Doreen had poured the wine instead, her theory as to how Rita had poisoned Mimi didn't hold water. So, did that mean Rita was off the hook? Only if the police were right, and only if Rita and Karen had told the truth, she finally concluded.

"So what was Doreen's motive?" Charlotte asked. "And his — her husband's motive?"

"We're still gathering evidence, but it seems that Doreen got on Mimi's bad side. We figure she was afraid that Mimi was out to get her husband fired. Seems Gordon Adams once ruined another man on Mimi's say-so, and the Mireses were afraid he'd do the same to them."

"Probably Don Landers." The second the words popped out, Charlotte immediately wished she'd kept her mouth shut.

Judith's eyes narrowed. "And just how did you know about Don Landers, Auntie?"

"Well, I-ah-I might have overheard something to that effect." She hastily added, "But it was just gossip."

"Is there anything else that you 'might have overheard' that you'd like to share?"

"Well, actually, there was something I wanted to talk to you about, but —" She shrugged. "I guess now it doesn't matter, since you've made an arrest."

"Something, as in what?" Judith asked.

A sudden, sharp rap at the front door interrupted them, so Charlotte simply said, "Maybe we can talk later. That's probably Carol and Hank. Would you go let them in?"

Judith nodded. "I'll go, but Aunt Charley —" She leveled a no-nonsense gaze at Charlotte. "If you think of anything else, you will tell me, won't you?"

Rain was forecast for Monday, and as Charlotte drove to work, the sky was already overcast with dark gray clouds. She never did get the chance to question Judith further about Doreen and George Mires on Sunday. Halfway through the meal, Judith's beeper had gone off and she'd had to leave.

In spite of all the so-called motives that Judith had listed, Charlotte still couldn't believe that the Mireses had conspired to murder Mimi. Doreen Mires just hadn't struck her as the type who could do such a thing. Then again, after she'd thought about it, she'd remembered the scene between Doreen and Mimi after the HHS meeting, with Doreen begging Mimi not to hold George responsible for what she'd done.

Charlotte shook her head. Even so, Mimi was already ill by that time, which meant that, in all likelihood, she had been poisoned before the meeting. And Doreen's concerns were a result of what had happened during the meeting.

Charlotte pulled over in front of the Adamses' house and parked the van. As she unloaded her supplies, thunder rumbled in the distance. She glanced up at the sky, then decided to add her umbrella to the supply carrier.

At the front door, Charlotte knocked first as a precaution, just in case Gordon happened to be home. She waited several minutes, and when no one came to the door, she unlocked it and let herself inside.

Once she secured the deadbolt and disarmed the security system, she left the vacuum cleaner and supply carrier in the entrance hall. Then she took her lunch bag into the kitchen and left it on the cabinet.

Charlotte glanced around the kitchen assessing what needed to be done. Though it wasn't as clean as it had been on Friday, it wasn't the worst mess she'd ever seen either.

As she walked around the rest of the downstairs to check out what needed cleaning, she made up her mind to phone Judith and set up a meeting to discuss the arrests of Doreen and George Mires. If they were truly guilty, that was one thing, but if they weren't, then Charlotte didn't want the real murderer to get away scot-free.

For the most part, the rest of the rooms downstairs were just cluttered, and once she toured the downstairs, she returned to the entrance hall, picked up the supply carrier, and went upstairs.

She'd just set the supply carrier down outside the master suite when she heard a noise downstairs. Frowning, she walked to the top of the stairs, tilted her head, and listened for several seconds. Other than the hum of the air conditioner running and the faint sound of the case clock ticking, there was nothing but silence.

"Strange," she murmured, and with a shake of her head she walked back toward the bedrooms. The house was old, and old houses creaked as they settled. Besides, she'd made sure that she had bolted the front door.

But what about the back door?

"Oh, for pity's sake," she grumbled, remembering how spooked she'd been the last time she'd cleaned. "Just get to work and stop being so paranoid."

Though still somewhat bothered by the noise she'd heard, she checked all of the rooms on the second level to see what needed to be done, saving the master bedroom and bath for last.

Emma's and Justin's bedroom suites and the guest bedroom suite looked exactly the same as when she'd left after cleaning on Friday.

As Charlotte headed for the master bedroom, she made a mental list of what she intended to do first. Laundry was at the top of the list, which meant stripping the bed in the master bedroom. Once she put the sheets in to wash, she'd make up the bed in the master bedroom with a clean set. Then, starting with the master bath, she would clean all of the bathrooms and dust the furniture in all of the bedrooms. The final chore would be vacuuming.

When Charlotte walked into the master bedroom, the first thing that caught her eye was the king-size bed. Unlike the last time she'd cleaned, when only one side had been rumpled, this time, both sides were. From the looks of it, she decided that either Gordon had had a really restless weekend and had slept all over the bed, or he hadn't slept alone.

Charlotte shook her head and felt ashamed for immediately jumping to such a conclusion. Though she couldn't think of any reason offhand, there could be other explanations for both sides being in disarray.

She set down the supply carrier, approached the bed, and grabbed one of the pillows. As she tugged off the pillowcase, she caught a whiff of men's cologne and breathed more deeply. The scent was one that she recognized immediately: it was the same kind that Hank wore. But when Charlotte reached across and picked up the other pillow, she caught a whiff of a different scent. She held the pillow closer and sniffed. The odor was too flowery for a man's cologne. She sniffed again. It smelled more like a woman's perfume.

"The man has some nerve," she muttered, as she yanked off the pillowcase. Gordon had had company over the weekend all right, specifically, bedroom company. She'd suspected as much but hadn't wanted to believe it. Thoroughly disgusted, Charlotte flung back the comforter and the blanket, then wrestled the sheets off the bed.

In the bathroom, Charlotte found further evidence that confirmed her suspicions. There were way too many dirty towels and washcloths in the clothes hamper for one lone man to have used by himself. And there was an extra tooth-brush in the toothbrush holder.

Charlotte glared at the marble counter-top to the bathroom vanity. Not only was there an extra toothbrush, but there was also a suspicious-looking beige smudge and what looked like bits of loose face powder on the countertop. Using her fore-finger, she reached down and rubbed the smudge. Yep, just as she'd suspected. The smudge was makeup.

Growing more disgusted with each pass-ing moment, Charlotte washed her hands, then gathered up all of the dirty clothes in the bathroom. On her way out, she added the pile of sheets to her bundle and then took everything down to the laundry room. Once she turned on the washing machine and added the laundry detergent, she stuffed everything inside the machine, then returned to the upstairs master bedroom.

After she made up the bed with fresh linens, she went back into the master bath-room. It was while she was scrubbing out the shower that she found the most damning evidence of all.

"Yuck," she complained, and using a paper towel, she wiped up the long hair that had collected around the shower drain. Charlotte stared at the hair a moment before tossing the paper towel into the trash. Unless she was mistaken, either Gordon had bleached his hair and had had a world-record growth spurt over the weekend, or the blond strands of hair belonged to a woman.

As Charlotte went about her chores cleaning the rest of the house, she grew more and more outraged by what she'd found — outraged and suspicious. If Gordon could sleep with another woman so soon after Mimi's death, then it didn't take much of a stretch of the imagination to conclude that he could have murdered Mimi to get rid of her.

There was only one problem with her conclusion, she decided, as she was scrubbing out the sink in the kitchen. One big problem. The police had already arrested Mimi's so-called killers.

Much later, as Charlotte prepared to eat her lunch, it suddenly occurred to her that she'd been so disgusted by what Gordon had done that she really hadn't given much thought to the woman he'd been sleeping with.

She unzipped the insulated lunch bag and took out the salad she'd prepared earlier that morning.

The most likely candidate was June, she decided, given the way June had stepped in and completely taken over after Mimi's death. But the fact that June had long blond hair wasn't conclusive evidence in and of itself.

As Charlotte carried her salad and thermos of tea to the kitchen table, she thought of the day of Mimi's funeral. Rita Landers, the woman Mimi had suspected of having an affair with Gordon in the first place, had shown up sporting a new hairstyle that had been freshly bleached blond. And didn't Sally Lawson have blond hair as well?

Charlotte forked up a bite of salad. When she began to chew, she wrinkled her nose. Something in the salad had a bitter taste, but she kept chewing and finally swallowed it. Probably the purple cabbage, she thought, forking up another bite. "That's what you get for being lazy and buying those prepackaged salads instead of making them yourself," she muttered.

She placed the forkfull of salad in her mouth and, ignoring the bitter taste, turned her thoughts to Sally Lawson. If she remembered right, Sally had said something about Gordon and her being old friends. Just how close were they? she wondered.

Maybe there was more to the feud between Sally and Mimi after all than just a couple of dead trees. Maybe Mimi had sensed that there was more to Sally and Gordon's so-called friendship, and the feud over the trees was just a smokescreen. Mimi's suspicions could also be the reason why she had rejected Sally's attempts at friendship.

Charlotte sighed as she chewed another bite of the salad, and after she swallowed, she made another face. Though she'd only eaten about half of the salad, she pushed it away. Enough was enough. She reached for her thermos and took a long drink of the tea in an attempt to get rid of the bitter taste of the salad. All the while, her mind kept going back to Mimi and Sally.

Even if her suppositions about Sally were right, Mimi would have had more motive to murder Sally than Sally had to murder Mimi. Besides, she never had figured out how Sally could have pulled off poisoning Mimi without poisoning others as well.

Charlotte gathered up her dishes and took them to the sink. She dumped the remainder of the salad into the trash. Squirting a bit of detergent on a sponge, she washed and rinsed the dishes.

In the long run, it didn't really matter who was sleeping with Gordon or what she thought, Charlotte decided. The police had already drawn their own conclusions and arrested Doreen and George Mires.

The police could be wrong.

Charlotte dried the plastic container that had held her salad. Yes, the police could be wrong, and deep in her gut, she knew they were wrong. But who was she to suggest such a thing? Just the maid, came the answer. Merely the hired help. Before anyone would believe her, she'd need proof, not just her conclusions and gut feelings.

Charlotte repacked the dishes in her lunch kit and was still mulling over her suspicions when her cell phone rang. Praying that the caller wasn't Bitsy again, she pulled the phone out of her apron pocket and answered the call. "Maid-for-a-Day, Charlotte speaking," she said.

"Oh, Charlotte, you've got to come quick," Madeline cried. "I don't know what to do. I-I need help."

Chapter 19

"Whoa, hold on, Maddie. What's wrong?"

"It's Nadia!" Madeline cried. "She's in labor — she's having the baby, and it's too early. Oh, Charlotte, I told you — I told you she was working too hard. I told you to —"

"Madeline, stop it!" Charlotte ordered, fighting her own panic. "Where is Nadia right now?"

"For crying out loud, she's at the hospital. Where else would she be?"

"Which hospital, Maddie?"

"Ochsner, but —"

"Is Daniel there?"

"Yes, of course, but Charlotte, what if something goes wrong — I mean, it's too early. She wasn't due for at least another six weeks. What if —"

"I'll be there as soon as possible," Charlotte cut in.

"Please hurry," Madeline begged. "I just don't think I can handle it if-if —"

"Madeline!" Charlotte snapped. "Get hold of yourself. Just take a deep breath and calm down. The sooner we hang up, the sooner I can leave and the sooner I can get there."

Charlotte didn't wait for Madeline's reply. She immediately switched off her cell phone and dropped it into her pocket. Near the phone on the counter was a notepad and pen. Charlotte hurried over to the counter and snatched up the pen, but her hand was trembling so badly that she could barely write.

She clutched the pen even tighter, and taking her own advice, she took a deep breath, and then another one. Feeling a bit more in control, she scribbled a hasty note to Gordon explaining that she'd had a family emergency and had to leave. She left the note in plain sight on the counter-top near the coffeepot, and in record time, she quickly gathered her cleaning supplies.

Outside, the sky was gray, and a fine mist was falling as Charlotte quickly loaded her supply carrier and vacuum cleaner into the back of the van.

Ochsner Hospital was located on Jefferson Highway in the bend of the Mississippi River, not far from the Orleans–Jefferson Parish line. Charlotte comforted herself with the thought that Ochsner was one of the finest hospitals in the South, and the doctors there were top-notch.

Traffic was light, and she was making good time until she came to the first of the three sets of railroad tracks that crossed Jefferson Highway.

"No," she groaned, as she pulled up behind the line of vehicles waiting for a train to pass. To add to her anxiety, the train was moving so slowly that she decided she might as well put the van into park.

As she shifted the lever into park, she checked her watch. Fifteen minutes had passed since she'd left the Adamses' house. Again she took several deep breaths. Then, she began to pray.

A full ten minutes later, the last of the train finally passed, the cross arm lifted, and she shifted into drive. A few minutes later, when she finally reached the hospital's cavernous parking garage, she had to drive all the way up to the fifth level before she could locate an empty parking spot.

Charlotte found Maddie standing outside the baby nursery. She was staring through the glass partition. Charlotte walked up behind her sister and placed her hand on Madeline's shoulder. "Which one is she?"

Madeline shook her head, and when she turned to face Charlotte, her eyes filled with tears. "She's not in there, Charlotte. She was born right after I talked to you, and they had to transfer her up to the neonatal intensive care unit. She weighed just a little over four pounds and was having some breathing problems."

Charlotte squeezed Madeline's shoulder. "I'm sure she's getting the best of care, Maddie. It's fortunate that Nadia chose this hospital. And speaking of Nadia, how is she holding up?"

Madeline shrugged. "Not too great. She's exhausted . . . and frantic with worry. The doctor had to give her something to calm her down, and she's dozing right now."

"And Daniel? Where is he?"

"He's talking to the pediatrician."

Charlotte put her arms around Madeline and hugged her tightly. "It's going to be okay, Maddie," she murmured. "Just have faith." She released her sister and smiled. "Besides, that little girl comes from sturdy stock, and if she's anything like her mom and dad and grandmother, then she's a fighter."

"I wish I could believe that," Madeline whispered. "Dear Lord in heaven, how I wish I could believe that."

"Believe it," Charlotte said firmly. "Now, why don't we go to the waiting room, where we can sit down while we wait for Daniel. I think I saw a coffeepot in there. I don't know about you, but I could use a cup. And some aspirin," she added.

"Headache?" Madeline asked.

Charlotte nodded. "Just a small one."

When Daniel finally joined Madeline and Charlotte in the small waiting room, Charlotte's heart went out to him. He looked haggard and worried. She hugged him tightly. "And how's my favorite nephew holding up?"

"I'm okay . . . I guess. I'd be a whole lot better if . . ." His voice trailed away.

"What did the doctor say?" Madeline asked.

Daniel straightened and squared his shoulders. "He said that if she makes it through the night, she'll have a good chance of surviving." He sighed, then bowed his head. "What am I going to tell Nadia, though?"

"The truth," Charlotte said. "You tell her the truth." Charlotte reached out and took Daniel's hand in hers. "She's stronger than you think, hon." In an attempt to lighten the tension, Charlotte released Daniel's hands, then poked him in the chest with her forefinger. "And by the way, young man, I have a bone to pick with you. When did she go into labor and why wasn't I called right away?"

A faint smile pulled at Daniel's lips. "Nice try, Auntie, but to answer your questions, Nadia began complaining about a backache last night. Then, about seven this morning, she began having contractions."

Charlotte turned to Madeline. "Why didn't *you* call me, then?"

"She didn't call you because she didn't know," Daniel said. "Since it was so early and all, Nadia wanted to make sure it was the real thing before we alerted the family."

When Charlotte finally left the hospital around four-thirty, baby Danielle was still holding her own, and Charlotte's headache had gotten worse.

Charlotte hadn't wanted to leave at all, but Daniel and Nadia had dropped Davy off at day care that morning on their way to the hospital, and someone had to pick him up. They had called Judith, but she couldn't leave work. Knowing that neither Daniel nor Madeline wanted to leave the hospital, Charlotte had volunteered to pick up Davy.

Nadia had already prearranged for Davy to stay with a neighbor that evening, so after Charlotte picked him up from day care she dropped him off at the neighbor's house.

With Davy settled, Charlotte fully intended to return to the hospital. She had just pulled up at the stop sign and was waiting for an opening in traffic on South Claiborne when she suddenly groaned.

"Oh, just great!" she grumbled. "Just terrific!"

In her haste to get to the hospital earlier, she'd left clothes in the washing machine at the Adamses' house. If the clothes were left too long, they would mildew for sure.

For several seconds Charlotte debated on what she should do. After what she'd discovered about Gordon, she was sorely tempted to let the silly clothes mildew. And she was sorely tempted to drop Gordon from her client list altogether.

But then she suddenly remembered that she'd left her lunch bag there as well. Besides, she reminded herself, what Gordon did or didn't do was none of her business. Her business was doing the job she was paid to do.

"Yeah, yeah," she grumbled, feeling unreasonably irritated. Her headache had worsened, and her mouth felt like cotton. Finally, she spotted a break in the traffic.

A few minutes later, Charlotte parked the van in front of the Adamses' house. She didn't expect Gordon to be home yet, but as a precaution she knocked on the door anyway. Key in hand, she waited a couple of minutes and was just about to insert it into the lock when she heard the lock click, and suddenly the door swung open.

"What are you doing back here?" June demanded.

Charlotte had to bite her tongue to keep from retorting that it was none of the woman's business, and she had a good mind to ask June the same question. But why ask when she was already pretty sure that she knew the answer. For one thing, the silk lounging pajamas June had on weren't exactly what someone paying a casual visit to their best friend's grieving husband would wear. Besides, Charlotte figured asking would just be a waste of time. June would never admit to the real reason for being there anyway.

"I had a family emergency earlier," Charlotte explained, and when she realized that the tone of her voice was a bit sharp, she immediately apologized. "Sorry, I'm just tired and a bit frazzled. I didn't plan on returning, but then I remembered that I'd left some clothes in the washing machine, and I knew they would mildew before I returned to work on Friday. And I also left my lunch bag."

June nodded, and when she stepped back, Charlotte figured that was her invitation to come inside. "I saw the note you left for Gordon," June said. "And I saw your lunch bag sitting on the cabinet. I just came by to drop off some food for his dinner."

Yeah, right. Sure you did, and I'm the Queen of Mardi Gras. Charlotte simply nodded, stepped past June, and headed down the hallway. *Just do what you came to do and get out.* "I won't be but just a minute," she called out over her shoulder.

Out of habit, as Charlotte walked past the entrance to the dining room, she glanced into the room, and for the briefest of seconds, her steps faltered. But ever aware that June was behind her, and ever aware that more than likely June was watching every step she made, Charlotte forced herself to keep on walking.

June had outright lied about the reason she was there. Charlotte had suspected as much, but now she knew so for certain. June hadn't come by just to drop off a meal for Gordon. She'd come by to share one with him. Charlotte's glimpse of the dining room revealed that, the dining room table was set with Mimi's good china, table linens, and candles. And there was a bottle of wine chilling in a wine bucket — all evidence of an intimate dinner for two.

In the kitchen, Charlotte saw even more evidence that June had lied. A large pot simmered on the stove, something was heating in the oven, the countertop was littered with various ingredients for cooking, and dirty dishes were in the sink. June hadn't simply dropped off a meal. She was actually cooking the meal in Mimi's kitchen.

Charlotte felt her insides churn with outrage. Poor Mimi was barely cold in her grave, and already June, Mimi's so-called best friend, was playing house with Gordon, Mimi's husband. The whole matter was despicable enough to disgust even a maggot.

When Charlotte reached the laundry room, she paused. Expecting June to still be behind her, watching her, she glanced over her shoulder. But June was nowhere in sight. With a shrug, she walked over to the washing machine, jerked open the lid, then yanked open the door to the dryer. Grabbing a handful of wet clothes out of the washer, she stuffed them into the dryer, and as she transferred the rest of the clothes, her mind raced.

The panties. No wonder June had acted so strange when she'd mentioned finding the panties. The stray pair of panties belonged to June.

Charlotte shook her head in disgust. All along she'd had her suspicions about June, but all along she'd tried to convince herself that Rita was the guilty one, mostly because of what June had told her about Rita, she now realized. All along June had been the one who had encouraged everyone to believe that Rita was so jealous of Mimi and so vindictive that she was capable of murder. Then, just in case no one believed her about Rita, Charlotte figured June had tried to hedge her bets by using her venomous tongue to malign Sally Lawson as well. June had probably been the one who had put the bug in Mimi's ear about Sally killing Mimi's trees to begin with. June also could have talked Mimi into believing that Gordon was having an affair with his old friend Sally.

"Some friend," Charlotte whispered in

disgust. The same "friend," Charlotte was sure, who had encouraged Mimi to plant the toxic jimsonweed.

In retrospect, Charlotte could see it all as plain as the nose on her face. June had deviously and purposely set up the other women as likely suspects in order to cover up her own duplicity.

After going to so much trouble, how surprised June must have been when the police had arrested Doreen and George Mires instead of Rita or Sally.

Charlotte frowned. Or *had* she been surprised? she wondered. Were Doreen and George victims of June's treacherous scheme as well?

Charlotte pulled a dryer sheet out of the box and threw it into the dryer, then slammed the dryer door.

All along she'd had her suspicions about June and about Gordon, but she'd made excuses for both of them, excuses that seemed reasonable at the time. But that was then and this was now. That was before she had proof that the two were having an affair.

An affair. Charlotte swallowed hard as she stared at the dryer settings. Closing her eyes, she reached up with both hands and massaged her temples with her fingertips.

Her head felt as if it were about to split open.

Another thought suddenly occurred to her, and her eyes sprang open. Had Gordon been a part of everything all along? Had he done more than just have an affair with June? Was it possible that he'd conspired with her to rid himself of his wife, or had June acted alone?

Charlotte clutched the edge of the dryer, as she thought back to what she knew about Gordon, and she tried to recall what she'd heard the three men in the kitchen discussing on the day of Mimi's funeral.

It was possible that Gordon had conspired with June, she supposed, but other than the gossip she'd heard about the insurance policy, his losses in the stock market, and his philandering, there was no real evidence that he'd been part of a murder plot.

With a sigh, Charlotte set the timer on the dryer. She turned the dryer on, then stood there for several minutes, staring at the laundry room wall. How long had June and Gordon been having an affair? Her mind still racing, Charlotte felt her stomach tighten in a knot.

She should have told Judith about the brownie incident, about how June had insisted that Mimi sample one of the brownies the morning before the HHS meeting and about how Mimi had complained to Charlotte that the brownie was bitter.

"It was bitter alright," Charlotte muttered. Bitter with the jimsonweed. And she should have told Judith about the gossip she'd heard about Gordon as well, instead of worrying what Judith or the police would think about her meddling.

Charlotte reached into her pocket for her cell phone. "No time like the present," she whispered, as she punched in Judith's phone number. "Please, oh, please be there," she murmured, as the phone began ringing.

When Judith answered on the second ring, Charlotte let out a sigh of relief. "Oh, Judith, thank God I got you," she said.

"Aunt Charlotte? What's wrong? Is it the baby? Has something happened to the baby or Nadia?"

Charlotte groaned, and guilt reared its ugly head. Not once in the past twenty minutes had she even thought about little Danielle. "No, hon," she quickly reassured her niece. "I'm not calling about Danielle or Nadia. Last I heard, your little niece was holding her own and Nadia was still sleeping. I'm calling about Mary Lou Adams's murder. You've arrested the wrong suspects, and I have to talk to you —"

Charlotte heard a noise. "Wait a second, hon," she whispered into the phone and tilted her head forward. After listening a moment more, sure enough she heard the distinct sound of footsteps . . . footsteps headed her way. June's footsteps.

Now what?

Charlotte figured she had two choices. She could either play it safe, hang up, and get out of there or — "Judith, don't hang up," Charlotte whispered. "Please just hang on and listen."

"Aunt Charley, don't you dare —"

Without waiting for Judith to finish and praying that she wouldn't hang up, Charlotte dropped the cell phone into her pocket. With all of the real evidence conveniently disposed of, there was only one way of actually proving that June had killed Mimi.

Swallowing hard and taking a deep breath for courage, Charlotte turned, faced the doorway, and waited for June to appear.

Chapter
20

Within moments, June appeared in the doorway of the laundry room.

She knows that I know she killed Mimi, Charlotte thought, as she stared at June. Fear mingled with sudden anger, and both settled in the pit of her stomach. It was there in June's smug, amused expression as well as in the hard, knowing glint in her eyes.

But of course she knew. Only a moron would think that no one would notice the little tryst June had set up for the evening. And only a moron would think that no one would put two and two together. If Charlotte's suspicions were correct — and she was ninety-nine per cent sure that they were — June was certainly no moron. Far from it. But even worse, even more terrifying, Charlotte could tell that June didn't care that Charlotte knew. Why didn't she care?

Charlotte's heart raced as she contemplated all of the reasons that June wouldn't care; she took deep, even breaths in an effort to calm down. Of all the reasons, one in particular kept popping into her head. June didn't care because she planned on getting rid of Charlotte.

Weapons? Make sure she doesn't have a weapon. Charlotte glanced at June's hands.

As if she'd read Charlotte's thoughts, June held out her hand. Other than Charlotte's lunch bag, June's hands were empty. "I didn't want you to forget this," June told her.

When Charlotte took the lunch bag, June crossed her arms and a sinister smile pulled at her lips. "Are you finished snooping yet?"

Shock rippled through Charlotte. She had suspected that June was deceitful and evil. She'd have to be to poison her best friend. But her brazenness was unbelievable. The woman not only thought she could get away with murder, but she intended to flaunt it as well.

Shock quickly yielded to anger, and Charlotte tightened her grip on the lunch bag. No one should get away with murder. But June would. She would unless someone did something about it. With no evidence to speak of and Doreen and

George Mires in jail for the crime, the only way to trap June would be to get her to confess. June might think she was clever, but Charlotte figured if she played her cards right, she just might be able to use June's arrogance to trip her up.

Taking a deep breath, Charlotte sent up a quick prayer for strength to do what had to be done, and another prayer that Judith was listening.

"I'm almost finished," Charlotte finally answered evenly. "What I'm having trouble understanding is why? Mimi thought you were her friend."

June didn't even try to pretend that she didn't know what Charlotte was talking about. She laughed. "Why did I do it?"

Charlotte nodded.

"Hmm, let's see now." Suddenly her eyes flashed with pure venom. "Because she had it all," June snapped, her voice rising. "She had the house, the two perfect kids, the money, the social standing, and she had Gordon. Worst of all, she didn't deserve any of it — took it all for granted, thought it was her due." June dropped her arms and her hands curled into fists. "A man like Gordon deserves more. He deserves a woman who really appreciates him, someone who truly loves him, not some simpering weakling who doesn't have sense enough to come out of the rain."

"But she thought you were her friend," Charlotte repeated.

"Ha! No one, but no one was Mimi's friend. She didn't know the meaning of the word."

"That's a little like the pot calling the kettle black, given the circumstances, don't you think?" The moment Charlotte uttered the words, she wished she had kept her mouth shut. Antagonizing June was not the way to keep her talking about the murder.

June glared at Charlotte. "There are two kinds of people in this life: givers and takers. Mimi was a taker, a selfish, silly woman who thought the world and everyone in it owed her a living."

"The poison," Charlotte injected, in an attempt to keep June from going off on a tangent. "You baked two batches of brownies that day, didn't you? One laced with the jimsonweed for Mimi to taste test, and another batch to serve at the meeting."

"Well now," June sneered. "Aren't you the clever little maid? Figured that out all by yourself, did you?" She laughed. "But then I suspected you had when you found my panties. Too bad, though, and a fat lot of good it's going to do you. In case you haven't heard, the police have already arrested Mimi's killers, and you can't prove diddly-squat. It's your word against mine."

"No, I guess I can't," Charlotte replied, praying that her face wouldn't give her away and wishing that she had the nerve to shake her cell phone in June's smug face.

June stepped back and motioned for Charlotte to exit the room. "You can leave now, and if you have any ideas about running to the cops, I'd think twice about that if I were you."

Clutching her lunch bag, Charlotte took a step forward, but June held up her hand to stop her, and Charlotte tensed.

"Just one more thing." June laughed again. "Under the circumstances, your services won't be needed any longer. You're fired! Oh, and don't expect any references either." Again she motioned with her hand. "Now you can leave."

Charlotte didn't waste time. Keeping an eagle eye on June, she hurried past her. With a prayer on her lips and feeling as if the hounds of hell were nipping at her heels, she hotfooted it through the kitchen, down the entrance hall, and out the front door. Too easy, she kept thinking. June had let her go too easily.

Once outside, she ran down the porch steps and jogged all the way to the van. June might be arrogant, but she had to know that there was no way Charlotte would keep her mouth shut.

Charlotte's hand shook as she unlocked the door to the van. When she finally opened it, a rush of pent-up heat hit her, and for a moment her legs went weak as a feeling of vertigo washed over her.

She grabbed the steering wheel to keep her balance and threw the lunch bag in. Ignoring the heat, she pulled herself inside, slammed the door, and hit the automatic locking mechanism. Once she heard the comforting click of the door locks, she felt a bit safer. Only then did she venture a glance back at the house.

What she saw chilled her to the bone despite the heat. June was standing in the doorway, her arms crossed against her breasts, and she was laughing! "Have a nice day," June called out. Then she waved and burst into laughter again.

"We'll just see who gets the last laugh," Charlotte muttered, as sweat trickled down her face. But in spite of her bravado, she still couldn't shake the feeling of imminent danger, a nagging feeling not unlike waiting for the other shoe to drop.

With a shiver of fear and trembling fingers, she jammed the key into the ignition, cranked the van, and peeled rubber.

Once Charlotte was safely several blocks away, she pulled the van over and shoved the gearshift into park. Still fearful that any minute she'd see June coming after her, she left the engine running, just in case she needed to make a fast getaway.

Breathing heavily and checking the rearview mirror, she adjusted the air conditioner vent to blow on her face. Her head felt as if a jackhammer was inside working overtime. The cool air from the vent helped, but dear Lord, she was tired. And thirsty. Her mouth felt like she'd tried to chew a wad of cotton.

No time to think about that now, though. She fumbled in her pocket for the cell phone. Once she finally got a grip on the phone, she put it to her ear, and praying that Judith hadn't hung up, she said, "Please tell me you heard what was said."

"Every word, Auntie. When I realized what you were doing, I grabbed a tape recorder, and I've got every damning word on tape. We were just lucky that you were so close to her. Now — please tell me that you've left that house."

Charlotte's vision suddenly blurred, and she blinked several times in an effort to clear her eyes. Something was wrong, something —

"Auntie? Are you still there? Answer me!"

Charlotte nodded, then realized that Judith couldn't see her nodding. Got to answer Judith. "Yes, I-I'm parked — Oh, Judith, something's wrong. I — I feel —"

"Aunt Charlotte!"

Suddenly, with the speed of a runaway freight train, Charlotte knew exactly what was wrong. Headache . . . irritability . . . thirst . . . All the same symptoms that Mimi had had. But when, and how?

She gripped the phone tighter. "I — I've been poisoned," she whispered. "She poisoned me." And though her thoughts were growing more confused with each passing moment, she tried to think back over the day, tried to pinpoint a time that June could have poisoned her.

"Auntie, you're scaring me!" Judith cried. "Who poisoned you? Where are you?"

"The salad," Charlotte whispered. "And the noise I heard."

"Aunt Charley, you aren't making sense. Where in hell are you?"

"Don't curse," Charlotte mumbled, her mind growing fuzzy. "I think I'm near Prytania and Washington. Hurry, Judith. Please hurry."

Chapter 21

"Aunt Charley! Wake up! You can't go to sleep!"

Charlotte didn't want to wake up. Her head still hurt. Besides, what was Judith doing in her bedroom? she wondered. And why was her bed moving?

"Go away," she tried to whisper, but her mouth didn't want to work. Thirsty, so thirsty. And something was covering her mouth. Dear Lord, was Judith trying to smother her?

"She's coming around," a gruff voice said, a gruff male voice. "Hey, Ms. LaRue, just take it easy now. I've got an oxygen mask on you. No-no, don't pull it off. Leave it on."

Charlotte forced her eyes open. Above her were Judith and a doctor. Outside, a siren screamed. No, not a doctor, Charlotte decided. The man was a paramedic. "Wh-what happened?" she tried to ask, but her voice was muffled by the oxygen mask.

"You've been poisoned, Auntie. You told me you were poisoned. Remember?"

Charlotte felt as if she were wading through a fog, but the second Judith said "poisoned" it all came back. June . . . Mimi . . . the confrontation in the laundry room . . . the noise she'd heard downstairs . . . the bitter salad . . .

"Who poisoned you, Auntie, and what did they poison you with?"

Charlotte blinked, trying to clear her blurry vision. "June," she muttered. "June Bryant. Same as Mimi."

"Jimsonweed, Auntie?"

Charlotte nodded. "In my salad," she murmured. "Should have known . . . salad in the garbage . . . couldn't eat it all." Her voice trailed away.

Though Charlotte was semiconscious during the ambulance ride to the hospital, and she was conscious when she was treated for the poison, most of it was a blur. By the time she was finally admitted to a room, Hank had shown up.

"Just take it easy, Mom," he said, as he smoothed her hair away from her face. "You're going to be just fine."

"Where's Judith?" she asked.

Hank's hand stilled on her forehead. "Judith said to tell you that she'd be in later to get a statement from you. Right now, though, I'm pretty sure she's arresting that woman who did this."

Charlotte nodded. "Good. No one should get away with murder."

"Don't worry about all of that right now. Just rest."

Charlotte nodded again, then shook her head from side to side. "Can't rest yet. Need to find out how the baby is."

"The baby's holding her own," Hank reassured her. "I just called a few minutes ago."

Charlotte closed her eyes. "Good," she murmured.

When Charlotte opened her eyes again, Judith was standing over her. "What time is it?" Charlotte asked. Out of the corner of her eye, she saw Brian Lee standing by the door.

"It's late, about eleven. So how are you feeling?"

Charlotte frowned. "Actually, pretty good, I think. My headache is finally gone, thank goodness."

"That was a pretty close call, Aunt Charley. What am I going to do with you? Haven't you learned yet that you can't go around conducting your own little investigations. One of these days you're going to get yourself killed."

"Now, Judith, I really don't want to hear a lecture right now. I know you're upset with me, but I do not, as you say, go around conducting my own investigations. Can I help it if I hear things?"

"No ma'am, I suppose not, but when you hear something that's relevant — relevant to an ongoing case — you need to report it, not jump in the big middle."

Knowing it was pointless to argue with Judith, Charlotte sighed. "So what happened?" she asked. "Did you arrest June, I hope?"

Judith nodded. "You bet. We hauled her butt in. Of course, she denied everything and demanded an attorney right off the bat. But once her attorney got there and heard the tape, and once he learned about you and your salad, he talked to her and she changed her tune. She wants her lawyer to try plea-bargaining for manslaughter. But she went too far when she tried to murder you too." Judith pursed her lips. "I don't think the DA will go for it. And by the way, we found the remainder of your salad outside in the garbage can."

"And?"

"And just as you suspected, there were traces of jimsonweed in it. Not a lot, mind you. But enough."

"Not a lot," Charlotte retorted, "because, like an idiot, I ate some of it."

"Never mind that for now. One thing, though. Why did she suspect that you knew?"

"As best as I can figure, it was the panties." When Judith frowned, Charlotte explained about finding the panties in the dryer.

"That's pretty flimsy," Judith commented.

"Yeah, I suppose so," Charlotte agreed. "But she also noticed that there was a resemblance between you and me, and she commented on it more than once." Charlotte shrugged. "The only thing I can think of is that she found out that you were my niece, then put two and two together."

"One more thing, Auntie. How did she get hold of your salad?"

"I was upstairs cleaning," Charlotte explained. "And I thought I heard a noise but didn't pay it much attention. You know how those old houses creak and settle. Anyway, I figure that's when she did it."

"But how did she get inside? You did lock the doors, didn't you?"

"Yes, Judith. I always lock the doors. But June has her own key."

Judith nodded knowingly. "Well, why don't we go ahead and get a formal statement from you — that is, if you're feeling up to it."

When Charlotte nodded, Brian stepped closer to the bed. In his hands were a small tablet and pen.

"Glad you're doing better, Ms. LaRue," he said. "Just go over what happened."

As Charlotte recounted what had happened, Brian took notes, only interrupting a couple of times to clarify a point.

"Well, guess that about does it," he finally said. "You were lucky, Ms. LaRue — this time." He then added, "And Judith's right. Next time you overhear something that's relevant to a case, you need to report it."

Charlotte shuddered. "The good Lord willing, there won't be a next time." She turned to Judith. "A couple of questions, hon, if it's okay."

Judith shrugged. "It's okay by me."

"Did June happen to say anything about Gordon being involved — I mean, like, did he conspire with her to kill Mimi?"

"Why are you asking?" Brian interrupted. "Do you have information that could implicate him?"

Annoyed at Brian's interruption, Charlotte shook her head. "Not really, nothing other than the fact that he and June were having an affair. And the reason I'm asking is because I work for him."

"We know about the affair," Judith said. "June included that in her confession. But to answer your question, she denied that Gordon Adams had anything to do with poisoning his wife. And so far, we haven't found any hard evidence to implicate him in any kind of conspiracy."

Charlotte found that hard to believe, and from the look on Judith's face, she figured that Judith didn't quite believe Gordon was completely innocent either. "Another question. Other than what June said to me — what you recorded — did she offer any other reasons for killing Mimi?"

Judith shook her head. "Not really. But we did find out that she's been planning this for a long time, almost a year. And I have to say, as murders go, she was pretty devious. She covered most of her bases. Spreading rumors about Mimi having an affair with Rita Landers's husband was a stroke of genius. Then aggravating an already touchy situation between Mimi and her neighbor Sally Lawson, as well as rigging that HHS election." Judith laughed. "She didn't admit it, but I wouldn't put it past her to have rigged that business with Doreen and George Mires as well. Too bad she didn't count on my aunt being such a snoop."

"Judith Monroe, you take that back. I am not a snoop." When both Judith and Brian began laughing, Charlotte said, "That's okay. Go ahead and laugh, make fun of me, but I love you anyway, even if you are a royal pain sometimes. Now —" Charlotte pushed herself up in the bed. "Hand me my clothes."

"Whoa, hold on there, Auntie. Where do you think you're going?"

"I'm going to check on my grand-niece."

The door leading into the hallway swung open, and Hank and Carol walked in. "What's going on?" Hank asked, when he saw Charlotte sitting on the side of the bed.

"Your mother wants to get dressed and go to Ochsner to check on Danielle."

"Mother, you can't —"

"Oh yes I can," Charlotte shot back. "One way or another I'm going. Maddie, Daniel, and Nadia need all the support they can get right now. So either help me or get out of my way."

For several seconds Hank stared at his mother; then, with a sigh, he nodded. "In that case, we'll all go. Just let me make a couple of calls first."

"And not a word to Madeline, Daniel, or Nadia about any of this," Charlotte warned them. "They've got enough on their minds without worrying about me too."

It was well after midnight by the time they got to Ochsner and located Madeline and Daniel in the waiting room.

"How is she?" Charlotte asked Daniel.

"So far, so good," he replied.

"And Nadia? How's she holding up?"

As if the very mention of Nadia's name had summoned her, the door to the waiting room swung open. Standing in the doorway with one hand gripping the door frame and the other hand gripping the edge of the door was Nadia.

"I'm okay, Charlotte, but I'll be a lot better once my little girl makes it through this night."

Nadia's face was as pale as the white walls of the waiting room, and Daniel immediately rushed over to her.

"Aw, honey, what are you doing out of bed?" he said, wrapping his arm around her waist to lend support.

"They said I could get up and walk around if I felt like it."

"Well at least sit down," Daniel urged, motioning toward the sofa.

"Okay, but just a minute till I catch my breath. Then, I want to see our little girl."

After Daniel helped Nadia over to the sofa, Judith approached him. "Hey, big brother." She wrapped her arms around him, and for several moments, simply held him within her embrace. When she released him, she said, "I'm so sorry. I would have been here earlier, but it was impossible to get away."

As Charlotte watched the two of them together, her throat grew tight and she was reminded of when they were children. Madeline had been battling depression over her divorce from their father, and Charlotte had been forced to step in and take over the care of Daniel and Judith. Daniel, just a young boy, had been waging his own battle, trying to come to terms with the fact that his father wasn't around any longer. He'd wanted to talk to his father, but his father wouldn't return his phone calls. Then, too, Judith had wrapped her arms around her brother, and had, in her own childlike way, tried to comfort him.

"Daddy's just mean, Daniel," Judith had told him, patting him on the back. "We don't need him 'cause we've got Aunt Charley, and she's better than any old daddy any day."

"Aunt Charley? Earth to Aunt Charley."

Charlotte blinked at the sound of her name, and when she glanced up, Judith was standing in front of her.

"Are you okay, Auntie?"

"Just daydreaming, hon."

"How about something to drink?"

Charlotte nodded. "A Coke would be great. Thanks, hon."

"Anyone else?" Judith asked.

Chapter 22

Charlotte folded the Monday *Times-Picayune* and took it into the laundry room, where she kept a basket to collect the papers for recycling. A week had passed since June's arrest, and for a change, there had been nothing new in the newspaper about the scandal surrounding Mimi Adams's murder or about June Bryant.

When Charlotte reentered the kitchen, she glanced at the clock on the microwave. Since it was only seven, in all likelihood, Gordon wouldn't have left for work yet. Charlotte tapped her foot impatiently. What to do . . . what to do . . .

She stared at the telephone on the cabinet. Using the excuse of an ongoing family crisis, she'd called and canceled work on Friday, but over the weekend she'd decided that canceling on Gordon yet again was simply delaying the inevitable. Knowing what she knew about Gordon, there was just no way she could continue working for him.

Though nothing could be proven and there was no evidence that he'd had a part in poisoning Mimi, in Charlotte's opinion, his affair with June made him just as morally guilty. By continuing his affair with June, he'd given her false hope and he'd encouraged her to think that if Mimi were out of the way, she would have a future with him.

Charlotte didn't believe in chance. For the most part, she believed that everything happened for a reason. And she'd thought long and hard about her circumstances. First, Marian had moved, leaving her Wednesday slot open, and now this. Was it possible that this was a sign, a sign that maybe it was time for her to finally retire? Then again, the Wednesday slot had already been filled by Sandra Wellington, and, of course, she still had Bitsy for the Tuesday slot. Without Gordon, though, she'd have Thursdays through Mondays off.

Was it possible that she was getting a sneak preview of things to come, a time when she wouldn't have to go to work at all? Charlotte didn't know the answer, and she was tired of trying to figure it out. But for now, she still had unfinished business to take care of.

With a resigned sigh, she walked over to the phone and dialed the Adamses' number. The phone rang four times, and then the answering machine kicked in.

Closing her eyes, she whispered, "Thank you, thank you," as she listened to the recorded greeting. Resigning the job didn't bother her, but she had truly dreaded having to personally talk to Gordon. It was the coward's way out, and she knew she should be ashamed, but this way was oh-so much easier.

Charlotte opened her eyes just as the beep sounded in her ear. "Hi, Gordon," she said. "This is Charlotte LaRue. I'm sorry for not giving you more notice, but I won't be able to continue working for you. According to my records, you still owe me for two days' work. If you would just mail my final check to my post office box address, I would appreciate it."

The moment she hung up the phone, it was as if the weight of the world had been lifted off her shoulders. Though it felt a bit strange not having to get dressed and rush off to work, it was kind of a nice feeling — no hurrying, no following a strict schedule, and no having to face a dirty mess made by other people. Maybe she would take a nice leisurely walk around the block for a change, and maybe she would finally have time to begin painting her house inside and out, a project that she'd been thinking about for some time.

It was midmorning and Charlotte had just walked into the kitchen to check on the pot of beef stew that she was cooking when the phone rang.

She reached for the new portable phone she'd recently purchased and pressed the TALK button. "Maid-for-a-Day, Charlotte speaking."

"Today's the day, Charlotte. Davy and I are expecting them any minute now."

Charlotte smiled. "Oh, Maddie, that's wonderful," she said, as a warm feeling spread within. Cradling the phone receiver between her chin and her shoulder, she reached for a wooden spoon and stirred the pot of beef stew.

It had been almost a week since little Danielle had been born, and though she had been small and had had breathing difficulties in the beginning, she'd survived with flying colors.

"Miracles still happen," Madeline continued more soberly. "Lots of prayers went up for that baby girl." A moment passed, and then suddenly she giggled. "Want to hear something funny? Before the doctor signed the release forms, he told Daniel that he'd weighed her with a wet diaper on and she made the weight cut with half an ounce to spare."

Charlotte laughed. "I can't wait to get my hands on that little doll."

"Well, you'll have to stand in line. And, by the way, you are still bringing over their dinner, aren't you?"

"It's almost done." Charlotte tapped the wooden spoon against the top of the pot, then turned off the burner. "Beef stew, biscuits, and a salad."

"Yum yum, that sounds wonderful."

"Just as soon as the stew cools, I'll bring everything over."

"Thanks, Charlotte. We'll be waiting."

"See you then. Bye." Charlotte clicked off the receiver and placed it on the countertop, then began cleaning up the mess she'd made while preparing the stew. She'd just loaded the last dirty dish into the dishwasher when the phone rang again.

With a frown, she picked up the receiver and pressed the TALK button. "Maid-for-a-Day, Charlotte speaking."

"Hi, Charlotte, this is Sally Lawson."

Charlotte's frown deepened. "Hi, Sally."

"I guess you're wondering why I'm calling."

Charlotte was wondering, but she figured it would be impolite to just come right out and ask, so she didn't reply.

"I just got a call from Gordon," she explained. "And he said you'd quit. Not that I blame you, not after what he did, what with carrying on with that June Bryant right under poor Mimi's nose, but since you're not working for him any longer, I was wondering if you might consider working me into your schedule. All I need is one day a week, and any day you choose would be fine with me. And I'd pay you well. I know what Gordon paid you, but I'd be willing to pay . . ."

As Charlotte listened to Sally quote a price, temptation began to grow. She had liked Sally the first time she'd met her, and she had been truly relieved to find out that her very first impression of the woman had been right on target. Besides, the money that Sally was offering for one day of work was as much as she had made working two days a week for the Adamses.

Was Sally's offer yet another sign, she wondered, a sign that she shouldn't retire just yet after all?

"That's a very generous offer," Charlotte

told her. More than generous, she thought, and before she had time to talk herself out of it, she said, "How about Mondays, say from nine to three-thirty? Mondays are a good day for me."

A Cleaning Tip From Charlotte

Always clean from the top of a room to the bottom of a room, especially when dusting, and always vacuum last.

About the Author

Barbara Colley is an award-winning author whose books have been published in sixteen foreign languages. A native of Louisiana, she lives with her family in a suburb of New Orleans. Besides writing and sharing her stories, she loves strolling through the historic New Orleans French Quarter and Garden District, which inspired the setting for her Charlotte LaRue mystery series. Readers can write to Barbara at P.O. Box 290, Boutte, LA 70039 or visit her Web site at http://www.cclectics.com/barbaracolley-anne-logan.

We hope you have enjoyed this Large Print book. Other Thorndike, Wheeler or Chivers Press Large Print books are available at your library or directly from the publishers.

For more information about current and upcoming titles, please call or write, without obligation, to:

Publisher
Thorndike Press
295 Kennedy Memorial Drive
Waterville, ME   04901
Tel. (800) 223-1244

Or visit our Web site at:
www.gale.com/thorndike
www.gale.com/wheeler

OR

Chivers Large Print
published by BBC Audiobooks Ltd
St James House, The Square
Lower Bristol Road
Bath BA2 3SB
England
Tel. +44(0) 800 136919
email: bbcaudiobooks@bbc.co.uk
www.bbcaudiobooks.co.uk

All our Large Print titles are designed for easy reading, and all our books are made to last.